Love
WITH
THE
Viscount

AMERICAN
HEIRESS
TRILOGY

JULIANNE
MACLEAN

In Love with the Viscount
Copyright © 2020 Julianne MacLean Publishing Inc.

Print edition ISBN: 978-1-927675-64-9
Ebook edition ISBN: 978-1-927675-63-2

First edition published by Avon/Harper Collins under the title:
My Own Private Hero Copyright © 2003 Julianne MacLean

Cover and Interior Design: The Killion Group, Inc.

I like the Americans very well, but there are two things I wish they would keep to themselves—their girls and their tinned lobster.

—Lady Dorothy Nevill
England, 1888

Prologue

May 1884

*I*NSIDE THE LAVISH INTERIOR OF the *SS Fortune,* steaming smoothly across the deep, dark Atlantic at night, Adele Wilson stood in her first-class stateroom and gazed uncertainly at her reflection in the mirror.

A heavy lump formed in her belly. Why? Everything was as it should be. Her mother was in the adjoining cabin to her left, her sister Clara to her right. Adele had just eaten a delicious supper at the captain's elaborate table and was about to undress for bed and read a most thought-provoking novel before turning down the lamp and going to sleep.

She removed a pearl and diamond drop earring and watched it sparkle in her hand. She closed her fist around it, then looked up at her reflection again.

She felt oddly disconnected from the floor, as if she were in someone else's body. A stranger was staring back at her—an elegant, sophisticated heiress who wore a jewel-trimmed Worth gown from Paris made of the finest silk money could buy, and around her neck, an antique, pearl-and-diamond choker to match the earrings.

She turned away from the mirror and looked around. Suddenly, even the room seemed wrong. *Wrong.* There was no other word for it. Carved mahogany panels covered the walls, the ceiling was painted gold with extravagant ornamentation around a dazzling crystal chandelier. The sheets on her bed boasted the ship's monogram, and all the fixtures, from the door-knobs to the lamps, right down to the nails in the bulkhead, were polished brass, pompously gleaming.

Sometimes it seemed as if she were living someone else's life. She had not been born into this wealth. She didn't even know how to feel comfortable with it. At the moment, she felt as if she shouldn't touch anything.

Adele sighed. What she wouldn't give to be riding bareback through the woods as she used to do when she was younger, before they'd moved to the city and ventured into high society. Oh, to smell the damp earth and the leaves on the ground, and the green moss around the lake....

She inhaled deeply, longingly, wanting to remember, but smelled only the expensive perfume she wore. Feeling absurdly deprived, she exhaled.

It's nerves, she decided, crossing to her bed and removing the other earring and setting both of them on the night table. Tomorrow she would greet her future husband, Lord Osulton. An English earl. The newspapermen would probably be there to greet the ship and take her picture. No wonder she was nervous.

She would get through it, however.

Adele removed the combs from her honey-colored hair and shook out her long, curly locks until they fell loose upon her shoulders. That was better.

The door to the adjoining stateroom opened, and Adele's sister Clara peered inside. Clara had married the handsome Marquess of Rawdon the year before and had left her London home a month ago with her new baby daughter, Anne, to visit her family in New York. "You're still awake?"

Adele faced her sister. "Yes, come in."

Clara, still in her glittering evening gown, her mahogany hair swept into a flattering knot, entered the room and sat down on the chintz sofa. "You barely touched your supper. Are you all right?"

"I'm fine." But Adele knew she couldn't fool Clara who always strove to see beneath the surface of things.

"Are you certain, Adele? You're not having second thoughts, are you? Because it's not too late to change your mind."

"I'm not having second thoughts."

"It would be perfectly normal if you were. You barely know the man. You've met him so few times, usually at dull assemblies with Mother breathing down your neck. You've danced with him only once, which is essentially the only time you've been alone with him. And what was that, three or four minutes?"

Adele sat down next to Clara. "I'm just a little nervous, that's all. But I know in my heart that this is right. I'm sure of it. He's a good man."

"But you haven't had a chance to know for sure if

there is any true intimacy between you. Some form of attraction. A spark that leads to a flame. Maybe you should think about enjoying the London Season just once before you marry. Imagine who you might meet. A dashing white knight, perhaps."

Adele shook her head. "I'm not like you, Clara. You and Sophia were the adventurous ones, while I've always been prudent and practical. Isn't that what Mother and Father said every time you and Sophia got into trouble?"

Clara smirked. "I can hear Father now." She put a finger under her nose like a mustache. "Why can't you two girls be more like your younger sister? We can always depend on Adele to behave herself."

Adele smiled and rolled her eyes. "The fact remains, I don't wish to suffer through an entire London Season, being speculated about, forced to wear diamonds every night and flirt in crowded drawing rooms. The thought of it, quite frankly, makes me ill. I'd much rather be in the country—outdoors with the fresh air, which is exactly where my future husband is at this moment."

"You might enjoy the excitement of a Season," Clara said, sounding a little frustrated.

Adele shook her head again. "No, I would not. I am content with my decision to marry Lord Osulton. He is an agreeable gentleman and a very good match for me. From what I understand, he doesn't enjoy the city, either. He prefers his country house."

"But aren't you afraid you might someday wonder what extraordinary adventures you might have missed?"

Adele squeezed her sister's hand. "I don't seek adventure, Clara. In fact, I loathe the idea of it. I prefer a carefully laid out plan, free of the unexpected. Besides that, I believe that sometimes, the best marriages are sensibly arranged. Love comes later, when it has time to grow and become something more substantial, based on admiration and respect rather than a spark and flame. Fire can be unpredictable, and it often burns."

"It can also be wonderful, Adele."

"Can it? Funny, I do recall when it was not so wonderful last year, when you thought your husband was going to leave you. You were miserable. I don't want to be miserable like that. I prefer a sense of calm without any of those difficult emotional ups and downs."

"But Seger did devote himself to me," Clara said, "and we are very happy now. What we have today was worth every minute of misery, no matter how excruciating it was at the time. Some things are worth fighting for, no matter how unpleasant the task. Are you sure you don't wish to postpone the wedding, and suffer through just one Season? You might discover the greatest romance of your life."

Adele sighed and stood up. She crossed to the wardrobe and began to unbutton her bodice.

"You would think," Clara continued, "being bookish, you might have read something about love."

"I've read plenty about love," Adele said with her back to her sister, "and I could never relate to those simpering, lovesick heroines stuck in towers, who stake their happiness on white knights. There are no towers or white knights in real life, Clara. There are only realistic men, and I am quite content to have found a most agreeable one for myself. Besides, it makes me happy to please Mother and Father. You should have seen Mother's face when I told her I had accepted Lord Osulton's proposal. I'd never seen her so proud."

"You cannot live your life to please others, Adele. You must think of yourself and your future. After the wedding, Mother and Father will return to New York, and you will be left in England on your own— no longer a dutiful daughter, but a married woman. You will be responsible for your own happiness and be free to choose what you want to do with your life. You should marry whomever you wish to marry."

"I wish to marry Lord Osulton. *Harold,*" she added, deciding she should probably start referring to him by his given name now that they were betrothed.

Clara smiled lovingly at Adele. "I daresay, you will do as you wish, won't you?"

"As long as it is the right thing to do. I have chosen my path, and I have made a commitment. I will not veer from it."

Clara raised an eyebrow, stood up, and walked to the connecting door to her own stateroom. "I suppose there is no arguing with you. You always were determined to do the right thing, even when Sophia and I tried to convince you to do otherwise. You missed some fun, you know."

Adele tipped her head at her sister. "I also missed many hours standing in the corner."

Clara shrugged. "Adventure has a price."

"And you and Sophia were always willing to pay it."

Adele's maid entered and began preparing the bed.

Clara opened the door. "We'll be docking overnight to pick up some extra passengers, then it won't be long before we reach Liverpool. The captain says we should be disembarking by mid-morning. It sounds to me like you're sure."

"I am."

"Then I am satisfied. I must go and check on little Anne. I'll see you in the morning." She walked out and closed the door behind her.

Adele smiled at her maid and reached for her nightgown.

London's Savoy Theatre
Shortly after four a.m. the same night

It was a well-known fact among certain circles in London that Frances Fairbanks—celebrated actress and hailed by some as one of the most beautiful women alive—enjoyed lying about naked. Especially on the soft, bearskin rug on the floor of her dressing room, when the room smelled of wine and French perfume, and she was gazing at a lover.

Or rather, one lover in particular. Damien Renshaw, Viscount Alcester.

He was by far the most fascinating man she'd ever met—tall and darkly handsome with broad, muscled shoulders and facial features that could have been sculpted by an artist. He was rugged and wild and unpredictable, and what's more, he was the most ingenious, instinctive of lovers. He knew just how to move to give her the most intense intimate experiences she'd ever known.

Yet there was tenderness in his lovemaking.

Frances stretched out like a cat and rolled over onto her stomach, resting her elbows on the fur. Swinging her bare feet back and forth behind her, she watched Damien sit down on the deeply buttoned settee by the door and pull on a boot.

He glanced up at her briefly with dark eyes that usually promised pleasure and seduction, but at the moment revealed only impatience.

He was in a hurry to leave, Frances realized suddenly with a frown, which was extremely out of character for him. Because Damien Renshaw—the irresistible black lion—never hurried *anything* in the bedroom.

Frances stopped swinging her feet. "You left your shirt on when you made love to me tonight."

She had to work hard to sound confident. It was not something she was accustomed to—working hard at it, that is. She was always absolutely sure of herself where her lovers were concerned. *They* were the ones who did the scrambling.

She swallowed uncomfortably and made a conscious effort to swing her legs again. "You're not angry about the bracelet, are you?"

Pulling on his other boot, Damien didn't look up. "Of course not. As you said, you fell in love with it."

Indeed, she had. So much so, she'd purchased it herself and had the bill sent to Damien.

She sat up on her heels and spoke with pouty lips, hoping to kindle his flirtatious nature. "It was only a small bracelet. I didn't think it would matter in the larger scheme of things."

He rose to his feet, tall and beautiful as a Greek god in the flickering shadows of the candlelight. He searched the shambles of the room for his waistcoat. He spotted it in a heap on the floor—on top of some purple feathers and Frances's colorful costume from her performance that evening.

He picked up the waistcoat, slipped it on, then reached down to cradle Frances's chin in his hand. He grinned, his eyes sparkling instantly with the allure that reassured Frances that she was still the envy of every hot-blooded woman in London. His voice was husky and sensual when he spoke, but at the same time commanding.

"Next time try to resist the urge. You know my situation."

She did, of course, know. *Everyone* knew. Lord Alcester was in debt up to his ears and had been forced to lease out his London house to a German family and take up residence with his eccentric cousin.

It didn't bother Frances, however. She didn't want Damien for his money. There were others who served that purpose. Damien's talents lay elsewhere.

He dropped his hand to his side and pulled on his overcoat. "My apologies for leaving my shirt on."

"You're not yourself these days, Damien," she said. "I hope it's not me."

"It's not you." He kissed Frances good-bye, leaving her ever so slightly distressed by this unexplained change in him.

It was still dark when Adele woke to the sound of a thump in her cabin. She remembered they were stopping briefly on the coast of England to pick up a few new passengers. She rolled onto her back, wondering how long they would be docked.

She stared up at the ceiling in the darkness and thought about the conversation she'd had earlier with her sister. Clara had suggested that Adele should be reckless for once in her life. This was not a new conversation. They'd had it countless times before as children and young women. Clara and Adele's oldest sister, Sophia, often tried to lure Adele into their mischief.

Adele rested the back of her hand on her forehead and recalled a summer afternoon when they were girls, not long after they'd moved to New York. Clara had gathered them together in the attic of their new house and said, "If we want to grow up, we must have an adventure. And everyone knows that an adventure must always start with running away from home."

Sophia's eyes sparkled, while Adele had been horrified. She had refused, of course, and argued the point of such foolish horseplay, and threatened to tell their parents.

Clara told Adele that if she breathed a word of their plan, they'd string her up by her heels, so Adele promised to keep it secret. Which she did. For about an hour. Then she told her father, who promptly marched out onto Fifth Avenue and brought the girls home and put them to bed with no supper. Adele, conversely, had been given an extra slice of blackberry pie.

Clara and Sophia didn't speak to her for a week after that, but then they forgave her—as they always did—

and told her they supposed it was her job to keep them out of trouble because she was the sensible one.

But even now, as women, Clara was still trying to talk Adele into misbehaving. Adele smiled and supposed it would never change. She'd be an old lady with a cane and spectacles, and Clara would try to convince her to dance in the rain. Adele smiled again and shook her head.

Just then, she heard another thump, almost as if there were a monster under her bed. Her heart leaped with panic, but she quenched the sensation because she'd stopped believing in monsters under beds many years ago.

Nevertheless, she tossed the covers aside to check. Her toes had just touched the floor when a man rose up in front of her. Adele gazed at the dark figure in terror and tried to cry out, but before she had a chance, a cloth soaked in a strong-smelling chemical covered her mouth.

Heart now blazing with terror, she struggled and tried to scream, but couldn't make her voice work. Then she felt weak and dizzy, and lost all sensation in her body before she gave up the fight and remembered nothing more.

Part One

The Adventure

Chapter 1

Somewhere in Northern England

THREE DAYS. IT HAD BEEN three long days, and now it was beginning to rain. A storm was brewing.

Adele rose from the hay-filled tick that served as her bed and walked across the creaky plank floor to the window. All she could see in every direction were endless, rolling hills of grass and rock beneath an angry gray sky, swirling with the oncoming threat of bad weather. Hard raindrops pelted against the glass.

It was barren and lonely, this part of the world, wherever it was. She hadn't seen one person. Not even a lone goat or sheep. There were no trees, and the wind never stopped blowing. It pummeled the stone cottage on top of this sadly forsaken hill, rattled the windowpanes, and whistled eerily down the chimney. The door to the stable knocked and banged constantly. All day long. That—combined with the musty, damp smell of this room—was enough to drive a person to the brink of madness.

Adele made a fist and squeezed it. She had been steered off course into fierce, treacherous waters, and she wanted her calm life back.

If she still had a life to go to…. She wasn't even sure Harold—or any man, for that matter—would want her after this, because she had no idea what her kidnapper had done to her. All she knew was that he had undressed her at some point, because when she woke up, she was wearing someone else's shabby, homespun dress. Beneath it, she wore petticoats and a shift with ivory stockings, but no corset and no shoes. She had no idea what happened to her nightgown, nor did she know why her abductor had undressed her. To be less conspicuous, perhaps, in delivering her to this place of custody? She hoped that was the reason.

Adele breathed deeply in an effort to keep a cool head. She must not panic or lose control. That would do her no good. She had tried everything to escape this room in the past few days. She had pounded on and shaken the door, shouted for help, used all her strength at the window, but her efforts had been futile. All she could do now was wait for something to happen—something she could act upon. Or for someone to find her. Surely her mother was searching, and the police were investigating.

Just then, the front door of the cottage opened downstairs. Heavy footsteps entered the house and pounded across the hard floor. The door slammed shut and Adele's heart quickened with fear. She stood quiet and still, listening.

Voices. It was more than one person, which wasn't the usual routine. There had only ever been one captor here to bring her food and water. What was happening?

Suddenly, a commotion erupted. There was a frenzy of footsteps. A piece of furniture fell over. Or it was kicked over. Was someone here to rescue her? Harold? But Harold would never face a kidnapper on his own. Or would he?

Her father? If only it could be him! But no, he was at home in America. He wasn't due to arrive in England until the wedding. Perhaps it was a constable. Or a neighbor who had discovered what was happening and had come to her rescue!

Footsteps pounded up the stairs and Adele's breath caught in her throat. Every particle of her being froze with fear and dread. Was someone here to ravish her? Murder her? Her eyes searched for a weapon, but there was nothing. Nothing but a chair. She picked it up. It was heavy, but she would swing it if she had to.

The lock clicked and the door swung open. Two men walked in. One held a pistol to the other's head. The one holding the gun was tall and dark and his eyes smoldered with fury. He wore a heavy, black greatcoat that matched his black hair. Adele feared him instantly.

Was he her captor? She had never seen the man in daylight.

"Your name!" he barked.

"Adele Wilson." It didn't occur to her to ask why he wanted to know. Or to ask anything at all. All she could do was answer the question because he expected an answer.

In that instant, the other criminal—a short, stocky

fellow with rotting teeth and thinning hair—whirled around and grabbed the pistol, lunged forward, and took hold of Adele around the waist. He pressed the cold, steel barrel to her temple. She dropped the chair as fear shot through her. She'd never faced a gun before.

"Now the ransom!" The man's high-pitched voice revealed his desperation.

For the first time, Adele looked fixedly at the other man—the dark, wild one—and understood that he was her rescuer.

He held up his hands in a gesture that invited calm, but it wasn't easy for Adele to relax because his dark eyes and windblown black hair gave him the look of the devil, or something worse. Masculine to the core, rough around the edges, he looked as if he'd been traveling for three days straight and hadn't taken the time to shave or bathe or even sleep, because he'd been hell-bent on reaching this house.

Who was he? Where had he come from?

"Harm her and you will die," he said.

His English accent caught her off guard, for he didn't have the look of a polite English gentleman—at least not the type she'd ever met in New York. This man was pure, unleashed aggression.

"Or you can take the ransom and run," he continued. "I recommend the latter."

Adele felt the other man's grip tighten about her waist. She sucked in a breath.

"You won't let me leave," her kidnapper said shakily.

Her rescuer stepped out of the way of the door. "I

will let you leave when you let the lady go. But be quick about it because my patience is dwindling fast."

The man pressed the pistol harder against the side of Adele's head. "I don't believe you will let me go."

Paralyzing fear twisted around her heart. This man was not going to simply walk away. Why should he risk them following?

By the dark calculating look in her rescuer's eyes, Adele sensed he was thinking the very same thing.

In an instant, survival instinct took over. Adele dropped to the floor and sank her teeth into the man's thigh. While he screamed out in pain, her rescuer dashed forward and propelled the man to the wall, where they smacked into it, hard. They wrestled for a few seconds, both grunting as they tried to gain control of the pistol.

It would have been prudent for Adele to run for safety, but some other reflex took over. She darted at the pair of them and leaped onto the shorter man's back. He swung around and threw her to the floor, then aimed the pistol at her heart.

"Damn you!" Her rescuer tackled the man just as he fired. The noise was deafening, the pain shocking. Adele grabbed hold of her thigh and curled forward.

The two men rolled around on the floor until her rescuer swung the handle of the gun and struck his foe on the head. The man's body went still, while thunder rumbled in the distance.

Clutching her throbbing leg, Adele stared numbly at the two of them.

Her rescuer looked up. "You're shot."

"Yes," she rasped.

He crawled across the floor and without so much as a second's hesitation, tossed up her skirt.

Adele leaned back on her hands, trying not to show her sudden ridiculous sense of modesty in these circumstances. She had been shot. He—whoever he was—needed to examine the wound.

She looked down at her leg. Her ivory stocking was stained red on the inside of her thigh. The whole area burned like nothing she'd ever experienced before. It was as if someone were branding her with a red-hot poker.

Her rescuer wrapped his hand around her calf and moved her legs apart to get a closer look. Adele stiffened. She had to fight the urge to squeeze her legs back together again.

"I must remove your stocking," he said, "to get a better look. May I have your permission?"

"Of course."

Her reply came intuitively, but after she'd said it, she felt her modesty return. She swept the petty notion aside, for now was not the time to worry about decorum. She squeezed her eyes shut and focused on overcoming the pain.

The man's hands were swift as he rolled the stocking down her leg. He barely touched her skin. His touch was light as silk. He eased the stocking to her ankle with great care, as if he were handling something very precious. Adele held her breath the entire time.

"This looks painful," he said.

It was. Her whole leg throbbed, and the pounding sensation reverberated all the way up to her shoulders.

Adele opened her eyes and watched the man's face. His dark brows drew together with concern as he inspected the gash. He slid a hand over her bare thigh as he touched all around the wound.

"It's just a graze, thank God," he said, sitting back on his heels. "We'll bandage it and you'll live." He stood up and glanced around the room.

Looking up at him, so tall and serious, Adele had to fight the sense of embarrassment and intimidation that made her almost afraid to speak. She had never let a man who was not a doctor touch her so intimately before.

"May I ask who you are? And how you found me?"

He considered her question for a moment. "I apologize, Miss Wilson. I should have identified myself."

Suddenly, he was transformed into a proper gentleman. At least his words were gentlemanly. His appearance was quite another matter altogether. He was unshaven, wild, and rough. His black wool coat looked shabby, dusty, and weathered, as if he'd rolled down a hill in it. There was intensity in everything about him, and it left her breathless and panicky.

Adele was nowhere near ready to relax. Especially when she found herself locked in his dark, gleaming stare.

"I am Damien Renshaw," he explained. "Viscount Alcester. Harold's cousin."

Harold's cousin? Yes...she knew of him. Her sister Sophia had met him in London and described him as the polar opposite of Harold. Lord Alcester had a terrible reputation with women, he was irresponsible with money and his mother had been a scandalous adulteress. He was following in his mother's footsteps, it was said, and led a careless life with a string of mistresses of questionable repute. The current one was a famous and beautiful actress.

"The ship's master at arms informed Harold of your kidnapping," Lord Alcester said, "as there was a ransom note left in your stateroom. Harold informed me of the situation, and it was deemed that I should take care of things."

Deemed? By whom?

"I assured Harold that I would bring you home quickly and quietly," Lord Alcester added. "We will leave here in the morning, after the storm has passed, and travel under assumed names to meet your mother and sister in two days' time, in a village between here and *Osulton Manor*. It has all been arranged. She will then escort you the rest of the way, as if nothing ever happened."

Adele was in shock. She was to travel alone with this man?

Still fighting the excruciating pain in her thigh, she struggled to collect her thoughts and understand the situation. "No one knows about my kidnapping?"

"Besides the ship's officer, no one except your family and Harold's mother and sister. I suggested he not even tell them, but by the time he contacted me, he had already informed them. They have since been advised to keep quiet."

"To avoid a scandal," Adele said.

"Yes."

She glanced uneasily at her rescuer—a rake of the highest order—then at the unconscious man lying on the floor beside them, who had done God-only-knew-what to her while she was unconscious.

Adele felt sick and dizzy.

Lord Alcester followed her gaze, then crossed the creaky floor to where her kidnapper lay. Kneeling down, he pressed two fingers to the man's neck. The wind from the storm outside moaned like a beast inside the stone chimney and the draft lifted the clinging cobwebs around the hearth.

When at last Lord Alcester spoke, his voice was low and subdued. "He's dead."

Adele swallowed hard as Alcester pinched the bridge of his nose. All the color left his face and he looked as if a severe headache had just taken root inside his skull.

"Are you all right?" she asked.

As soon as he met her gaze, his color returned. "Yes."

He stood up and she found herself trying to read his thoughts but couldn't.

"I'll need to wrap your wound." He was gone before she had a chance to utter a single word.

A moment later he returned with a cloth in a bowl of water and a bottle of whiskey. He shrugged out of his long black coat.

"This house was abandoned long ago. There's nothing downstairs to use for bandages. My shirt will have to suffice."

Adele sat forward to protest—partly because she couldn't fathom the idea of this man walking around shirtless—but the movement caused a stabbing sensation in her leg.

"Sit still," he said. "You'll worsen the bleeding." His voice seemed strained and impatient. Was he annoyed with her?

"I'm sorry," she replied apprehensively. "I wanted to tell you that we could use my petticoat for bandages. It has a bullet hole in it anyway."

He considered that for a moment and nodded.

Adele swallowed. "If you would be so kind as to avert your eyes while I remove it?"

"Do you need assistance?"

Assistance! Her pulse drummed at the suggestion. Based on his reputation, he was probably a master at removing women's underclothes.

Adele was astonished by the sudden depraved direction of her thoughts. It was exhaustion, surely. She'd hardly slept in three days. *Think clearly, Adele. He is merely offering to help in order to spare you pain.*

"I can manage, thank you," she replied.

He left the room but remained just outside the door while she struggled to reach up under her skirts and free the ribbons at her waist. With more than a little discomfort, she slid the garment down over her hips.

"You can come in now." She held the petticoat out to him.

He took it and began to tear it into strips. "If you're in pain, you're welcome to take a few swigs of that whiskey."

She eyed it uneasily. "No, thank you." She wanted to keep her wits about her in the coming hours, for she didn't know what those hours might bring.

While Lord Alcester stood tall above her, ripping and tearing at the petticoat, he glanced around the bare room with assessing eyes. "You spent three days in here?"

"Yes."

He met her gaze. "After I clean and bandage your wound, we'll move you downstairs where you'll be more comfortable."

"I'm perfectly fine here," she replied.

The sound of fabric ripping filled a long, drawn-out silence between them. Adele felt a great need to add conversation to that silence, for she needed to distract herself from her anxiety.

"I don't even know what it looks like downstairs," she said. "I was unconscious when I arrived, and sick when I woke up."

Lord Alcester stopped ripping. "Sick and unconscious?"

"Yes. I was drugged on the ship. He kept me drugged until I woke up here."

"Were you hurt in any way?"

She understood his meaning. He was wondering if she had been violated. She was wondering that herself, with more than a little concern. She knew nothing about such things regarding the female body.

"I'm not certain," she replied. "I didn't feel...." How could she put it? "I felt no pain anywhere. Except for a headache. But I suppose a lady couldn't be sure about a certain kind of pain. Or could she?"

What kind of question was that?

Alcester's expression revealed no hint of awkwardness. He knelt beside her, dipped the cloth into the bowl of water and gently squeezed it out. His eyes lifted to meet hers and he responded with composure.

"It depends," he said softly. "Pardon my candor, Miss Wilson, but did you notice any bleeding when you woke up?"

"No, but couldn't he have...?" *Lord, this was awkward.* "He disposed of my nightgown. Couldn't he have...tidied up afterwards?"

She'd never had a conversation quite like this before.

"I suppose, if he were an exceedingly neat person." Lord Alcester smiled gently at her, and Adele knew he was trying to minimize her concerns.

Continuing to rinse the cloth in the bowl, he said, "My suspicion is that you are probably fine. I believe you would know if something was wrong. But if you wish to be certain, a physician can examine you."

"He'd be able to tell?"

"Yes."

"Would he be able to tell if I was—" She stopped. She couldn't go on.

"If you were what, Miss Wilson?"

"If I was with child?" The idea was unsettling, to say the least, but she had to ask.

"I believe it would be too soon to ascertain the answer to that particular question, but let us deal with one problem at a time, shall we?"

Grateful that Lord Alcester was direct and honest with her about this awkward topic, she considered what she knew about the English aristocratic code. A woman was expected to be a virgin upon marriage to ensure any child born of the union was the true heir to the man's title. Perhaps Harold was worried. Perhaps Lord Alcester was worried, too. He was a member of that family, after all.

"I would like to be examined officially," she said, remembering that she was to become an aristocratic lady herself. It would be her code, too. Best to follow the rules.

Lord Alcester held the cloth above her wound and squeezed water over it. "The Osulton family physician is a very good man," he said. "I would trust him with my life, and you can rest assured that he will be discreet. I hope you are not unduly worried?" Alcester's eyes met hers again. He often seemed to be assessing things.

"I am, but I will do my best to be patient."

He nodded, appearing satisfied, then turned his attention back to the task of treating her wound. The droplets of water tickled her skin. A few times, her leg jerked upward from the intensity of the dribbling sensation—the odd combination of pain and tickling. She wished she could keep her leg still, but it was no use.

"Try to relax," he whispered, glancing up at her again. "Breathe deep and count each breath."

She did as he suggested, keeping her eyes locked on his. All the knots in her muscles began to untie themselves, while she stared at him.

Slowly, the blood washed away, along with the tension in her neck and shoulders. Her breathing slowed.

Lord Alcester bent to look more closely at the gash, then he reached for the bottle of whiskey. "This is going to hurt, but it must be done."

"I understand."

"Squeeze my arm if you have to."

She didn't want to.

He paused to give her time to prepare herself, then poured the alcohol over the wound. He might as well have poured liquid fire on her. Adele clenched her teeth together to keep from crying out.

As soon as he tipped the bottle upright, she leaned forward and squeezed her thigh. "Sweet Mary!" she ground out.

"Apologies." He set the bottle down and reached for the long bandage he'd fashioned from her petticoat. "I'm going to wrap the wound now."

Adele nodded in agreement. He tried to press a smaller bandage to the gash, but she had unconsciously pressed her legs together at the knees. She was clenching her teeth together, too.

He cupped her other knee in his hand and gently pushed her legs apart, again keeping his eyes fixed on hers the entire time. "It's important to do this properly," he said. "Relax if you can."

She struggled to still her racing heart—for no man had ever parted her legs before—and forced herself to surrender to the gentle pressure of his hand.

"Perhaps you could bend your knee slightly?" he politely asked, then he reached for the bandage and wrapped it around her thigh.

His movements were swift and efficient. Before she knew it, he was tying a knot and sitting back. "There. All done. You can breathe now." He lowered her skirt to cover her leg.

She hadn't even realized she was holding her breath until he mentioned it.

He helped her rise but as soon as she attempted to walk, pain flooded through her. She felt suddenly nauseated.

"Let me help you." He wrapped his arm about her waist. "Lean into me. That's it."

She began to limp beside him, and felt the thick, firm muscles of his shoulder and the solid, steady support of his body. He did not waver or lose his balance.

"It will be difficult to walk for a few days," he said.

"But how will we ever get me away from here? For one thing, I don't have shoes. And it will be torture to ride."

"No shoes?" He paused. "Leave that to me. I will ride out at first light and return with a coach and driver for the journey, and I will bring shoes for you."

"What about him?" She gestured toward her kidnapper.

"I will alert the authorities in the morning and have someone come to collect him. Don't worry about a thing. I'll make sure our names are not connected. We'll be long gone by the time they arrive."

They hobbled together into the hall and reached the top of the staircase. Adele stopped and looked down. "This might be a challenge."

"Allow me." He held out his arms.

He meant to carry her? Her heart did a little nervous flip at the thought of it.

Before waiting for her reply, he scooped her into his strong, able arms and descended the narrow steps effortlessly. When he reached the bottom, he carried her to the kitchen, where a faded upholstered chair faced the fireplace. Other than that, the room was unfurnished. There was only a small pile of kindling, some cooking utensils, and provisions to prepare a few meager suppers.

Lord Alcester set her down on the chair. Lightning flashed outside the window. Thunder rumbled almost immediately afterward as darkness began to descend.

"If you will excuse me," he said. "I must take my horse to the stable before the storm is fully upon us."

"Of course." Yet she did not want him to go. She had been trapped alone for three days, helpless and locked in a room. She had just been shot. She was an ocean away from her home, and he was all she had.

Lord Alcester raised his coat collar up around his neck and picked up the hat that lay on the floor. He must have torn it off quickly when he'd first arrived. She remembered the violent commotion that ensued when he'd entered and could only imagine what had occurred.

Settling the hat on his head, he faced her. "The worst is over now."

It was exactly what she had needed to hear. Had he known? He seemed very intuitive.

He opened the door and let in a powerful gust of wind carrying a pattering of cold, hard rain. The gale swept into the cottage and whirled like a tempest, but the room calmed quickly when he slammed the door behind him.

Adele sat alone in the silent kitchen, staring at the door and trying to come to terms with her situation. She couldn't believe that she had been kidnapped and shot. Bookish Adele Wilson, who avoided adventure at all costs....

Her sisters were sure to be shocked when she told them her tale of woe—how she'd been abducted, trapped and finally rescued by a proverbial white knight.

It was embarrassing, actually, to think of him that way. She had always considered those fairy tales to be silly and unrealistic and would have preferred to read about heroines who rescued themselves.

Either way, Lord Alcester was hardly a white knight. He was more of a dark knight. She remembered how intense and angry he had appeared when he burst into her room. Her knees had turned to jelly.

Then he'd killed a man. *For her.*

A cold shiver moved through her as she replayed that horrific moment when she'd gazed into that dark barrel of death. She had been impossibly lucky. If her kidnapper had fired a fraction of a second sooner....

She was immensely grateful to be alive.

And she owed a tremendous debt to Damien Renshaw—her future cousin. True, his reputation was concerning, and she would never get over the embarrassing fact that he had seen her naked thigh. But he had come to her rescue, galloping across England to what felt like the ends of the earth. He had been her champion, when despite her own efforts, she had been unable to rescue herself.

Adele inhaled deeply, glanced at the door and considered the night ahead, trapped in this isolated cottage with such a man.

All at once, she found herself wishing that the man who had come to her rescue had been Harold instead.

Chapter 2

Osulton Manor

"HAROLD SHOULD NOT HAVE SENT him, Mama. It was an unwise decision."

Eustacia Scott, Lady Osulton, lifted her impatient gaze from her embroidery and glared at her daughter across the blue drawing room. "Contrary to what you might think, Violet, your brother is not an unwise man. He trusts his cousin."

"I hardly know why, considering Damien's reputation with women."

"You *do* know why," she replied. "They are the closest of friends, and they share a bond of many years. Damien has always been very protective of Harold, and Harold knows it. He knows Damien would not betray that loyalty."

Violet shook her head at her mother. "That may be true, but this American girl—Miss Wilson.... Can *she* be trusted? Damien is a very attractive man, and you know what they say about those Americans."

"No, I do not know what they say."

"Oh, Mama, don't be so provincial."

"I am not being provincial. I simply do not listen to gossip or idle generalizations."

Violet harrumphed. "The Americans are passionate, Mama. How do you think they won at Yorktown? They were feral and wild, overtaken by a blazing fire in their veins—not unlike Damien can be sometimes. When they want something, they spare nothing to get it. They are like stubborn, unstoppable rams."

Lady Osulton began to stitch faster. "From my understanding, what Miss Wilson wants is *Harold*."

"She wants a title. And Damien has one, too. Plus good looks."

"A lesser title."

Violet raised a severely arched eyebrow. "I don't think it matters to these Americans. One is as good as another."

Lady Osulton laid down her embroidery and gazed across the room in shock. "Surely that cannot be true."

"Oh yes, it is. Most of them don't even *know* that an earl outranks a viscount, or that a marquess outranks an earl. I heard it from the Countess of Lansdowne, and she herself is an American, though no one seems to remember that. She changes her voice, you know, and copies our accents."

Lady Osulton lifted her embroidery again, though she had not fully recovered from the inconceivable notion that *anyone* could think one title was as good as another, American or not. She could barely hide the tremor of incredulity in her voice.

"The Countess of Lansdowne does not concern me. All that matters is that Harold has finally chosen a wife when I thought he would never look up from his silly scientific experiments long enough to even think of it. And if Damien is our most reliable courier to bring her home, then Damien it shall be, because I want that girl delivered to us."

"Oh, Mama. You know her money is her only recommendation."

She laid down her embroidery again. "I know no such thing, and shame on your vulgar tongue!" She pressed the back of her hand to her forehead. "Sometimes I wonder how you and Harold could possibly be brother and sister. He would never say such a thing to torture me. Harold is such a polite boy."

Violet had to work hard not to roll her eyes at her mother's melodrama. "I'm only being honest, Mama. I agree we need the influx of capital... The estate is not performing as it should, and I can't bear another reduction in our spending."

Lady Osulton picked up her embroidery again and resumed her stitching. "Don't talk about that, Violet. You know I don't like it." A moment went by before she spoke again. "The fact is, Harold has taken a fancy to someone, and I am greatly relieved. I don't care where she comes from, and I have every intention of welcoming her into this family like one of our own. She will provide us with an heir, after all. I only want what's best for this family, Violet. That's all. I don't care about the money."

"Of course you don't, Mama."

But it was generally understood by all members of

the prestigious Osulton household that Violet—wanting a substantial dowry of her own to snare the very best husband possible—most certainly did.

The storm raged on, and the cottage creaked and groaned like an old ship. Damien sat on the floor, slouching against the wall while sipping coffee out of a tin cup, his long legs stretched out in front of him, one bent at the knee.

He gazed at Miss Wilson's profile in the firelight while she sat before the hearth watching the flames dance, and wondered why Harold had neglected to mention that she was so beautiful.

"I have found the perfect woman," Harold had said with a dumbfounded, besotted smile upon his return from America. "She is so good, I believe she must be a saint. She is polite and obedient with her parents. She is agreeable and genuine. I don't believe she is even capable of having a bad thought. She is purity and goodness and perfection personified, and her favorite thing in the world is books. Do you hear that, Damien? Books. What were the odds that I would find such a woman?"

For some reason, Damien had imagined Miss Wilson would be plain. She was many things, but not that.

Regarding the other qualities Harold had described, Damien couldn't argue. Harold was right. There was something sweet and angelic in her nature. Damien knew it now, even after meeting her only hours ago in the most disturbing and extraordinary circumstances. The woman exuded virtue.

He disregarded the virtue for a brief moment, however, to let his experienced gaze roam over her beguiling physical attributes. She had long, graceful legs and a curvaceous figure. With freckles and full lips and honey-gold hair, she was the sort of woman who could make a man dream of things that were— in a polite manner of speaking—quite the *opposite* of pure and saintly. Which was ironic, he thought, feeling slightly amused as he imagined the men who must have salivated over her in the past—and gone to confession straight afterward, whether they were Catholic or not.

Damien took another sip of his coffee. Truth be told, if she were any other woman than his cousin's virginal fiancée, he would likely be sharing the chair with her right now...holding her on his lap, offering comfort in the form of gentle caresses and softly spoken words. They were stranded alone in a remote cottage, after all, and she had suffered a terrible ordeal. Surely she was in need of solace.

As he continued to watch her, however, he came to the opinion that she was made of sterner stuff than that. There had been no tears today. No hysterics. She'd remained calm and clearheaded through all of it. In fact, she'd earned his respect the instant she'd announced her name, while holding a chair up over her head.

A gust of wind whistled down the chimney and shook the flames. Miss Wilson sighed. Damien looked at the tattered dress she wore and imagined what she might look like in her opulent Newport mansion, wrapped in silks and jewels. She was probably desperate for her maid.

"I suppose this is not the sort of lodgings to which you are accustomed," he said as he raised his coffee cup to his lips. "Let me guess. You are dreaming of your gold-plated bathtub back in New York."

She tilted her head at him. "I beg your pardon, Lord Alcester. You are mistaken if you presume I am over-indulged and have never known hardship."

Enticed by her unexpected response, Damien rested an elbow on his knee. "You're not?"

"No," she replied somewhat tentatively.

How damnably charming she looked. He raised his eyebrows, waiting for her to continue.

"I don't mean to sound defensive," she said, "but I wouldn't wish you to be misinformed about your cousin's future wife. Or to entertain prejudices about Americans in general."

He narrowed his eyes, suddenly in the mood to goad her a little. "But I thought all American heiresses were overindulged."

She paused, as if taken aback. "No. That is not so, my lord. Not so at all. In fact, I'll wager that I've survived worse circumstances than you have. I can't imagine you've ever gone hungry or went around without shoes on a regular basis each summer— indoors *and* out."

"Without shoes?" He had to concede. She had him with that. She also surprised him with her "wager." Perhaps there was a touch of an adventurous spirit lurking somewhere in the depths of this perfect angelic creature after all.

She seemed to suddenly comprehend the implications of her argument, and squeezed her eyes shut. "I shouldn't have said that. You English already think we are beneath you as it is."

"*You English?*" he repeated, drawing his dark brows together, feeling very pleasantly intrigued by their conversation. "Clearly *we English* are not the only ones with prejudices. *Tsk tsk*, Miss Wilson. What is the world coming to when people of different nationalities cannot get along, I ask you?"

She stared at him for a few seconds, looking surprised until she realized he was teasing her. Then she smiled. It was a dazzling smile—sweet and scintillating at the same time, and so very genuine.

It was the first time Damien had seen her smile. She'd been nervous and uncomfortable until this moment, looking at him as if he were something to be feared. Perhaps now she might relax.

He, on the other hand, felt his own sense of ease slip.

Damien dropped his gaze to his coffee, suddenly understanding very well why Harold had been so taken with her. Not only was she splendid in every way a woman could be in the physical sense, but there was something elusive and indefinable about her as well—a sensual, earthy nature that seemed to glow with warmth. A man like Harold, who was shy around women, would be seduced by such natural charisma.

When their smiles died away, she returned to the thread of their conversation. "I suppose Harold described my summer home in Newport to you," she explained, "and it didn't sound at all like I had to go without shoes."

"He told me about your diamond-studded champagne glasses."

She was suitably embarrassed and lowered her gaze, shrugging as if to apologize for the glasses.

Damien seized the opportunity to glance down at the lovely fullness of her bosom beneath her thick, wool bodice. He experienced a pang of guilt, because she belonged to his cousin, but that was quickly overcome when he returned his gaze to her face and made a solemn vow to keep it there.

"We didn't always have money," she said innocently, which charmed him, because she was not even remotely aware of his interest in her bosom. "Papa earned his first fortune on Wall Street when I was ten." She stared pensively into the fire. "Sometimes when I look at my life, it seems like it's divided into two. Before the money, and after. So you see, I am not quite as overindulged as you think. At least, I wasn't always." She inhaled and let the breath out slowly, as if reminiscing.

"I miss those old days," she said. "I used to enjoy running about barefoot. I still do on occasion, when I'm alone in the woods, which unfortunately is very rare. But *please,*" she said, her bright smile returning, "keep the part about my running about barefoot to yourself."

He inclined his head, trying not to become too diverted by the enticing image of her doing *anything* barefoot.

"But perhaps I owe it to Harold to tell him," Damien said. "He doesn't know he's about to marry a wood nymph."

Her responding smile made his breath catch.

She let her head tip onto the chair back and gazed into the flames again, looking tired. Damien allowed her some peace, though he couldn't tear his gaze away from her enchanting profile. As he watched her in the firelight, he contemplated their situation.

If she were a different woman, and these were different circumstances, he would probably find a way to have her tonight. In his arms. Crying out his name as he took her to the heights of passion.

But she was *not* another woman—she was his cousin's intended—so he would not have her. Tonight, or any other night. He should not even think about it.

"It's getting late," Lord Alcester said, rising to put another log on the fire. "You must be tired. I can help you up the stairs if you wish."

Adele watched his broad back as he set the log on the charred remains of another and used the poker to stir the heat. She felt a tremor of panic. She did not want to go back upstairs. She'd been locked in that room for three days, and her kidnapper was still up there. Dead.

Lord Alcester leaned the poker against the stone hearth and turned to face her. He stared down at her for a long moment. "I'll move the body," he said, as if he'd read her thoughts.

She considered it, but the sickening dread remained. "I would rather not go back up there. Could I sleep down here?"

He gazed at her for another few seconds, and she recognized a flicker of sympathy and compassion in his eyes—an expression that eased the tension in her shoulders.

"Of course. I'll bring the bedding down."

He immediately went upstairs, and she listened to the sounds of his movements across the floor, then his boots tapping slowly back down the stairs. He reappeared with the hay tick, dragging it across the floor and setting it down a safe distance away from the fire. He took the blankets and shook them out on the other side of the room, then spread them on the tick.

"Sleep here," he said. "I can go upstairs to give you privacy, or sleep in the chair, whichever you prefer."

"The chair, if you don't mind," she told him.

He nodded, then held out his hand. "May I assist you?"

She allowed him to help her up, then crawled onto the makeshift bed and pulled the rough wool blanket over her.

"I'll be glad to leave this place," she said, lying back and looking up at him where he stood tall over her.

"That is understandable." He turned and knelt in front of the fire again and used the poker to move the log, making sure it was catching the flame. Then he sat down in the chair.

Adele closed her eyes and tried to go to sleep. The only sound in the room was the crackling of the fire. After about a half hour, Adele opened her eyes and looked at her rescuer.

"I can't sleep," she said. "I haven't been able to sleep at all over the past few days. Could we talk a little longer?"

"Of course. What would you like to talk about?"

She thought about it, then rolled onto her side and rested her cheek on her hands. "Tell me about Harold's home—*Osulton Manor*. Have you been there?"

"Been there?" he said, sounding surprised at her question. "I was raised there."

She rose up on her elbows. "You grew up with Harold?"

"Yes. We're like brothers. You didn't know that?"

"No. Harold and I didn't have much time together in New York," she explained. "Do your parents live at Osulton as well?"

"My parents died when I was nine. That's why I was sent to live with Harold's family until I was old enough to take over my father's estate."

"I'm very sorry."

He looked into the fire. "I suppose my life is divided in two, as well."

Adele nodded compassionately. "Do you visit Osulton often these days?" she asked.

He seemed to require a moment to think about how to answer that question. He tilted his head from side to side. "As it happens, I am residing there again—temporarily—because I've rented out my London house for the Season, and I'm looking for tenants for my country house as well."

Because of money problems, she presumed.

The conversation died for a few minutes. The wind whistled through the chimney, and the flames danced chaotically.

Lord Alcester leaned his temple on a finger and stared down at her. "Tell me about how you met Harold."

Adele was happy to resume their conversation. She had spent too many days alone upstairs to enjoy any kind of silence now. "We met in Newport," she replied, lying back on her side again. "As you know, he had taken a holiday in America over the winter, and my mother heard of his visit and arranged a ball in his honor. It was quite the affair," she added, smiling. "Every Knickerbocker in New York was scrambling for an invitation."

"Knickerbocker?"

Adele smiled again. "Would you like the long, drawn-out explanation?"

He gestured with his hand. "We certainly don't have much else to do."

She sat up. "All right then. Let me describe the social hierarchy of America to you. There is a very defined line between Old Money and New. I—as you may have guessed—am *New* Money. My father earned his fortune almost overnight, and as I mentioned before, took us from our one-room cabin in Wisconsin to a mansion on Fifth Avenue quicker than you can blink. To get to the point, Old Money is inherited, and those who have it are called Knickerbockers because most of them are descended from the early Dutch settlers who wore knee-length trousers. Like you, they can trace their family's heritage back through generations. They live in Washington Square in plain brownstones, and consider themselves the social elite, while people like us are vulgar because we build showy mansions in the newer neighborhoods. And I will admit, our house is obscenely showy, but that's my mother. She loves everything to be grandiose."

Lord Alcester's lips turned up in a grin.

"I think you'll like her," Adele continued, lying back down. "Or at the very least, you'll find her amusing. She doesn't put on any airs and sometimes ignores or protests certain social graces that have no practicality, which I suppose is why the Knickerbockers give her such a difficult time."

Lord Alcester leaned forward to rest his elbows on his knees, his gaze intent upon hers. "I had no idea there was such a pecking order in America. I thought it was a classless society."

"On paper, perhaps," she replied, tossing an arm up under her head again, "but if you could walk in my shoes in Newport for one day, you would feel the divisions as clearly as you feel your own here in England. It's like walking into a brick wall sometimes."

He leaned back again, his dark eyes studying her with a serious intensity that unnerved her. "I am much enlightened, Miss Wilson. Was Harold aware of all this when he attended your ball? I can't imagine he was."

"No, I don't believe so. And I certainly wasn't about to tell him." She recognized her blunder as soon as she said it and felt her cheeks drain of color.

Lord Alcester chuckled softly and crossed one booted leg over the other. "Don't fret. Your secret is safe with me. It wouldn't have mattered to him anyway. In his eyes, you're either English or you're not."

It should have been Lord Alcester's turn to go pale, but he brushed it off with a clever retort. "In your case, you are most decidedly *not* English, and thank goodness for that, or I would be immensely bored right now."

The flattery came a little too close to a flirtation, and a flock of butterflies invaded Adele's stomach. She was reminded of Lord Alcester's scandalous reputation and felt a sudden measure of unease.

"How did you go from a ball to a proposal?" he asked, bringing the conversation back around to her and Harold.

Adele looked up at the ceiling, determined to focus on the questions instead of the man. She thought about how quickly she and Harold had become engaged and could attribute it to one very obvious catalyst.

"When you meet my mother," she explained, "I'm sure you'll notice that she is very ambitious and often impatient about getting what she wants. She has spared nothing to be accepted by the Knickerbockers in New York—and she's managed to accomplish that since my sisters married a duke and a marquess. When she decided Harold was the one for me, she was equally determined."

"*She* decided?"

Adele tried to explain. "Well...yes, she was the one to suggest that he would be a good match for me. My father came into the equation then. He was impressed with some of Harold's ideas about science, and I believe he would like to be involved in one of Harold's experiments—something to do with a new type of dye. He sees business potential there."

"Does he indeed? Harold didn't mention that to me."

"Well, it's all just in the idea stage. At any rate, my mother held a few more assemblies and invited Harold, and it wasn't long before we both realized that she was right, and we were very comfortable with each other. I liked his sense of tradition, and he liked my—"

"Yes?" Alcester leaned forward, radiating an intensity she'd never encountered in a person before. This cousin was a very potent human being, she realized, and she supposed that was why he had a reputation. Women were no doubt attracted to such strength, with a handsome face to go along with it. Even Adele found him intriguing, and certainly unnerving as well. He was her future cousin by marriage, however, so she would have to get used to him.

"Well...." Her insides jangled. "He said he thought I would fit in very well in England, and I believe that is why we were drawn to each other. Compared to most other American women my age, I am perhaps more reserved than most. Perhaps he liked that about me."

He studied her for a moment. "You don't seem sure that's the reason."

"Well, I suppose I can only guess at why Harold thought I would fit in. He didn't actually *tell* me."

Lord Alcester sat back again. "He told *me*. Would you like to know what he said?"

She felt instantly wide awake. "He told you?"

"Yes. We're not only cousins, we are friends as well."

Adele found it odd that they were so close, considering how different they were in every way. Harold was shy and slightly awkward and never threatening, while Lord Alcester had an unmistakable hard edge to him. He was very confident. Especially around women. Reputedly, according to her sister, Sophia.

Lord Alcester rested his temple on a finger again. "Harold told me that he admired your goodness. He even went so far as to say you might be a saint."

Adele plucked at the woolly blanket over her legs. "Ah. A saint."

"That doesn't please you?"

Adele wet her lips. "Lord Alcester, it's strange. People have always told me how good I am, how agreeable and dependable. They look at me and they think I can do no wrong. Even my parents have always thought that. I don't know why. I don't know where it started. I certainly didn't *try* to be a well-behaved child. I just was. At least, compared to my sisters, who were always trying to get me to join them in their mischief. The point is, I don't know why I am perceived that way. I don't consider myself overly righteous. Sometimes I even feel like an impostor."

"Have you ever done anything you knew was wrong?"

She considered the question carefully. "Not really. I've made mistakes, of course. Everyone has."

"Have you ever *wanted* to do anything wrong?"

A vivid memory of a red candy stick came swirling into her mind. She had seen it at the mercantile in Wisconsin when she was very small, but she'd had no money.

"I once thought about stealing something when I was a child," she said. "A piece of candy."

"But you didn't."

"No, I didn't. It was very tempting, though," she added with a smile. "It was the brightest, most colorful candy stick I'd ever seen, with a cherry drawn on the tag. I knew it would fit perfectly into my pocket, and no one would know if I was sneaky enough. I kept staring at it, imagining how I would hide it and keep it secret from my sisters. I picked it up and held it in my hand."

He smiled and nodded, seeming to understand. "But you didn't take it," he reminded her.

"No, I put it back. So maybe I *am* a saint," she said, mocking his insight. "If you could have seen that candy stick—"

"I'll bet it was delicious."

She sighed. "I've always wondered."

They watched the fire for a few more minutes until Lord Alcester stood. He picked up the cushion from the chair and tossed it onto the floor close to the fire, but a few feet away from where Adele lay. "I think if I am to sleep, I'll need to stretch out," he said.

Adele shifted to get more comfortable. "The floor won't be too hard? Or too cold?"

He lay down on his side, facing her. "Not at all. This is a fine pillow, and my coat is warm. I expect to sleep quite well, in fact, because I found you today. Now I can finally relax and close my eyes." He stared at her for a few seconds. "Good night, Miss Wilson."

"Good night." Adele snuggled into her makeshift bed but continued to watch him in the firelight. She had to admit she was intrigued by him. He was so very different from Harold, yet they were close. She would like to know why and how.

I expect to sleep quite well because I found you today. Now I can finally relax and close my eyes.

She pondered that and imagined him riding across England on a mission to rescue her. He'd had to contend with the prospect of facing a kidnapper, or the prospect of finding her harmed. Or dead. He had likely worried over that prospect.

And now, he had fulfilled his duty to Harold. His cousin and friend.

Adele could only assume that Harold had been worried, too. She did not know because he had not come himself, but surely, he had lost sleep over her abduction. She certainly had. She was exhausted. Yet tonight, like the past three nights in a row, she did not want to close her eyes.

This ordeal had been very difficult. She would be happy to return to her normal, safe life.

Waking to the budding light of dawn the next morning, Damien opened his eyes. He lay on his side and looked at Miss Wilson across from him. She was asleep, facing him, her cheek resting on her hands, the blanket pulled up to her chin. Her lips were parted slightly, and her breathing was slow and steady. It would be best, he decided, if he could rise without waking her, and simply leave to fetch a coach and driver.

He rose up on an elbow and looked around. The fire had gone out sometime during the night, and the cottage was cold. Damien blew into his fists to warm his hands. Miss Wilson made no sound, so he quietly rose to his feet.

He stood gazing down at her in the early light of the morning. She was impossibly beautiful. Harold must have been distracted by something substantial to have forgotten to mention such a thing. Damien wondered if Harold realized how lucky he was, and if his cousin had been fighting lustful thoughts ever since he'd met her in America last spring.

It was difficult, however, to imagine Harold having lustful thoughts about anything except his chemistry experiments. He had never described Adele—or any other woman, for that matter—in such a way. But he got a certain hot and bothered look in his eye when bubbles started to form in a beaker.

Harold should have come, Damien thought suddenly with a slight twinge of reproach as he considered what Adele had suffered. How could Harold have trusted this important task to someone else, even if that someone was Damien, his cousin and best friend? How could Harold sleep at night, not knowing if his beautiful fiancée was dead or alive? At the very least, he could have accompanied Damien.

But Damien supposed that Harold had always preferred to keep his head in the sand, and likely always would. Damien and the rest of the family even helped Harold to bury his head on occasion. They often dealt with certain household problems themselves, keeping Harold in the dark, knowing that he preferred it that way because he loathed anything that got in the way of his experiments.

In the very next instant, Damien felt guilty for being critical of Harold, his friend, who was a kind-hearted and principled person. Like Adele. Perhaps they were a perfect match.

When it didn't appear that Miss Wilson would stir

any time soon, Damien combed his fingers through his hair and rubbed his face. He went outside and fetched a fresh bucket of water for Adele from the well and set it down quietly in front of the chair. He stared at her for another few seconds, admiring the slender curve of her hips and the feminine shape of her hands. He imagined her as a girl, staring long-ingly at that candy stick, and felt an odd mixture of amusement and pity. He wondered how many cherry candy-sticks she had resisted in her life, how many she had never tasted. Then he thought of Harold again. Harold would probably be very pleased that she had not taken the candy.

Damien, on the other hand, wished he could get her one. He wouldn't steal it, of course. He would pay for it. He would just like to see her face when she tasted it. He would enjoy watching her expression.

He shook his head at himself and silently headed for the door. It was probably a good thing that they were leaving and heading back to civilization. Because Damien was beginning to find Miss Wilson far more appealing than he should.

Chapter 3

SHORTLY BEFORE NOON, ADELE WENT outside to meet Lord Alcester, who rode into the yard on his big, black horse. He swung down from the high saddle and landed gracefully on the ground. A coach was behind him, rumbling slowly up the hill.

His hair was like a wild mane around his face, his coat blowing in the wind. It was difficult to imagine that this man was related by blood to her fiancé, for they were remarkably different in every way. Harold had red hair, and though he was tall, he was very slender, with small hands. Damien's hands were large and strong.

"You shouldn't be out here," he said. "You'll catch your death."

"I've been stuck in there for three days," she replied. "I couldn't bear it anymore."

He glanced down at her feet, which were bare. "Isn't it a little chilly to be a wood nymph this morning?"

She met his smiling eyes and recognized the power of his charm. It was no wonder he had so many eager lady friends. "You know I have no shoes."

"I have not forgotten. There are stockings and shoes for you in the coach."

She turned and watched as it slowly rumbled up the hill. Lord Alcester was very good at taking care of things, she realized. It was easy to rely on him.

"Thank you."

She limped beside him while he led his horse to the trough.

"I know this is unpleasant business, Miss Wilson," he said, "but someone will be along to collect the body after we're gone, and we'll have to speak to the magistrate tonight. He's given me his word that he'll keep it quiet, and I trust him. Will you be able to discuss it?"

"Of course."

"How is your wound, by the way?" he asked.

A vision of his hands on her leg jolted her. She forcefully pushed the recollection away. "It feels a bit better this morning. It's not so difficult to walk. But I didn't sleep well."

His eyes were downcast as he watched his horse drink from the nearly overflowing trough. The wind blew a part in his thick, black hair and revealed dark brows against his sun-bronzed skin. If Adele were an artist, she would paint him as Michael, the warrior angel. She had seen a statue of Michael in Paris once, when she had spent time there with her sisters, learning to speak French. She never forgot it. She often dreamed about that statue.

For some reason, she thought of Lord Alcester's mistress at that moment, the famous actress. From what

Sophia had said, the woman was very beautiful and liberal. She enjoyed taking lovers, and by all accounts, she was just the sort of woman Lord Alcester desired. Theirs was purportedly a passionate love affair.

It was difficult for Adele to imagine any woman being so free, not worrying about duty or correct behavior. To even *think* about such a woman—to have any connection to her whatsoever—seemed strange for Adele, who had led an exceedingly sheltered and proper life. She didn't know a single person who'd had a "lover" and spoken about it.

"I also sent a wire to Harold," he said, "to inform him that you're safe and he can expect you in two days."

"I hope he'll pass that message on to my mother," Adele said. "She must be worried sick."

"From what I understand, your mother will be traveling by train to meet us. You and I will travel by coach and check into an inn this evening. We'll tell everyone we encounter that you are my sister." Lord Alcester tethered his horse to the post next to the trough. "And I am pleased to announce that you can anticipate a hearty dinner by a warm fire this evening."

"I can hardly wait."

Lord Alcester walked to the edge of the yard. "Here is the coach."

A moment later, it pulled up and Adele limped toward it. She climbed in, pleased by the interior of the vehicle with its soft blue upholstery. A box tied up with a ribbon sat there on the seat.

Lord Alcester stood at the open door, his large frame

casting a shadow as the sun came out from behind a cloud. "Shoes and stockings."

"Thank you."

While she gazed at his handsome face in the sunlight, she felt almost entranced. In an effort to distract herself, she peered out the window at his horse, still tethered by the trough. "You're lucky you get to ride."

"Do you like to ride?" he asked, sounding surprised.

"Yes. I sold my hair when I was seven to keep my father from selling our pony when we couldn't afford to keep her. I just couldn't live without her, or without the freedom to explore the woods where we lived."

He lifted his chin, gesturing toward his own horse. "We have something in common. I've been leasing out my London house to keep *him*."

Adele's eyebrows lifted.

"Do you still have that pony you loved so much?" he asked.

"No. She died when I was nine. I explored the woods on foot after that—until we moved to the city."

He hesitated at the door. "You'll like *Osulton Manor*. It's surrounded by forest, and the stable is stocked with thoroughbreds."

"Really? Harold didn't mention that. I can't wait to get there."

He nodded. "Signal if you need anything."

"I will."

Lord Alcester closed the door. She watched him from the window as he waved to the driver and strode toward his own horse. He swung himself up into the saddle and led the way out of the yard.

The coach slowly turned around, and before Adele

knew it, she was rocking back and forth on the seat as they made their way down the hill and back to real life. Though she wasn't sure anything would ever be completely normal again.

Osulton Manor

"He found her! She's safe and on her way home!"

Eustacia waved the telegram over her head as she dashed into the brightly lit conservatory. Or rather, the brightly lit laboratory, as it had been cleared of plants a number of years ago and lovingly dedicated to the ambitious pursuit of chemical science.

Harold lifted his gaze from the beaker of bubbling liquid that stood before him. His protective eyewear was covered in steam, so he pushed the large glasses off his face to rest on top of his curly, red hair. "I beg your pardon, Mother? Did you say she was safe?"

"Yes!"

"Are you referring to Miss Wilson?" he asked.

His mother skidded to a halt before him. "Of course I am, you silly, silly man! She's safe! Damien found her!"

Harold took the telegram from his mother and read it. "Well, that is indeed good news. I told you Damien was the right man for the job."

"Yes, you were right as always. He no doubt put that despicable kidnapper in his place and.... Well, let us not go into that. We know how Damien can put up a good fight. The point is, they're on their way home! They'll be here in two days."

"Two days. You don't say."

"I do say, Harold. You'll have to get a haircut."

"Yes, I believe you're right."

"And we must plan a special dinner in Miss Wilson's honor. She is the future Lady Osulton, after all. Would roast lamb do? Or do you think she would prefer beef? I believe Americans are beef eaters, are they not? You were there. You should know. Or perhaps they eat so much of it, it's become a bore. Oh, Harold, what should it be?"

Harold looked down at his beaker. The bubbles had disappeared. "I don't know, Mother. You decide." He slid his protective eyewear back down and leaned close. "What the devil happened?" he muttered to himself. "The bubbles were there a minute ago."

That evening at the inn, after Adele had bathed and spoken to the magistrate, she prepared for supper. She had to don the same homespun dress she'd been wearing for the past three days, but at least she felt clean.

She left her bedchamber and went to the dining room. A movement to her left caught her eye, and she spotted Lord Alcester making his way across the room to greet her. He offered his arm. "Good evening, Miss Wilson. Our table is this way."

He had bathed, too, and shaved. His hair, still damp, was slicked back off his face. He looked.... Well, he looked....

Different.

He escorted her to a table in the far corner. It was covered with a white tablecloth and there was a vase of fresh daisies next to a decanter of wine. A candle burned in a small jar.

Adele stared down at it. "I can't begin to describe

how good it feels to be among civilized people again, and to look at such a lovely table laid out with such care." She gazed up at him. "I've been eating nothing but bread and turnip for the past three days."

He nodded with understanding, then moved behind her to pull out her chair. "Then it will be my pleasure, Miss Wilson, to provide you with what you've been missing. I'm happy to report that the food here is excellent." He took his seat opposite her. "I took the liberty of ordering the wine. I hope you'll join me in a toast."

"I'd be delighted."

He poured her a glass, then lifted his own. "To life and marriage."

"To both."

Over the next hour, they discussed light topics—the artwork in the dining room, the population of the village and surrounding areas, the weather, of course, and the route they would take to reach *Osulton Manor*.

Soon the food arrived, and they enjoyed their dinner while the pink hue of twilight streamed in through the lace-covered window and lent a relaxed, magical atmosphere to the room. Their conversation relaxed as well, as it drifted toward more personal topics.

"So you know how Harold and I met," Adele said, recalling her curiosity about this man the night before when she had watched him falling asleep. "Now tell me a little about yourself, Lord Alcester. You wear no wedding ring. How have you managed to avoid marriage for so long?"

It was a bold question, she knew, but she didn't feel quite herself. This was not her life, she supposed. It was "Adele on an Adventure."

"It's been no small feat, I assure you," he replied. "Both my aunt and my grandmother would like to see me attached as soon as possible, and they become more and more determined each year. I predict my aunt and your mother will get along famously. They'll be kindred spirits, matchmaking to their heart's delight."

Adele imagined what his life was like as an English nobleman, where a sense of duty was probably fed into his veins from infancy onward. "I suppose it's your goal in life, isn't it, to make a good marriage and produce heirs?"

Good God. Produce heirs? She was feeling bold, not scandalous. Perhaps she'd had too much wine.

"Yes, exactly. Not to put too fine a point on it, but I had best get to it. I'm not getting any younger." With a wicked grin that made her squirm in her chair, he picked up the bottle and tipped it over her glass, but she firmly held up a hand.

"No, thank you, I've probably had enough. Please feel free to finish it."

He didn't argue. He poured the rest of the wine into his own glass and took another sip. He didn't seem the least bit affected by it. Quite unlike her.

"Don't get me wrong," he said, "I adore my aunt and grandmother, and nothing would please me more than to make them happy, but I have yet to discover the one woman who makes me...." He paused. The candlelight flickered between them. "The one who makes me want to be a husband. I don't want to marry just anyone and be miserable. That doesn't do anyone any good."

"Well, happiness is indeed an important part of life to consider," she said, feeling a great need to bring her fiancé into this conversation. "Harold, for instance, has made me indescribably happy on so many occasions."

"Has he indeed? In what way, may I ask? Perhaps I should consult him in matters of romance. It sounds as if he could provide some helpful advice."

Adele stared at the electrifying glimmer in the viscount's eyes which almost seemed to challenge her. She noticed suddenly that they were both leaning forward with their elbows on the table. She sat back and couldn't help reaching for her wine again.

"I hardly think you need advice, my lord. I know about your reputation." She surprised herself with that comment.

"Do you, now? Where in the world would you hear such a thing? Does news like that reach America?"

"My sister told me. She mentioned it in a letter when Harold was still in America."

"I see." He took a deep swig of wine, then casually shrugged.

"You're not denying it," Adele said, shocked in some ways, but not in others. Lord Alcester didn't seem all that concerned with what was proper. He was like no one she'd ever met.

"No, I am not denying it, because it's all true. I am without a doubt the worst scoundrel in London. You had best keep your distance."

He smiled with riveting splendor, and *boom,* there it was in full force. The pounding allure that her sister had described, and she herself had witnessed on so many occasions leading up to this one. The sweet, seductive power that even Adele—inexperienced as she was with men—could recognize. The very qualities that made him notorious. A strangely pleasant, dizzying haze moved over her thoughts as she stared at him.

The server came and took their plates away. As soon as she was gone, Adele became aware of her heart beating shockingly fast. An unfamiliar thrill was rippling through her veins and she didn't like it.

Feeling shaken by her body's response to Lord Alcester, she thrust the haze away and forced her thoughts back to their earlier conversation. "Perhaps you're right. You haven't married because you simply haven't met the right woman yet," she said, struggling to recover her calm. "When you do, everything will seem effortless, and you will defy your reputation and find the happiness that you seek."

She saw his Adam's apple bob. "I'm not sure," he said, his voice low and husky, "that I will ever be able to know true happiness, Miss Wilson, even if I encountered Venus herself."

She stared at him across the table, bewildered by this surprising declaration, and more than a little curious about his meaning. "Why would you think such a thing?"

He said nothing for a moment, then he drummed his long fingers on the tabletop. "There is no good reason for me to think it, Miss Wilson."

The server appeared and asked if they wished to have dessert—almond cakes and cream.

Lord Alcester leaned back in his chair. "That sounds

rather delicious."

Adele held up a hand. "I couldn't eat another bite."

"Tea? Coffee?"

She shook her head and the server went away. Lord Alcester rested both hands on his thighs. "It seems our dinner has come to an end."

Though she couldn't possibly eat any more, Adele had to confess, she didn't want the night to end. She wanted to keep talking to him. Proper decorum, however—and the sensible, warning voice in her brain—required her to politely agree and take her leave.

He helped her from her chair. "We'll get an early start tomorrow," he said, "and meet your mother by noon the following day if the weather holds. Is seven too early for you?"

"Seven is fine. Thank you, my lord, for everything you've done."

His eyes were warm. The seduction was gone now. "It has been my pleasure, Miss Wilson."

She smiled one last time, then retired to her room.

Damien lay in bed that night with his arms up under his head, staring at the ceiling and remembering the conversation he'd had with Harold less than a week ago...

"I've never given you advice before, Damien. God knows it's usually the other way around. I feel clumsy even thinking of it, but here it is: Your creditors have been getting more aggressive lately, and things seem to be coming to a head. Maybe it's time you looked for a bride."

Damien had known that was coming. He'd been considering it himself. "A wealthy bride, you mean."

"It wouldn't be difficult. Not for you, with all your appeal with the ladies. Certainly, if I could do it..."

"You think I should go to America," Damien said.

"Yes, I do."

"But you know how I feel about marriage for profit."

Harold stiffened. "Unfortunately, it's my duty as your closest confidante to try and convince you that not all arranged marriages end badly like your parents' did. Some can turn out very well. I'm sure mine will."

"I would prefer not to leave anything to chance," Damien told him.

Harold sank into a chair. "All that aside, I know how wretched your financial situation has become, and that's perhaps the point of this conversation. There was another creditor here today...."

Damien rolled over on the bed as the weight of the world settled on his shoulders. He reconsidered his cousin's suggestion. If there were other women like Adele Wilson in America, perhaps Damien should consider it. It would solve a host of problems, to be sure. Money problems, for one.

And after today, there were other problems, too. More than once that evening, Damien had found himself staring across the table at Adele and wanting her for himself. Not only was she beautiful, but she was virtuous and honorable as well. The perfect woman. Nothing like Damien's own mother.

He wondered selfishly how much Harold really wanted Adele. How disappointed would he be if he lost her? Was there a chance her father's business interest in his experiments was what fueled their hasty engagement? Or had Harold, for the first time in his life, fallen in love? It was not unlikely, Damien thought, now that he had met Adele and seen for himself the full measure and depth of her beauty, both inside and out.

Damien shook his head at himself. He should not even be pondering such questions. Harold's happiness mattered to him deeply. Though perhaps at times, a little too deeply because he was extremely protective of Harold. Everyone said so.

Regardless of his feelings of loyalty toward Harold, however, his thoughts darted back to Adele. He imagined her in her bed. He imagined going to check on her. What would happen if he did? Would he stay very long? Would she be glad to see him?

He cupped his forehead in his hand and squeezed his eyes shut. "Bloody hell."

You should not have sent me, Harold. You should have sent someone else....

Chapter 4

*D*AMIEN WOKE TO THE SOUND of a scream in the night. He was out of bed and into the hall before he even thought to put on a shirt. Another scream rent the air—a woman shouting, "Get out!"

Adrenaline sped through his veins as he ran to Adele's door and jiggled the knob, but it was locked. He slammed his shoulder against it, again and again, until it gave way and opened, smacking against the inside wall and bouncing back.

Damien crossed the dark room in two swift strides and took hold of Adele, who was flailing on the bed. He wrapped his hands around her upper arms. "Adele, it's me. It's Damien."

She sat up and shoved him away and began to slap at him, smacking his face and arms and shoulders until he had to restrain her.

"You're dreaming. Wake up!"

She fought him for a few more seconds, then stopped suddenly. She sat very still, staring at him, and it was only then that Damien noticed the sound of footsteps in the hall and raised voices.

He watched her face in the bluish moonlight that beamed in the window and recognized the look of terror in her eyes. She bowed her head and covered her face with her hands. "It was just a dream."

His body began to ache with the most unsettling desire to draw her onto his lap, cocoon her in his arms and press his lips to hers to kiss away the terror. Then he sensed the presence of others in the doorway behind him.

"Are you all right, miss?" a male voice asked. "Do you know this man?"

Damien quickly stood while Adele nodded and sat back. She wiped the sweat from her face. "Yes, I know him. I'm sorry. I didn't mean to cause such a disturbance."

"Do you need assistance?"

"No, thank you." She looked into Damien's eyes. "This man is my protector."

There was a curious silence, then whispers as the spectators returned to bed. Adele's breathing slowed, and she wiped the perspiration from her face again.

"I should leave you now," Damien said as he made a move for the door, but Adele grabbed hold of his hand. Her grip was tight, her palm clammy.

"Please don't go yet."

He gazed down at her in the moonlight, and his chest heaved with dread. There was some truth to his reputation, after all. He enjoyed making love to beautiful women, and Adele was, in no uncertain terms, beautiful. More than beautiful. She was exquisitely lush and fresh and innocent. She was nothing like

Harold's terribly deficient description.

He glanced down at her slender hand on his arm and felt the warmth of her fingers. He was glad she had stopped him because he didn't want to leave.

But pleasure turned quickly to concern as he found himself speculating again about Harold's true feelings for her. Would he be all that disappointed to lose her?

It was a selfish thought. Things would get complicated if he didn't soon smother this attraction and leave the room.

Adele gazed up at him with pleading eyes. "Please stay for a while, until I fall asleep. I'm frightened. I don't want to be alone."

Damien shook his head. She had no idea what she was asking and who she was saying it to. He was a man of questionable repute. A man who could desire her. She should not be so trusting.

His gaze fell to the top of her shift and the smooth expanse of her neck, and he imagined how he would explain an indiscretion to Harold. He imagined Harold's reaction. Then all at once, Damien was overcome with shame. It came out of the past, from a day when he was only nine.

Damien remembered the look on his father's face when he'd told him what his wife—Damien's mother—had been doing and where she had gone. He remembered his father's sobs and tears at the betrayal. Then he remembered his own tears, not long afterward, when his mother and father were each lowered into the ground.

No. Seducing Adele was not something Damien could ever do.

Then he noticed she was squeezing her hands together in her lap, and he knew she was still afraid of the nightmare. He felt a stirring of compassion and tried to focus all his attention on that.

He told himself he would try to ease her fears, but he would make it clear that he could not, under any circumstances, spend the night in the same bed with her. Neither his conscience, nor his integrity, would allow that.

Moonlight streamed in the windows and gave the room an unearthly glow as Adele waited for Lord Alcester's reply. She gazed up at him standing shirtless before her.

A strange mixture of fear from the dream and memories of statues of nude men she had seen in Paris stirred in her mind. She recalled the muscular curves that had mesmerized her, the width and breadth of the shoulders, and the finely chiseled faces. Damien was no less magnificent standing before her now. He could be a god. A great work of art.

For a few awkward seconds, he stared down at her. When he finally spoke, his voice was deep and quiet. "It wouldn't be right for me to stay, Adele."

She wasn't sure if he referenced the strict code of behavior they both lived by, where an unmarried lady such as herself would be irreparably ruined if the people in the inn discovered she'd had a gentleman in her bedchamber at night—or if he referred to something else more specific. More personal. Something unspoken. Something to do with the open way they had interacted at dinner.

"I don't care," she said, thinking only of what she needed urgently: Him. His protection. His calm.

She took hold of his bare arm and found his skin was smooth and warm. She wanted to run her thumb over the tight bands of muscle, but she resisted the urge. It was only the second time in her life she'd had to fight hard against something she wanted, something she knew she shouldn't have—something that would be wrong.

He sat down and gently pried her fingers off his arm, then set her hands on her lap, away from him. He was going to tell her she would be fine if only she would lay her head down on the pillow and draw up the covers. That's what her mother used to say when Adele had nightmares as a child.

But he didn't say that. "What was the dream?" he asked.

She wet her lips. "I dreamed he came back."

"Your kidnapper?"

"Yes. He took me out of my bed on the ship, and since that night, I haven't been able to sleep."

"He won't be coming back," Damien assured her. "You can be confident of that."

Looking down at her hands on her lap, she nodded. "I know. At least my mind knows it, but when I dream, it feels real. How will I ever feel safe enough to fall asleep again?"

"You've been through a terrible ordeal and it's only natural to feel the way you do, but it will pass. Your peace of mind will return a little more each day, every time you wake up safe in your bed."

"How long it will take?"

"It's difficult to say."

"But I'm exhausted," she replied, and her voice broke.

Damien's hand came up to rest on her cheek. Feeling as if she were floating in someone else's body, she closed her eyes, while he stroked her cheek with his thumb and stirred unfamiliar longings inside her body.

She didn't want him to stop, but she knew, any second now, he would. Because this was wrong. Wrong, wrong, wrong, and they both knew it.

When he tried to draw his hand away, she took hold of it and clung to him.

"Adele," he whispered, "we shouldn't."

It was a gentle but clear warning.

"I'm sorry," she replied, feeling as if a glass of water had been splashed in her face. She shouldn't have clutched at his hand like a woman starving for affection. He had meant to offer her comfort and understanding, and she had tried to take more.

She forced herself to think of Harold. She was engaged to Harold. She wanted to marry Harold.

"I'm just upset," she said. "That's all. And scared."

"Yes. You need to get some sleep." He said it as if it were an explanation for her behavior just now.

She knew he was about to leave—which was of course what he had to do. He couldn't stay with her all night.

He continued to stare at her as if he were struggling with what to do, then he laid a hand on her upper arm. "Try to get some rest. No one is going to harm you."

Anxiety pooled in her belly. "You're not going to stay?"

"You know I can't do that."

"But you stayed with me last night."

He regarded her with unease. "Last night was different."

She wanted to ask why, but she knew why. They hadn't just spent an entire evening together enjoying a delicious dinner at a private table and drinking wine and talking and discovering things about each other, and he hadn't been shirtless.

"You'll be fine," he said, standing. "I'll be right down the hall, sleeping with one eye open."

She nodded because she had to, but her hands were still shaking.

He walked to the door and took hold of the knob to close it behind him, but the knob fell off. He tried to move the door. One of the hinges dropped to the floor with a noisy clang.

Adele sat up on her heels. "It won't close?"

"No."

Practicalities sank in. "I can't sleep here without a lock on the door."

He glanced back at her briefly and she could see he was not pleased. He returned his attention to the broken door, swinging it to and fro, then shook his head. "It'll need a new hinge."

"A new hinge?"

His voice was low and controlled. "You can have my room."

"But—"

"No buts. Come." From across the room, he held

out a hand to her.

She had no choice but to comply and was reminded of the way she had felt when she'd first seen him at the kidnapper's cottage. He was not to be reckoned with then, and he was not to be reckoned with now. He was tense and in no mood to argue with her.

Adele climbed out of bed barefoot and went to him. With his hand at the small of her back, he escorted her down the hall to his room. He opened the door for her, and she slowly walked in and looked around. Her gaze drifted to the bed, where the sheets and covers were tangled and spilling over the side, onto the floor. There was an indentation in the pillow. His clothes were tossed over a chair in the corner. There was an empty brandy glass on the bedside table. She could see the remaining traces of liquid in the bottom.

"You'll be safe here," he said, moving past her to pull the blankets up and tidy the bed. "The lock on the door works, and so does the one on the window. There's no one under the bed." He checked, just to be sure. "And I'll be listening."

He moved to the chair and picked up the shirt he'd worn at supper, and quickly shrugged into it. He relaxed a little after he did that, though he still seemed tense and a trifle impatient with her.

"Thank you," she said, not wanting him to think she didn't appreciate everything he was doing for her. But still, she wished he did not have to leave.

He crossed to the door and paused there a moment. "You'll be fine here, Adele. I promise."

Without another word, he walked out and left her alone.

She crossed to the door and turned the key in the lock. Struggling to remind herself that Damien was still nearby, she moved to the bed and pulled the covers back. She gazed down at the sheets in the moonlight—wrinkled and billowy in places from having been slept on. She swallowed hard and climbed in, pulling the heavy blankets up over herself and resting her arms on top of them.

She lay flat on her back and stared at the ceiling for a moment, then turned onto her side and closed her eyes. Damien's musky, masculine scent permeated her consciousness and swirled through her senses. She pressed her face into the soft feather pillow and breathed deeply, filling her lungs until she could hold no more of him, then she did it again and again and again, squeezing the pillow until she felt satisfied, and fell asleep.

But only for a little while. The rest of the night was a stressful affair filled with many swift, frightful awakenings.

Chapter 5

*A*DELE DESCENDED THE STAIRS THE next morning, her eyes burning from lack of sleep, and went to the dining room. Lord Alcester rose from the table they'd shared the night before and crossed the room to greet her.

She remembered with a shocking jolt to her senses how he had looked the night before in her bedchamber—shirtless and surreal, like a god in the moonlight.

"Good morning, Miss Wilson," he said coolly, with a slight bow. He escorted her to their table and as soon as they sat down, he asked, "Did you sleep at all?"

"Not much."

His chest rose and fell with a sigh, as if he felt he had failed her somehow.

"You will no doubt be relieved to join your mother soon and reach *Osulton Manor*," he said. "There was a telegram from her this morning." He reached into his breast pocket and handed it across the table. Adele read it quickly:

OVERJOYED TO HEAR YOU ARE SAFE STOP
WILL CELEBRATE SOON STOP
LOVE MOTHER STOP

Adele's heart relaxed a little as she read the words. It was a small connection to her reality—a reminder of her real life. She read the telegram two more times, then looked up to see Damien watching her, his brows drawn together with concern.

"What is it?" she asked.

"I'm sorry if I was short with you last night. It was inexcusable of me."

His apology surprised her, and she had to struggle to manage an appropriate reply.

"You weren't short with me. You were only trying to be helpful."

"You're being polite, Miss Wilson. The fact is, I shouldn't have left you alone when you were distraught. Last night you said I was your protector, but I was hardly that when I walked out on you like an irritable dog."

She inclined her head and spoke without thinking. "Why were you so irritable, Lord Alcester?"

He stared at her, speechless, from across the table.

Adele knew she shouldn't have asked that question—and with such an air of innocence, as if she had no knowledge of the fact that there was something improper budding between them.

Which was why she suspected he had been bad-tempered.

The server arrived and poured coffee. Damien leaned back in his chair, appearing relieved to be spared answering the question.

As soon as the server was gone, however, the question continued to dangle in the air between them. It could not go completely unanswered. That in itself would have revealed something was amiss.

Damien's gaze swept restlessly around the room, and she sensed he was displeased with her again.

"You did nothing wrong," he finally said. "I was the one who behaved badly. I was tired. Like you, I haven't had much sleep over the past few days. That's all."

Adele picked up her coffee cup and took a sip. It was probably best if neither of them acknowledged a mutual attraction. At least he was loyal to Harold, and she respected him for that. If he were not loyal, she would think him the worst human being in the world, and despite what she knew about his reputation, she did not think that of him. He had been nothing but a gentleman since the moment they'd met.

Though she herself had not always had the heart and mind of a proper, virtuous lady. A part of her had wanted something very improper, and she wasn't sure she would have the strength to put the candy back if she ever went so far as to take hold of it again.

All morning, the coach lumbered jerkily over moors and dales and hilly green pastures, stopping around noon to change horses in a quaint village inn, where Adele and Lord Alcester had a bite to eat.

In the afternoon, she dozed off a few times in the coach, but the slightest bump or jostle awakened her with a start, and each time it would take a good ten minutes for her heart to settle down again. When they stopped late in the afternoon, Adele sipped some wine, hoping it would help her sleep. She filled Damien's flask with a little extra to take with her as well and sipped it slowly for the next leg of the journey.

It was early evening when the vehicle rumbled into another little village and pulled up in front of an inn. As soon as they slowed to a halt, Damien opened the door of the coach and peered inside, offering his hand. "We've arrived. How are you?"

Adele took hold of his hand and felt the coach spin as she stepped unsteadily onto the dusty lane. "To be honest, I think I'm a little drunk. I slept a little though. Did it rain? I seem to recall raindrops pattering on the rooftop, but maybe I was dreaming."

Still holding her hand, he stopped in the street. "It didn't rain. But at least you slept."

"Small mercies," she replied, and found herself struggling to focus on the texture of his coat collar, and the details of the seam at his broad shoulder. She loved the way his thick black hair curled in a large wave at his neck.

"Your speech was slurred just now," he told her discreetly as he offered his arm.

She felt the heat of his breath in her ear, and it sent the most delightful array of gooseflesh down her left side. She closed her eyes and imagined what it might feel like to wrap her arms around his neck and just dangle.

"Slurred?" she asked, feeling rather giddy.

He held a finger to his lips. "*Shh*, my dear," he

whispered. "You're shouting. I believe lack of sleep has given that wine some extra kick."

My dear. That was all she heard.

The next thing she knew, she was blinking up at him, feeling dim-witted and completely unable to remember what he had said after *My dear.* His voice was like sweet syrup. Sweet and yummy. She would like to lick it.

He glanced over her head, up and down the street. "You need a bed, Adele, and it is imperative that you close your eyes when you get there."

She felt dazed, looking up at him. The strong line of his jaw was so lovely. Lovely, lovely, lovely. He would make a handsome statue on the chest of drawers in her room in Newport.

Ahhh, Newport. How she missed the gulls and the smell of the sea.

"It smells funny here," she said, wrinkling her nose. "Like sheep."

She felt a little nauseated suddenly. And dizzy. But still giddy.

Damien's arm slid around her waist, he scooped her up, and then she was floating toward the front door of the inn. No, not floating. She was being carried there. By a handsome black knight in not-so-shiny armor.

He smelled like the outdoors. Fresh and clean and manly—though there was a vague aroma of horse mixed in. Some horses were very manly. Yes. He was a stallion.

No, he was a knight. A knight with big, sturdy hooves.

She sighed and rested her face against the rough

wool of his black coat, feeling it rub roughly against her cheek. Her eyes were closed now. She sighed happily. Wasn't life wonderful?

Carrying Harold's snoozing, deadweight fiancée in his arms, Damien followed the innkeeper up the stairs to her room on the second floor. She was mumbling something about her sister, asking why she wanted the blue bowl, when the white one was closer.

Damien carried her into the bedchamber and laid her down on the bed, careful not to wake her. He sat down beside her and moved the fallen locks of hair away from her face. She moaned softly.

"She hasn't slept in four days," he told the innkeeper. "She's been ill." It was the only explanation he could come up with, as he didn't want to give away the details of their situation.

"Is she all right now?" the man asked.

"Yes, she just needs to sleep."

He gazed down at her freckled face in the gray light of the afternoon. She smiled and moaned again and rolled over on the bed toward the wall. The feminine sound of her voice and the gentle curve of her hips sent a wave of desire through Damien's tired, exhausted body.

He imagined for a moment what this moment might be like if she belonged to him. If she did, he would lie down beside her and hold her, and he would stay with her all night until she woke the next morning, feeling rested and more herself.

"Should I bring soup?" the innkeeper asked, startling Damien out of his thoughts.

He stood. "Perhaps later, after she's had a chance to sleep awhile." He reached for the wool blanket at the foot of the bed and covered her.

"She's your sister, you say?" the man asked with a hint of doubt.

Damien met his gaze squarely. "Yes."

The man inclined his head. "So, I presume you'll be wanting another room?"

The man was perceptive. He was checking to see if some other arrangement might suit Damien better. Another arrangement certainly *would* suit him better, but he would keep his room and hold tight to his integrity. Though it was squirming like a wet fish in his hands.

"Yes, another room would be most appreciated."

"Very well, sir. My wife will prepare one now." The innkeeper walked out and closed the door behind him.

Damien moved to stand over the bed where Adele lay sleeping, and let his gaze drift lazily over the exquisite, appealing length of her body. *Yes, if she were his....*

That very instant, something thumped in the next room—probably the innkeeper's wife making the bed—and Adele sat up. She gazed vacantly at Damien's face for a few seconds before she spoke.

"Did I sleep? Is it morning?"

"No. You've been asleep for only five or six minutes."

"Five minutes?" Her voice revealed utter disbelief. She was hopelessly discouraged. "Why can't I sleep?"

He ran his hand down her arm. "You need to relax

and know that you're safe."

"I'm trying. When I'm awake, I know he's not coming back, but when I go to sleep...." She took hold of Damien's lapel between two fingers.

She was touching him. Touching his clothes....

"Please stay with me tonight," she said. "No one will ever know. I won't tell. This is the last night of our travels, and tomorrow I'll be with my mother and sisters. Everything will be normal then. But I can't meet Harold looking and feeling the way I do. *I can't.*"

She gazed up at him with bloodshot, puffy, pleading eyes, and his blood burned like fire through his veins. It was all he could do to keep from pulling her close and pressing his lips to hers.

For a sizzling moment, he fought to subdue his desires. God help him, he wanted to kiss the warm, supple flesh of her body and hold her naked in his arms. He wanted to make love to her.

There it was. In plain terms.

He squeezed his eyes shut and pressed the heel of his hand to his forehead. He thought of Harold. Then he thought of his mother, who had betrayed his father. His father had died. His mother had died, too. So much of what happened that day had been Damien's fault. He had been the one to tattle on his mother. He'd had no tact; he was only nine. His father had not taken the news well. The situation had exploded.

Then he thought of Harold again, who trusted him completely. Harold, who, for the first time in his life, had not only fallen in love, but had found the courage to propose. Then he'd asked Damien to help him—to bring his fiancée home.

No. No! Nothing could ever happen between Damien and Adele. Not ever. She belonged to Harold. She was to become Damien's cousin by marriage. He could not permit himself to feel what he was feeling. He could not devastate Harold. He had to bury this desire.

"Please, Damien," she said. "All I need is one good night's sleep, then I'll be myself again. You need only spend one night in a chair, with a promise that you won't leave. A good night's sleep will cure me, I'm sure of it. I just can't think straight. My eyes hurt, and I can't seem to differentiate between what's real and what's a dream."

"Neither can I," he whispered, feeling more than a little exhausted himself. The past few days had been grueling—first with the disturbing news of the kidnapping from Harold, then with his own quest to find Adele and bring her home safe to his cousin.

His fight was gone. He couldn't do it anymore. He closed his eyes, tipping his head forward to rest upon hers.

"Please just stay in the room while I sleep," she whispered, and he reveled in her wine-scented breath on his face.

He couldn't argue anymore. Maybe it was exhaustion. Maybe it was adoration. Who would ever know?

But what did it matter *why* he couldn't argue? All that mattered was that if he slept in the chair in the corner, everything would return to normal in the morning. Adele would sleep well, then remember her life and again become the woman Harold had proposed to. She would be ready to go home to him.

Damien would deliver his cousin's fiancée to him as he had promised. Then he would be on his way.

He shook his head at the decision he was about to make. "All right. I'll sleep in the chair."

"Do you promise? You won't leave?"

"I promise."

She immediately fell back onto the pillows but continued to hold his hand. "Thank you, Damien. I swear I'll make it up to you somehow. Honest, I will."

She closed her eyes and fell asleep almost instantly, leaving him tense and worried, and wondering how he was going to resist collecting on that promise. Especially in the hours to come, after the sun went down and the moon began its rise.

Chapter 6

*T*HE INNKEEPER KNOCKED ON THE door a short time later and delivered a key to the other room, which had been prepared for Damien. Damien thanked him but requested that he and his wife refrain from knocking on Adele's door again through the night, as his "sister" was struggling to sleep and could not under any circumstances be disturbed. They would not likely be taking any supper.

The innkeeper gave a sympathetic nod toward the bed. "You have my word, sir. I hope she'll feel better in the morning." He walked out and closed the door behind him.

Damien spent the next fifteen minutes sitting in the blue chintz chair, grappling over his promise to stay and contemplating the worst temptation of his life: He desired his cousin's fiancée. He couldn't stop thinking of her; he wanted to be with her. Hold her. He wanted her in every possible way a man could want a woman, even while he knew it would betray the cousin whom he had always felt a need to protect.

Damien sat forward and covered his face with his hands. He despised himself. He knew he had to resist and bury this madness, but he had not yet done so.

Just then, Adele woke up again and sat up. Instinct pulled him out of his chair. The next thing he knew, he was sitting on the edge of the bed, wondering how the hell he had gotten across the room so fast before his brain had any say in the matter.

"Go back to sleep," he whispered, hoping, praying that she would.

"Is it morning yet?" Her eyes looked as if someone had poured salt into them.

"No. It's been only fifteen minutes since the last time you woke."

She rubbed her eyes. "You've been here the whole time?"

"Yes."

She tugged at the collar of her dress, buttoned tightly around her neck. "The bed is spinning. I'm not comfortable. I need to get out of this."

Perhaps this was some kind of test, Damien thought. If it were, he would pass it, no matter what it took.

"What do you need?" he asked.

She glanced around, looking almost confused, as if she didn't know where she was. "Nothing. I just need to take this off." She began to unbutton her bodice.

"Adele," he whispered quickly, curling his hand around hers to stop her. *"Wait."*

Her bloodshot eyes met his, and her forehead crinkled with frustration over her fatigue. Wait for what? he asked himself, realizing he needed her to stop only because he wasn't ready. Wasn't ready for this to be harder than it already was.

He told himself she probably wouldn't remember any of this. She was still drunk and half asleep.

"How can I help you?" he asked, because no matter how difficult this was for him, she needed his help and he would give it to her, because he wanted her to sleep, and sleep well, so things would be normal again.

"Help me unbutton this."

He took a deep, slow breath, then carefully reached down and put his fingers on the tiny covered button under her chin. One by one, he unfastened them.

"You're good at taking care of people," she said sleepily.

He said nothing. The bodice fell open in front, and he caught a glimpse of white undergarments beneath. He found himself comparing this moment to all the other moments in his life when he had gazed upon a woman's undergarments. There had been many times, but he had never felt like this.

"Would you be so kind as to look away?" Adele asked as she began to shrug out of the bodice, hardly giving him a chance to react.

He stood and went to the window, looking out at the darkening sky. He was completely worn out. He would be glad when night fell. Then he wouldn't be able to see her. He would go to sleep himself, then he would wake up and it would be morning and he would take her directly to Harold.

He heard the sound of clothes rustling and the bed creaking. "I'm finished," she said. He turned, and she was under the covers, lying on her back.

Damien returned to the chair. He sat for about an hour, trying to fall asleep, but couldn't. All he could do was watch Adele in the dim light and imagine with a deep, physical yearning what it would be like to lay beside her.

A short time later he heard footsteps in the hall. He stood up and opened the door. The innkeeper's wife was passing by.

"Pardon me," he said. "Would you send up a glass of brandy?"

"Certainly," she replied with a polite smile.

Five minutes later, she delivered a tray with two glasses and a full bottle. He had only wanted one glass, but he was very grateful for the bottle.

Chapter 7

*A*T SOME POINT IN THE night, Damien became
aware of a soft feathery kiss on his cheek. Still
half absorbed in what felt like a dream, the seasoned
lover in him responded with primitive instinct. He
turned his head on the pillow and met the sweet, teasing lips with a deep, sensual kiss. It was only then, as
his hand came up to brush the silky hair away from his
lover's face, that he woke and realized whose lips these
were and whose bed this was. Yes...he remembered....
He had stretched out beside Adele not long ago. He'd
only wanted to be comfortable for a moment or two.

Gracious lover that he was, he brought the kiss to a
polite and graceful finish before he spoke. "Adele," he
whispered, inching away from her while he struggled
to squeeze a tight fist around the neck of his desires.
"Wake up."

"I'm awake," she replied, and only then did she seem
to realize what had just occurred. "I'm sorry...I don't
know why I did that. I just wanted to thank you."

For a man who had shared beds with many interesting and experienced women, he found himself stumbling outside of his usual range. He was looking upon absolute innocence—virginal and naive beyond any imagining. And so beautiful, she knocked the wind out of him.

He raked a hand through his hair for he was problematically aroused.

"Please don't go," she said, "because I actually slept with you here. Finally."

He knew he should at least return to the chair on the other side of the room, but something prevented him from doing so. It was the part of him that wanted her, no matter the cost, no matter who he hurt in the process. He was incapable of rising from the bed. His body wouldn't let him.

He put his arm around Adele, and she snuggled close. Together they lay in silence while a voice in Damien's head warned him it was not wise. *You shouldn't be doing this.*

He was intensely aware of Adele's slender hand on his chest as she moved a finger back and forth over the rough wool of his waistcoat. Was she experimenting? Curious? Testing his limits? Or did she honestly have no idea how dangerous this was?

Damien clenched his jaw as she nuzzled his cheek with her nose. He didn't move a muscle.

For a moment more, he stared at the dark ceiling until the lover in him somehow gained a foothold. His blood quickened and before he had a chance to consider right from wrong, he was rising up on one arm and rolling on top of Adele in one smooth, fluid rush of movement.

If she had resisted, he would have stopped, but she wrapped her arms around his shoulders and welcomed his kiss. He devoured her soft lips, her sweet, silky tongue, and her deep, wet mouth. Damien lost himself in sensation, in the burning need to possess her, and was soon oblivious to the tenets of obligation and loyalty.

He pulled her closer, more snugly into his feverish, roused body, and reveled in the desperate quenching of his desires, until a thought emerged from somewhere in his consciousness. It came out of his childhood memories. He thought of his cousin and immediately sensed shame and disaster in the offing.

Forcing himself to drag his mouth from Adele's, Damien fought for control and exerted every effort to smother his passions. He rested his head on the pillow over her shoulder and breathed deeply and slowly, steeling his body against an impossible firestorm of desire.

"I feel safe at last," she whispered in his ear, and he wished she hadn't spoken.

"You're not safe," he replied. "Not from me."

"But I'm not afraid of you."

"You should be Adele."

They both stilled on the bed.

"I know this is wrong," she said shakily, "but I don't want to stop. I don't want to let go of you. I want to hold on tight."

He lay very quiet for a long, agonizing moment. "We have to stop this. I'm in your bed, and I'm not made of stone." He buried his face into the hair at her neck. "Push me away."

She made no move to do so. "Not yet. In a minute I will. I swear it."

He lay still, waiting.

Then he found himself bending to the whims of his sexual desires again, falling into a place where his principles lost touch with the workings of his body. He parted her thighs with his hips and gently thrust forward against the barrier of clothing between them. Slowly. Gently. Long and gradually.

If this were actual sex and he was not wearing trousers, he would be deep, deep inside her.

"Am I hurting you?" he whispered. "Your wound?"

"No," she replied breathlessly. "It feels good."

He was breathing harder now. Quite unable to stop himself, he slid his hand down to her knee and up under the cotton fabric of her shift, up the outside of her thigh to her bare, fleshy hip. She felt like heaven—soft and warm and succulent.

With his face still buried at her neck, and his eyes squeezed shut amid the battle that was raging inside him, he stroked her soft skin. How easy it would be to slide his hand around to the front, into the damp depths between her thighs, and discover for himself whether she was a virgin or not after the kidnapping. He could answer that question right here and now. Set her mind at ease.

If, on the other hand, she was *not* a virgin....

A host of possibilities—both glorious and horrendous—loomed in his brain. What if he made love to her, and they let people presume it had been the kidnapper?

No. He couldn't contemplate such a thing.

What was this woman doing to him?

Still breathing hard, he turned his face away from her again while his body trembled with need. He'd never wanted a woman like this before—perhaps because he wasn't used to waiting and wanting. He only ever engaged in this sort of activity with women who were ready and willing.

But no, it was more than that. Deeper than that.

Adele shifted slightly, making a cozy place for him between her thighs. She truly had no idea, not the faintest, of the peril she was placing herself in.

Damien knew, however. He also knew with a crushing sense of frustration that it was time to stop. "Don't do that, Adele," he said. "Push me away. *Now.*"

She tensed at the terse, commanding voice he used with her, and a second later she obeyed. Her hands moved to his chest, and she pushed.

He rolled off her onto his back. "I'll stay with you so that you can get some sleep," he said, his voice low, "but don't touch me again. Do you understand?"

"Yes."

He turned his back to her.

He was angry. Not with her. She'd been through an ordeal and all she wanted was to be held.

He was angry at the situation, and at himself for letting this go too far.

He was also angry with Harold for sitting idly back with his head in the clouds, while Damien saved the day as he always did. Harold should have saved it himself this time or accompanied Damien. He knew how beautiful Adele was. He should not have expected Damien to be made of stone.

Damien shut his eyes and vowed to keep his back
to his cousin's fiancée for the rest of the night. After
tomorrow, if Adele wanted to be held, it would be
Harold's duty to fulfill. Damien would have his own
problems to deal with. He would have to forget about
Adele Wilson and find a way to live with the regret
he would feel over his weakness and lack of honor
tonight—just like the adulterous mother he didn't
care to remember.

Adele woke gradually from the glorious oblivion
of a long, deep slumber. Conscious thoughts began
to form. It was morning. She had slept. But what a
headache she had.

She opened her eyes, blinked up at the ceiling and
remembered suddenly that she had kissed Damien
during the night, and he had lain on top of her in
the bed. The memory roused her senses and she felt
a heated fluttering in her belly, but the thrill was
quickly crushed by a guilty awareness of what she had
let herself do and what she had wanted. Thank heavens Damien had put a stop to things when he had.

Regardless, she would never be the same again.
She now possessed a more thorough understanding
of the true basis of attraction between a man and a
woman. She felt as if her eyes had been opened to a
whole new world—a world of handsome men and
their so-called charms. It was all about lips and hands
and the sweet promise of physical pleasure. Clara had
tried to explain all that to her on the ship, but Adele
had not been willing to listen.

Now she understood. She also understood Damien's

famous allure, and the reason he was able to have any woman of his choosing. There was something seductive in his eyes, in his body, and quite frankly, in everything about him. Last night, without lifting a finger, he had drawn her to him like a magnet, and she had been pulled in, much to her dismay. It was shocking to think that she had lost all sense of what was proper and hadn't found the strength to ward off temptation.

What would her parents think if they knew what she'd done? Could she blame it on the wine? No, it wasn't just that. It was Damien.

She glanced to her left and there he was. He sat in the rocking chair across the room, watching her with a dark, haunted expression in his eyes.

Her heart began to pound with apprehension. They were going home that very day. She would see Harold, her mother, her sister. Last night suddenly seemed like a delirious dream, now laden with regret—a dream they could not erase.

"I take full responsibility for what happened last night," Damien said, sitting forward in the rocking chair. "You are an innocent, I am not. I knew what I was doing, and from my perspective, I took advantage of you. You should, therefore, harbor no guilt."

She sat up. "No, that's not what happened. You did not take advantage of me. You were the one who put a stop to it. Remember? Therefore, you should harbor no guilt either." She paused as she tried to make sense of the events. "I was frightened and exhausted. That's all. You took care of me last night because I asked you to. I wanted you to."

He nodded reluctantly, rose from the chair and turned to the window.

"Should we tell Harold?" she asked.

He swung around immediately. "No. Definitely not. As far as I'm concerned, this never happened."

"But you and he are close," Adele said. "Can you live with a secret between you? Because I'm not sure that I can, not if I am to become his wife."

Damien frowned at her. "You would hurt him just to ease your own guilt?"

She swallowed uncomfortably. "No... I suppose I didn't think of it that way."

"Well, that's the way it is. Believe me. I've told you before that I am protective of my cousin, and I do not wish to see him hurt because of a temporary error in my judgment. We both had too much to drink, and I for one am willing to bear the guilt to spare him pain. Besides, this is not real life. Once we are back at *Osulton Manor*, things will be different, and I am certain beyond the shadow of a doubt that we will both deeply regret our indiscretion here and wish it never happened."

She nodded. "Yes. Of course. You're absolutely right. It was a terrible mistake."

"It would be best for everyone," he continued, "if you and I never spoke of this again, not even privately to each other. Especially privately. Such a rapport between us would not only be inappropriate, it would be...." He paused. "It would be dangerous. I'm a dangerous man, Adele. You think you are safe with me, but you're not. I'm not like Harold. He should not have sent me to bring you home. I should not have been the one."

She stared at him, speechless. "No, he was right to send you. I am alive, aren't I?"

Damien walked to the door, shaking his head. "I will return to my room now and arrange for breakfast to be sent up to you. Then I will see you downstairs in an hour." He paused in the doorway. "I will deliver you to your mother today, then you will be reunited with Harold a few hours later. I will not mention this again, Adele. I give you my word. As I said before, it never happened."

He walked out and shut the door behind him.

Adele was left behind to gather her composure and try to make sense of her feelings.

Part Two
The Reckoning

Chapter 8

THE OSULTON COACH, WITH AN impressive liveried driver at the reins, rolled swiftly and smoothly across the lush, green English countryside behind a thunderous team of galloping grays. Inside, Adele sat quietly with her mother, Beatrice, her sister Clara, and baby Anne, while a second coach followed with their maids, luggage, and Anne's nurse.

Adele had met her mother earlier that afternoon in the reception room of a small village inn somewhere. She had no idea where. As soon as Damien ascertained that she was reunited with her mother, he had taken his leave without waiting to be introduced and rode off into parts unknown.

In some ways, Adele had been relieved to see him go, but in others, she was mystified by the frustrating well of uncertainty that descended.

She should not be mourning their parting, she told herself for the umpteenth time as the coach passed through the village just north of *Osulton Manor*. She was promised to Harold, and besides, Damien was not the sort of man she would ever wish to marry. Yes, he had been her hero during their journey together, but in real life, he was in love with a scandalous actress and was known to be irresponsible with money. She had to keep her head on straight and accept what he said as true: They would deeply regret their indiscretion and wish it had never happened. She would approach the manor with the sensible view that she was at last returning to the real world. The adventure, thank heavens, was over.

Upon peering out the window, however, she discovered that one's expectations could often be lost in the wind. As the carriage passed through the massive stone gateway, which resembled the Arch of Constantine in Rome, Adele found herself facing another surprise. This place—this massive country estate—was not at all what she had imagined. She'd thought she would be living in a cozy stone cottage in the English countryside, cloaked in ivy, in the Tudor style perhaps, because Harold had described his home as a "quaint little country dwelling."

Quaint and little? Perhaps Harold needed a new dictionary.

Osulton Manor was no quaint country house. It was a great, white palace, baroque in style, with large flanking octagonal turrets and a spectacular center skyline of smaller cupolas and domes. It stood high on a hill, surrounded by wrought iron fences and ancient English oaks that watched over the property like great lords themselves.

It was a palace fit for kings and queens, and Adele would be mistress of it all. She felt an unexpected tightening in her chest, as if this entire continent pressed down upon her. A strict manner of behavior beyond her years and experience would be expected of her. How in the world would she learn all that she needed to learn to run a household on a scale such as this?

She pulled her gaze from the window and stared blankly down at the floor of the coach. Harold had not prepared her for this. He had made it sound like nothing. "You're very amiable," he had said. "That's all it takes, really."

She sincerely doubted it.

There was also the matter of her virginity. She had not forgotten about that. Every so often, the uncertainty hit her like a snowball in the face. She hoped it would not be an issue.

They drove past a rectangular pond that reflected the house and trees, then rolled to a stop in front of a central rotunda that served as the formal entrance. Adele noticed the large glass structure around the side of the house and reasoned it was a conservatory. She imagined what it might look like inside, filled with leafy green plants and colorful flowers. She felt her spirits lift slightly and told herself there would be other things to look forward to as well. Damien had mentioned the fine stables and the forest.

"Here we are, girls," her mother said, as if all the proud ancestral ghosts of Osulton were listening from above. "Sit up straight, now. Here they come."

"You're making her nervous, Mother," Clara whispered, trying not to wake baby Anne.

"I'm fine," Adele replied, which, of course, she was

not.

People stood outside on the steps, waiting for them. A footman wearing navy knee breeches, ivory stockings, and shiny buckled shoes opened the door and lowered the step, then reached in to take Clara's hand. Their mother was handed out next, and then Adele.

Adele peered out from under the wide brim of her green, plumed hat, and searched over the strange faces on the steps, all of them staring at her. Evaluating her.

Then she saw Harold. *Ah,* familiar Harold.

She was back. Centered. Her fears and tensions drained away at last. She met his gaze and smiled. He smiled with his usual exuberance, in return.

That's what she had admired most about him the first time she'd met him. He always looked so pleased to see her. He possessed the friendly excitability of a child, and he made her feel at ease.

He stepped away from the rest and descended the stairs to greet her and her mother and sister. "Lady Rawdon, welcome. And Mrs. Wilson, it is indeed a pleasure to see you again." He turned toward Adele and spoke more slowly, with more care. "And of course, Miss Wilson. Adele, I should say." With a flourish, he raised an arm to display his home. "Welcome to *Osulton Manor.*"

"Thank you, Harold. I'm so happy to be here at last."

"Yes, of course you are! Come and meet my family."

She followed him up the stairs to where the others were waiting.

"Lady Rawdon," he said to Clara, "may I present

my mother, Eustacia Scott."

The countess—a plump woman with curly red hair like her son—stepped forward.

"Please call me Clara." The two shook hands.

"It is a pleasure indeed," Eustacia replied. "And this must be baby Anne! What a darling!" She admired Clara's daughter.

"And Mother," he continued, "may I present Beatrice Wilson, and her daughter, my betrothed, Adele Wilson."

Adele paid careful attention to this English manner of introductions, for it was something she would be required to understand fully. Rank meant everything, which explained why Clara had been addressed first, before their mother.

Eustacia shook her mother's hand. "Welcome to our home, Mrs. Wilson." She clasped Adele's hand last. "And my dear, we are so very pleased to welcome you into our family."

Adele couldn't have predicted the relief she would feel upon meeting her future mother-in-law. Her sisters had both been forced to contend with women who despised Americans and did not approve of their sons' marriages. In time, Sophia had won the respect and love of her mother-in-law, the dowager duchess, but Clara had never been able to do so. Adele, it seemed, would not have to face that challenge.

"Thank you, Lady Osulton. I'm pleased to meet you, too."

"You are going to be my daughter-in-law, so you must call me Eustacia!" she said, with the same jolly enthusiasm that characterized her son. "Now come and meet Harold's sister. This is Lady Violet."

Violet was as dark as night, resembling a certain other member of the family. Adele shook hands with the young woman.

"Now let us go inside and get you settled," Eustacia said.

Adele walked into the house with the others but stopped in the center of the round entrance hall. All along the walls of the great rotunda stood classical busts and statues of Greek and Roman gods and emperors. Over her head was a frescoed dome depicting a man atop a black horse, holding a spear over his head.

Adele gazed in awe at the bright colors and the graceful, sweeping lines. There was such movement in the artistry. She could almost hear the thunderous clatter of hooves and the victorious battle cry of the warrior.

Harold moved to stand beside her. "It's the first Earl of Osulton," he said, "victorious in battle. He was awarded his title and this house in 1715 by King George I. Just think, America wasn't even a country then."

Adele smiled at her fiancé. "I'll look forward to seeing the rest of the house, Harold. Perhaps when you show me around you can tell me more about its history."

"You will learn every detail, as you should. But there is plenty of time for that. Now, we must see you all to your rooms to give you time to dress for dinner. We have invited a few other guests to celebrate your arrival. Some of the local squires. The Earl of Whitby is also here—who is a friend, I believe, to your broth-er-in-law the Duke of Wentworth," he said, referring to Sophia's husband. "My cousin Damien, Viscount Alcester, will be dining with us as well."

Adele stiffened at the mere mention of Damien's name. She had known that in order to avoid a scan-dal, they were all to behave as if nothing out of the ordinary had transpired. Adele was to meet Damien as if she were meeting him for the first time.

But she had not expected it to be that very night. She'd thought she would have more time to come to terms with what she had done and bury the memory of it.

Harold gestured toward the grand staircase, framed at the bottom by two massive, fluted columns. "I am sure you will approve of your accommodations, ladies. They are—may I be so bold as to say?—fit for queens. You shall have everything at your disposal as you prepare for a most exhilarating evening."

Adele made her way soberly to the stairs. If Damien was to be at the table that night, exhilaration was something she would prefer to avoid.

Chapter 9

*I*T WAS LATE AFTERNOON WHEN Damien finally emerged from his rooms. He had bathed and felt clean at last after far too many days spent sleeping in his clothes. He went immediately to see his grandmother.

As soon as he pushed through the door, she clapped her hands together and wheeled herself away from the table where she had been reading the newspaper. "At last! Give me a kiss, you devil."

Damien clasped her frail, trembling hands in his, and bent forward to kiss her on the cheek. He straightened, then tipped his head at her. "A new perfume, Grandmama?"

"Why, yes...." She fiddled alluringly with a tendril of snowy white hair that had fallen out of her chignon. "What do you think?"

"It's wonderful on you, but you've always had exquisite taste. I hope you realize you'll have to fight off the gentlemen this evening."

She slapped his hand. "Oh, you naughty flirt. Come and tell me about London. Are you still tangled up with that actress?"

His grandmother—who knew nothing of the kid-napping and thought he'd been in London all this time—wheeled herself back to the table.

Damien seated himself across from her and stretched out in a lazy sprawl. "Yes, and by God, she has talent."

His grandmother smirked. "You are a wicked scoundrel, Damien. Just like your grandfather. Until he met me, of course."

He smiled affectionately at her.

"So, tell me, what do you know about this heiress Harold has brought over from America? I told him not to go, you know. I told him he'd be purchased like a stud at market."

"And he was. For a very good price, I might add."

She clicked her tongue at him. "Have you met her?"

Damien hesitated. "Yes."

"I heard the girl's father wants to fund one of Harold's experiments. Is it true?"

"I believe so."

"Go into business together!"

Damien smiled and raised his eyebrows.

She leaned forward and rested an elbow on the table. "What about you? Isn't it time you took a wife, too? Essence House has been empty for too long. I understand Harold's American fiancée is related by marriage to the Duke of Wentworth. He has a sister, does he not? Lady Lily, I believe? A pretty little cup-cake?"

"I do like cupcakes."

"I'm quite aware of that, young man." She leaned back again, gazing into Damien's eyes with scrutiny.

"From what I understand, this particular cupcake has exceptionally rich frosting. The duke had become a very wealthy man since he married the American. Surely, you must be considering such a practical quality in a young woman. Times have been difficult lately, have they not?"

Damien stood and walked to the window. "Yes."

"It would be a very advantageous match."

Damien sighed. "I doubt that the duke would be pleased to marry his sister off to an impoverished viscount. She could aim much higher, I'm sure."

His grandmother grinned at him. "If Lady Lily has hot blood in her veins, she would probably make her brother's life miserable if she didn't get what she wanted. You have a powerful effect on women, Damien, and don't pretend you don't know it. You could have any woman you wanted if you set your mind to it."

Hands clasped behind his back, he continued to gaze out the window. "Not *any* woman, Grandmama."

She was quiet for a moment, then her eyes turned serious. "Promise me you will try this Season, Damien. I know you too well. These eyes may be old, but they can still see when you are troubled. I know the desperate state of your finances, and I've known it for quite some time."

With a sigh of resignation, he turned away from the window and faced her. "Yes." Though there was so much more to it than just that.

"I also know how you feel about marrying for money or position, and that cynicism has held you back."

He merely nodded.

"Please, promise me," she said. "You mustn't continue to let your parents' deaths stop you from living. You deserve happiness. You were just a boy when they died. It was not your fault."

Damien approached his grandmother, who looked so much older than she had the last time he'd seen her, only weeks ago. He bent forward and kissed her hand. "I promise, I will try." He meant it sincerely, because he loved his grandmother very much, and he knew she was right. "Now I must go and dress for dinner. I will see you later."

He walked out and returned to his rooms.

The green Huntington Room, where Adele was staying, overlooked the east garden and the celebrated Chauncey Maze.

It was a fascinating view, for the green hedges of the maze were unlike any other hedges she had ever seen depicted in photographs or paintings. All the mazes she had seen and explored were square or round but always symmetrical, while this one sported an indiscriminate, paisley design. It would be a challenge to the most enterprising of minds.

The loud dinner gong rang, and a moment later, Adele met her mother and Clara in the wide corridor to make their way to the drawing room.

"I liked Harold very much," Clara said, looping her arm through Adele's. "He's very genuine. Not at all pompous, like some people can be."

Adele pulled her sister close as they walked. "Oh, Clara, you have no idea how relieved I am to hear it. I was dreading the possibility that you might not approve of him. I didn't want to have to argue with you."

"Not approve?" their mother said haughtily. "Surely not!"

Clara smiled. "You won't have to argue with me, Adele. I admit that I pictured an older man for some reason. I'm pleased that he's young, and he seems lively. I believe the two of you will be very well suited. And I am thrilled that you will be close by. We will be separated by a short train ride, rather than the unbearable expanse of the Atlantic."

Beatrice quickened her steps to keep up with her daughters. "Oh, must you rub salt in the wound, Clara? The Atlantic will now separate me from my youngest daughter. The dearest, most sensible of my brood. How will I ever manage?"

Clara grinned playfully at her mother. "You will manage just fine, Mother, when Mrs. Astor sends you invitations and waits with bated breath while you take your time to reply."

They found their way to the formal drawing room and quietly entered. Eustacia was quick to greet them at the door. "Welcome!"

Adele looked around at the dark red velvet wall coverings that repeated the paisley design from the Chauncey Maze, the matching velvet chairs and set-tees, the spectacular gold ceiling carved with intricate swirls and leafy patterns. With her educated eye, she recognized the French style of Louis XV.

She didn't see Damien anywhere.

"Please come and meet our other guests," Eustacia

said, then she added with a whisper, "And Harold's grandmother is here—the Dowager Lady Alcester."

Adele glanced across the room at an elderly woman in a pushchair. Her snowy white hair was pinned up in a loose, elegant bun, and her black, high-necked gown complemented her coloring. She was slim, with high cheekbones, and she wore dainty drop earrings. Adele suspected she had been a great beauty in her youth.

Eustacia escorted them to her. "Mother, we have some new guests."

The older woman raised a long-handled pair of gold spectacles to her eyes with slender hands that trembled. "The Americans," she said cheerfully. Her head trembled as well. Eustacia was about to begin the introductions, when the dowager interrupted. "Do you young ladies know what a stir you and your fellow countrywomen have been causing in England?" She turned slowly to look up at Eustacia. "Times are changing, are they not?"

Adele and Clara exchanged smiles.

The dowager nudged Eustacia. "Well, get on with it. I want to know which one of these Yankees is to marry my grandson."

Eustacia made the introduction. When it was Adele's turn, the dowager raised her spectacles again to get a better look. She smiled and leaned back. "Now I understand what all the buzzing was about. You, my dear, are a cupcake!"

Adele laughed. "A cupcake?"

"Yes. Tell me...." She leaned forward, as if to ask for a secret. "Do you plan to raise your flag outside?"

Adele laughed. "No, Lady Osulton."

"Call me Catherine. And what about the country dancing you people do? Are you going to make us learn that? I understand someone shouts out the steps."

Eustacia bent forward to speak loudly in her mother's ear. "Adele is not like most Americans, Mother! She won't be *shouting!* She's very polite, you'll soon see! One would almost take her for an Englishwoman!"

Adele tried to take the remark as a compliment. She wanted to fit in, after all.

Catherine raised her shoulders to her ears and peered up at her daughter. "The only one shouting at the moment is you, Eustacia. I'm not deaf."

She winked at Adele, who decided she was going to like Harold's grandmother very well.

Eustacia led them across the room toward a handsome, golden-haired gentleman in the opposite corner, who was speaking with Violet.

"Lord Whitby, may I present Lady Rawdon, Beatrice Wilson of New York, and Adele Wilson, my future daughter-in-law."

"Ah, yes," he replied, turning and bowing toward them. "But we have met before, Mrs. Wilson, during the Season a few years ago, and of course at the wedding of your eldest daughter, Sophia."

Adele's mother beamed. "Yes, of course! Lord Whitby! I remember your charming toast at their wedding! And the beautiful red roses you sent to Sophia not long after her London debut."

Adele winced, for she remembered those roses. Sophia had described them in one of her letters. Whitby had clearly been making his romantic feelings for Sophia known, but he had lost out to his friend James, the duke, who had later become Sophia's husband.

Leave it to her mother to mention that.

Whitby smiled rakishly, unruffled by the reminder. "Your memory is most impressive, Mrs. Wilson. I believe at your daughter's wedding, I referred to our newest duchess as a rose, for which England was to benefit from the careful American transplantation."

Adele's mother blushed. "Oh, Lord Whitby. You are too kind. Too kind."

They discussed light matters for a few minutes, then Eustacia guided them toward the other corner of the room just as Harold walked in. He was not alone.

"And here with Harold," Eustacia said, "we have my nephew, Damien Renshaw, Viscount Alcester."

Adele—caught off guard by the shock of seeing Damien again—sucked in a breath. He looked so different. He wore a formal black dinner jacket with a white waistcoat and white bow tie, and his raven hair was slicked back in the most flattering fashion, complementing the strong, masculine lines of his cleanly shaven jaw.

He looked like the perfect London gentleman, devastatingly handsome as he bowed politely with his hands clasped behind his back. "Lady Rawdon, it is a pleasure," he said, bowing first to Clara. He greeted Adele's mother, then turned his attention to Adele. "Allow me to offer my best wishes on your engagement, Miss Wilson."

Adele was momentarily speechless, for it felt hypocritical to behave in this manner. She had woken up beside him in her bed that very morning, yet there they were, both of them, acting as if they had never met.

The most outrageous part of it all was that half the people in the room knew the truth. They were aware of her kidnapping and Damien's heroic rescue and escort across England. They knew that Damien had bandaged her thigh. They knew he had brought her to the inn where she had been reunited with her mother and sister.

What they did not know was that he had held her intimately in his arms and kissed her deeply in the night, and that she couldn't stop thinking about it, not even now when he stood beside her fiancé.

Adele tried to keep the color from her cheeks as she offered her hand to Damien and went through the motions of meeting him while her body came alive at his touch. Her heart beat fast with excitement and pleasure.

"I'm honored, Lord Alcester," she said, as indifferently as she could manage, realizing, however, that what she felt for Damien Renshaw was anything but indifference. Now—back in the real world and in the presence of all these other people—she felt a potent, inescapable attraction.

Chapter 10

AFTER A FORMAL DINNER, DURING which Adele gratefully sat at the opposite end of the table from Damien, the ladies retired to the drawing room for coffee while the gentlemen remained at the table to enjoy their claret and cigars.

"Come and sit with me, Adele," Violet said, patting the sofa cushion beside her. "It's time we became better acquainted. We're going to be sisters, after all."

Adele rose from the chair on the other side of the room to join her future sister-in-law, who looked ravishing in a low-necked gown of magenta silk, trimmed with black lace. Her dark hair was pulled up in a most flattering bun with loose tendrils curling around her temples.

"Harold is so happy you're here at last," Violet said, leaning to pick up her coffee cup. "He absolutely adores you. I've never known him to be so deeply in love."

"Thank you, Violet."

"You must be pleased to be reunited with him as

well."

"Oh yes."

Violet lowered her voice to a whisper and touched Adele's hand. "I can't imagine what you must have suffered the past few days. I said a prayer for you every night, and we were all so relieved to hear that Damien had found you. You must tell me everything. Was it as horrible as I imagined?"

Adele swallowed uneasily. "How horrible did you imagine it?"

"Well, to be kidnapped and held prisoner is one thing, but then to have to travel alone across England with a man like Damien. You must have been terrified."

Adele leaned forward to set her cup down on the table. "I wasn't terrified of Lord Alcester. Or...was that what you meant?"

She could have kicked herself.

Violet gazed intently at her for a moment, then waved a hand through the air. "Oh, of course you wouldn't be terrified of Damien. He's family. Though with his reputation, a lady can never be too careful." She sipped her coffee. "Oh dear. I apologize. I've shocked you."

"I'm not shocked," Adele replied, working hard to keep her composure. "My sister had mentioned that Damien was slightly—" she stopped. "Oh, I don't remember what she said. It's not important. All that matters is that I'm here now and I am safe, and Harold and I are to be married."

Violet squeezed her hand. "Yes, and I hope that you'll let me help with the plans. I can show you all the best shops where you can choose your flowers and everything else. It's going to be such fun." Her voice took on a playful tone. "I only hope we can keep Mother from insisting upon using the family seamstress. She'll want to make you look like a big glob of clotted cream with bows. But don't worry. I won't let her do it. I want everything to be perfect for you and Harold. He's my only brother, after all, and my favorite person in all the world. You couldn't ask for a better husband, Adele. He is the most decent man you will ever know. Don't ever forget that."

Adele picked up her coffee cup and knew that he was indeed the most decent man she would ever know, and she was very lucky. She also knew that she had to be sensible in the coming days, keep her desires in check, and be very careful about her behavior around Damien.

It never happened, she told herself. She must forget it. She must forget all of it.

"No, I don't know the Earl of Whitby very well," Clara said to Eustacia, who was glancing across the room at her daughter, Violet. "I met him at my sister's wedding, but I've not had the pleasure of his acquaintance since then. I was married just last Season, you see, and from what I understand, the earl has been in California until recently."

Eustacia handed Clara a cup of steaming coffee with cream. "Yes, that trip to California is what I am wondering about. I assume he was looking for an American wife." She met Clara's gaze. "Not that there's anything wrong with that, of course. You girls are charming and lovely. I only mention it because I think Violet might have caught his eye. She does look stunning in that gown, don't you think?" Eustacia gazed proudly at her daughter.

"Yes, she does. She'll do very well this Season, Eustacia. I wouldn't be surprised if she receives more than a few proposals."

Eustacia sipped her coffee. "One will do just fine," she replied with a anxious smile. "As long as it's the one she wants."

Later, the gentlemen joined them for an evening of music and entertainment—all except for Damien, who sent his apologies, explaining that he had a business matter to attend to.

Adele was relieved. She hadn't been sure she could keep up the pretense of never having met Damien before. Nor had she been looking forward to spending an evening beating down her feelings of attraction. That was going to take a very big stick.

Violet played the piano and sang a charming rendition of "Home Sweet Home." Shortly thereafter, a game of charades began, and much giggling ensued. Afterward, Adele found herself alone with her fiancé at last, in a quiet corner of the drawing room.

"Harold, I am so sorry to have caused so much anxiety for your family these past few days," she said. "I cannot bear the thought that I was such a bother."

"Nonsense," he said with a smile, in his usual friendly manner. "You're here now, and that's all that matters. Tomorrow I will take you on a tour of the house and gardens, and you'll feel like you've lived here your entire life."

She felt her shoulders relax slightly. "That would be very nice. Thank you."

"And I believe," he said, "that my mother is bursting with ideas about our nuptials. I hope you'll humor her by listening. She mentioned lilies in the church, and she was most curious to know what you Americans like to eat. I daresay, she's eager to please. She sees it as her duty to bridge the gap between our two cultures and smooth out your conversion."

Adele swallowed. "It's not as if I were changing religions, Harold."

He laughed awkwardly. "No, of course not. I only meant to say that some things will be very new for you. I hope you will feel free to turn to Mother with any questions you may have. It is imperative that you learn all about our English ways."

"I certainly will, but I hope I will be able to turn to you, as well, Harold, for we are to be husband and wife."

He blushed, then laughed out loud. "Quite so! I will be happy to answer any of your questions, Miss Wilson." His blush brightened. "Goodness me. Adele! I keep forgetting."

She smiled, finding his nervousness endearing. How comfortable she felt when she was in his amenable company. There were no nervous butterflies. He was everything she remembered him to be.

After the party ended, Adele and Clara walked together to their rooms, which were conveniently located across from each other in the Huntington Wing.

"Will you come in for a little while?" Adele asked,

hoping Clara wasn't too tired.

"Of course. We haven't had a chance to talk yet, have we? Not without Mother listening in. And Seger will be arriving tomorrow, so I will no doubt be pleasantly occupied most of the day."

They both smiled, for Adele knew all too well the fire that burned between her sister and her husband.

Adele led the way into her bedchamber and Clara sat down on the bed. Adele removed her pearl necklace and laid it down on her night table. "May I ask you something?"

"Of course," Clara replied.

After a pause, Adele said, "Why have you always tried to talk me into having adventures, when I've constantly told you that I don't want them?"

Clara smiled gently and thought about her answer. "I suppose I always wished that you would let go of your inhibitions every once in a while. I worried that you might be repressing your passions, and that you might eventually explode. Because I certainly would, if I were as perfect as you all the time."

"Explode?"

"Yes. Though you have never shown any signs of discontent. That is why I've tried to tell myself that you're not like me, and I shouldn't expect you to want to 'let go' like I must do occasionally. We're different, that's all, and I've learned to accept that."

Adele thought about the way she had felt in bed with Damien. She had definitely been repressing her passions during the night—passions she hadn't even known she was capable of.

"Yet, on the ship," Adele said, "you wanted me to

have a proper London Season."

Clara shrugged apologetically. "Old habits are hard to break."

Adele faced the mirror on her dressing table and pulled the pins out of her hair. "Maybe you still believe I'm repressed."

Clara didn't say anything.

"I've begun to wonder," Adele said, "why I have always been so well behaved, and so different from you and Sophia. Was I born this way, or did something make me this way?"

"Maybe you should ask Mother that question." Clara leaned back on the bed and put her hand on something. "What's this?" She picked up a note that lay on Adele's pillow and handed it to Adele.

It was written on the Osulton stationery.

> *Miss Wilson,*
> *I took the liberty of arranging for the Osulton*
> *family physician to visit you tomorrow at ten in the*
> *morning.*
> *D.*

Adele's pulse began to beat erratically, all because of a simple note. A note from *him*. "Oh my."

Clara slipped it out from between Adele's fingers. "Someone's coming to examine your leg," she said cheerfully. "That's very wise. You don't want to risk an infection. Wait—who's D.?" She stared at the note for a few seconds. "That must be Lord Alcester."

Adele felt a little breathless, which made no sense. It was just a note about a doctor's visit—a visit she had been readily anticipating.

But the note had been private, meant only for her, and it had been written in the finest hand, laid on her pillow....

"Oh," Clara said softly. "You were on a first name basis."

Adele knew that somehow, without her ever saying a word about Damien to her sister, she understood everything.

"I see." Clara gave the note back and stood up, pacing behind Adele. "I must admit, I was surprised when I met him this evening."

"Why?" Adele asked.

"Because he's so handsome. Why didn't you mention that?"

"Because I'm engaged to Harold. I don't notice whether or not other men are handsome."

Clara gave her a look, and Adele wasn't sure why she was denying something obvious when Clara wasn't blind. Perhaps it was because every instinct Adele possessed was telling her to deny it to herself as well. And she was so used to being good.

She continued to stand before her dressing table, slowly removing her earrings, until Clara stopped pacing behind her. "You don't have to be that way with me, Adele. I'm your sister."

Adele crossed the room to fetch her nightgown. "I'm not being *that way*. Honestly, I care nothing about what Lord Alcester looks like. Don't you remember what Sophia said about him? That he keeps mistresses with scandalous reputations? I certainly remembered, and I could hardly find a man like that attractive, no matter what he looks like. You know me better than that."

"But he rescued you," Clara argued, "quite heroically. Then he tended to a wound on your thigh."

"I'd been shot," Adele explained. "We had no choice about the thigh. Although it was just a small graze. But it still hurt. Believe me, I didn't feel a thing except for the pain."

Too late, she realized how defensive she was sounding. She faced her sister, who was watching her with a look of sympathy. Perhaps the "discontent" Clara had mentioned and feared was finally revealing itself. Perhaps this was a small spark before an explosion. Adele felt a sudden wave of apprehension move through her.

"Don't, Clara," she said firmly, holding up a hand. "I'm fine. I am in love with Harold, and he's the one I want to marry."

"But—"

"No buts. I know you have very romantic notions about passion and adventure—and I will be the first to admit that Damien is a handsome man—but we've had this conversation before. Damien might have come to my rescue, but he is not my knight in shining armor. Harold is. Harold sent him, after all."

"Yes, I know, but—"

"No buts!" she said again. "I don't want to talk about it anymore. Damien helped me, and I am grateful for that, but he's not the kind of man I would ever want to marry. That's the end of the story."

Clara—quite surprisingly—gave in. "All right. I won't mention it again."

"Thank you."

Clara yawned. "I think I'll check on Anne now, then go to bed."

She walked to the door but paused and glanced uncertainly at Adele before she left. As soon as she was gone, Adele picked up the note and read it again, then thought about Damien arranging for the doctor. He had spent some time thinking of her and her needs, in particular about her worries regarding a most intimate, personal matter. She imagined him taking the time to make the arrangements—riding to see the doctor, explaining things as discreetly as possible. He had not forgotten about her.

Warmth swelled inside her. She wondered curiously if he had told Harold about the examination. A part of her—a part that she didn't want to face—hoped he had not. She liked knowing it was a secret they shared, just between the two of them. And she couldn't imagine discussing something like that with Harold.

Chapter 11

*D*OWN BY THE LAKE—WHICH WAS dead calm in the early morning, reflecting the trees and sky with astounding clarity—Damien slowed his horse from a gallop to a walk.

He hadn't realized how badly he'd needed time alone in the woods to breathe the fresh air and the scents of new spring growth. It calmed him, it always had, and that morning, he had needed to ease some tension.

Two letters had arrived for him yesterday. One had come from Henderson, his steward at Essence House, informing him that one of the tenant farmers had packed up and left without so much as a note explaining why, and something had to be done because the rent was due and the estate couldn't weather another loss in income.

Damien had written back to Henderson, instructing him to manage the finances as best he could for a little while longer. Things would improve soon, Damien promised. He didn't say how, but he did ask Henderson to discontinue the search for a family to lease the house because Damien planned to return after the London Season. He assumed his steward would guess that he intended to bring home a bride.

As he wrote the reply, however, Damien envisioned himself wearing a stiff bow tie every night during the Season, attending dull London balls and assemblies, and bowing politely to dozens of simpering, bejeweled debutantes.

He had not enjoyed penning the note.

The other letter, doused in perfume, had come from Frances. She wanted Damien to return to London as soon as he could manage it, because she was "utterly bored" with her current theater production. She wanted a distraction.

Damien headed back to the house and spotted his grandmother's open carriage on the lane. She was out for her usual morning drive. He trotted up beside her.

"Damien!" she said. "I was hoping I would meet you. I have a bone to pick with you, young man."

"A bone, Grandmama?" he replied over the clatter of hooves and carriage wheels.

"Yes. You kept a secret from me yesterday. About your adventure."

Damien glanced uneasily at the driver of the carriage.

His grandmother tapped her cane. "Stop here, Regan. Would you fetch me some daisies? Just over there, that's right." The driver set the brake, hopped down, and left them alone. "Why didn't you tell me about the kidnapping?" the dowager asked.

Damien's horse took a few restless steps sideways.

"Who let it slip?"

"Adele's mother, Beatrice. She can't keep a secret, that one. Delightful sense of humor, though."

They both looked up at the house on top of the hill.

"It was nothing," Damien replied.

"Please, you needn't pretend it hasn't been intriguing for you, rescuing Harold's fiancée from a kidnapper and bringing her home like a hero to deliver her into the arms of her betrothed. Very romantic, don't you think?"

He shook his head at her.

She smiled mischievously. "I heard she was shot, too. Truly, it's the stuff of novels. And you were so good to bandage her leg. Her thigh, I should say. Good heavens, if you weren't future cousins, one might go so far as to call it scandalous."

"It was nothing, Grandmama."

"Of course. I'm sure you kept your eyes closed the entire time."

Damien grinned at her. "You know you're a thorn, Grandmama?"

"I do," she replied with a wink. "But you need a good painful prick every once in a while, Damien, to remind you that you're still alive." She turned toward her driver, still picking daisies. "Call him back, will you? He'll get stung by a bee."

"Regan!" Damien shouted, waving him back. He returned and handed the bouquet to the dowager, who patted him on the arm.

"Thank you. You're such a dear."

The carriage lurched forward, and they started back toward the house. "All right," she said, "let's change the subject. I had a good time last night."

"I heard you were up until two," Damien replied.

"Yes. We played charades and Violet sang and received a tremendous round of applause. She loved it, of course. It's a shame you missed it."

"I had things to do."

"Did you now?"

"I did."

He felt his grandmother's intrusive gaze digging into him.

"She is certainly lovely," she said.

"Who?"

His grandmother gave him a knowing, sidelong glance. "Adele, of course. I like her demeanor. She has no pretensions. She was nervous meeting us, but she didn't try to hide it under an aloofness that's so common among some people. She was very warm and friendly. I can see why the American girls are snatching up all our young men. Clara, her sister, was just as lovely."

"I suppose," he replied.

The dowager leaned over the side of the carriage to tap Damien's knee with her cane. "Oh, stop, will you? Didn't you get to know her?"

"Not really."

They looked up at a blackbird soaring, then rode in silence for a few more minutes.

"Do you think she'll be happy with Harold?" the dowager asked.

"I wouldn't know."

"She mentioned she loves to ride."

"Did she?"

"Harold hates it."

Damien shook his head again. "There are more important things in a marriage than a shared interest in horses and a love of the outdoors. People connect in many different ways."

"I didn't mention a love of the outdoors," his grandmother said. "I think you know her better than you let on."

Damien pulled his horse to a stop. "Have a pleasant morning, Grandmama."

She waved a hand and continued.

On any other day, he would have ridden the rest of the way back to the house with his grandmother. But today—given the subject matter of their conversation—he preferred to stay behind.

Adele sat up on her bed and watched the physician close his black leather bag. He must be a very skilled man, she thought, feeling more than a little impressed. After he'd checked her bullet wound and changed the bandage, he'd taken one brief look at her down there and said simply, "All is well." He hadn't even touched her.

"Thank you, Dr. Lidden," she said.

She escorted him to the door but could not let him leave without learning something first. "This is certainly good news. May I ask if you will report the results to Lord Osulton?"

The doctor paused and looked down at her. He had very kind eyes. "Lord Alcester requested the strictest confidentiality on my part. You are the only person to whom I am responsible, Miss Wilson. Unless, of course, you wish me to inform Lord Osulton."

Damien had indeed been discreet.

Adele gazed up at the doctor. Should she tell him to go and speak to Harold? Dear sweet Harold hadn't mentioned any concerns about this sort of thing, but how could he possibly initiate such an intimate topic of discussion?

He must be wondering, though. The whole family must be concerned....

"I believe, Dr. Lidden, I would prefer that Lord Osulton know all the particulars of my condition. We are to be husband and wife, after all. Please tell him why I was concerned—because I had been unconscious during a part of my abduction. If you could assure him that all is well?"

The doctor smiled. She sensed he was relieved to be spared the necessity of keeping a secret from the family. "I will go and speak to him right away." He bowed to her before he walked out.

"I beg your pardon?" Harold said, straightening from his bent-over position at his lab table and pushing his protective glasses onto the top of his head. "What did you say?"

Dr. Lidden cleared his throat. "I said, my lord, that Miss Wilson was not compromised during her abduction. I have just examined her, and you can be confident that there will be no questions regarding a male heir, if one were to be a product of your marriage in the near future. Do you understand my meaning?"

Harold laughed nervously. He pulled off his glasses,

dropped them onto the stool behind him, and moved around the long table to screw a lid onto a jar. He closed it tight, then laughed again.

"You can actually diagnose these things?" he asked. "I say, it's quite a science, isn't it? Though not a science I would likely enjoy." He gestured toward the bottles behind him, stacked on shelves against the glass wall of the conservatory. "Are you a man of science, Doctor?" Harold blushed and laughed again. "Of course you are. What a dimwitted question." He paused and shifted his weight from one foot to the other. "So... you say she is healthy? Well, that is good news, isn't it? Good news indeed."

Harold turned around to face the opposite wall, as if looking for something to do, then faced the doctor again and lowered his voice to sound more like the lord he was supposed to be. "That will be all, Lidden. Thank you for your time."

Dr. Lidden bowed and walked out, shaking his head as he climbed the steps that led back into the main part of the house.

Damien sat back in the saddle and watched the doctor's carriage roll by on the lane. It was done. He had examined Adele.

Bloody hell. Damien could not contain his curiosity, which was completely inappropriate. He had instructed the doctor to keep the matter private, but now Damien wished he had told the man to report back. Damien wanted the assurance that she had not been harmed when she had been unconscious, and it was killing him now—absolutely killing him—to leave the matter alone and stay away.

Chapter 12

*F*ROM HER WINDOW ON THE second floor, Adele watched Dr. Lidden walk out of the house, climb into his carriage, and drive away. She turned and looked at her door, expecting to hear a knock at any moment. Surely, Harold had been relieved to hear the news that she had not been violated during her kidnapping.

She waited, and waited, and waited some more. Still, Harold did not come. Perhaps he was afraid to. Perhaps he felt uncomfortable discussing such things.

Adele sighed, remembering what a sensitive gentleman he was. She remembered how he had rescued a spider in her Newport drawing room once, while the ladies were screaming, and had set him free out the window. That was the moment she had decided that Harold was the one for her. He had not squished the poor creature under his boot. He was a sweet, non-threatening man.

She decided to seek him out instead. She wanted to share her happiness with someone. Who better than her husband-to-be?

She met the butler in the main hall and asked where Lord Osulton might be.

"He is in the conservatory, Miss Wilson," the butler replied.

What a perfect place, she thought. She had been looking forward to seeing the plants and flowers.

She made her way through the gallery and down a long corridor, then finally found the entrance to the conservatory, flanked by graceful statues of the human form. She didn't let herself stop to look at them. She did stop, however, rather abruptly, at the top of the conservatory steps.

There were no plants. The entire room had been converted to a laboratory. There were five or six tables covered with bottles, scales, funnels, and flasks, and papers strewn about. Tall bookcases filled with reports and journals stood in front of the glass windows, blocking the view of the garden. It was not what she had expected—which characterized her life in general over the past week.

Slowly, feeling almost heartbroken, she descended the steps, looking around at the jars and bottles full of liquids and powders, all with hand-written labels. Adele cleared her throat. "Harold, I'm so sorry to disturb you, but could we have a word?"

His smile seemed strained. "What about, my darling?"

Adele tried to keep her voice casual when, in actuality, she felt very ill at ease. "Did Dr. Lidden come to see you?"

He raised his protective glasses to rest on top of his

head. "Dr. Lidden? Why yes, he did."

"And he told you that everything was fine?"

The smile disappeared from Harold's lips as he stared at her for a few awkward seconds. Then he picked up a crucible and moved it to a new spot on another table, keeping his back to her. "Everything is fine. Yes. That is good news indeed."

A wave of disappointment washed over Adele. She had imagined that Harold would take her into his arms and express his relief. She thought he might kiss her.

"What do you think of my laboratory?" he asked, swinging around to face her again. "I had it converted two years ago."

She had to work hard to recover from her disappointment and show interest in this passion of his. She moved more fully into the conservatory and looked up at the glass ceiling. "What did you do with all the plants?"

"To be honest, I'm not sure what they did. It wasn't my concern, really. I was more interested in where the tables would be placed. The light is excellent, isn't it?"

"Yes, it is."

He gave her a tour of the laboratory and showed her a chemical heating lamp that a local tinsmith had made, which Harold was very proud of. He showed her his alkalimeters, his acidimeters, his hydrometers, his eudiometers, and his pestles and mortars and gas tubes. He was particularly proud of his collection of scientific circulars.

As soon as he had shown her everything, an uncomfortable silence ensued.

"Well, I should leave you to your work, then," Adele said, laboring to sound cheerful. "Perhaps later, we could begin the tour you suggested."

"Tour?" he asked, looking slightly baffled.

"Of the house and gardens. You said you'd show me around."

His face split into a wide grin. "Oh yes! A tour! I would be most happy to do that, yes!" He glanced around at the papers lying about. "Just give me a few minutes to finish what I'm doing here. Why don't I come and fetch you in an hour or so?"

Adele nodded. "That would be very nice, Harold. Thank you."

She picked up her skirts and climbed the steps, telling herself that she would feel better in the days to come, after she and Harold had time to be alone together and talk, and become more acquainted with each other.

Adele stood on the front steps of *Osulton Manor* and watched Clara dash into the arms of her husband, Seger, who she had not seen since she'd left England over a month ago.

"I missed you!" Clara said as Seger swung her around. "Next time, you're coming with me."

"Next time, I most definitely will," he replied, pressing his lips to hers and kissing her passionately, for everyone to see.

Adele gasped at the shocking display of physical affection and felt the others gasp, too. Then they all looked away, pretending not to notice, except for two footmen, who enjoyed the spectacle and nudged each other.

Clara took her husband's hand and dragged him up the stairs to introduce him to everyone. Adele heard someone whisper, *"Those Americans."*

While Seger met the family, Adele noticed a rider coming up the hill. It was Damien. He circled around to the stables at the back of the house.

A short while later, Clara and Seger retired to their rooms to spend time alone with baby Anne, and everyone dispersed. Adele was left alone in the main entrance hall with Harold.

"Perhaps I could take you on the tour tomorrow," he suggested. "I'm in the middle of a very complex experiment and I would like to return to the conservatory. Tomorrow would be better for me."

Adele wondered why he continued to call it a conservatory when it was quite another thing altogether. She kept her opinions to herself, however. "Tomorrow will be fine, Harold."

He hurried off to finish what he had begun.

Adele stood alone in the center of the round hall and felt a tremendous longing to be outdoors. Though she was disappointed that Harold wished to work on his experiment, she was still very pleased and happy about the doctor's news earlier. She glanced toward the front door and remembered seeing Damien not more than a few minutes ago, riding toward the stables.

She also remembered what he had said to her at the inn—that it would be dangerous for them to speak to each other, especially alone.

But surely, she could just tell him this one small bit of news. She couldn't very well leave him to wonder about it.

For a moment or two, she dithered over what to do, then gave in and decided she would break the rule just this once. It wouldn't be such a terrible thing. She would just tell him the news, then return to the house.

She ventured out the front door and made her way around to the back, her leather boots crunching over the clean, white gravel. The air smelled of roses and clipped green grass. She glanced down the hill toward the woods and longed for the smells down there. A leisurely ride would certainly clear her head. Perhaps Harold would finish his work early and be willing to join her later.

She walked to the stables, didn't see anyone around, so quietly entered where the doors were flung open, letting the sun stream onto the wide, plank floor. Inside, the smell of hay and horses wafted to her nostrils, and she breathed deeply, basking in it. She had been too long in a cabin on a boat, and then trapped in a tiny cottage with no escape. Her bones were kicking to enjoy freedom, her heart longing to gallop.

Thinking of such freedoms made her remember her conversation with Clara the night before, when Clara had used the word "repressed." Adele realized that the only time she felt truly "free" was when she went riding or running in the woods. It was a natural place where everything was real. There were no expectations in the woods. No rules to worry about.

Adele wandered down the long row of stalls, stroking the horses' soft, silky noses, enjoying the sounds they made as they nuzzled her palm. Just then, she heard a familiar voice inside the next stall. It was Damien, and she stopped, her heart racing.

She contemplated her frustrating response. She had thought she would be able to control her feelings when she saw him, but there she stood, suffering from yet another attack of exhilaration—and she hadn't even seen him yet.

Perhaps this hadn't been such a good idea, after all. Feeling apprehensive and anxious, she turned quickly to leave, but then she heard him talking to his horse. She stopped again. What was he saying? His voice was too low to decipher. She listened for a few seconds, then couldn't help herself. She turned back and peered around the corner.

He was feeding an apple to the horse. She heard the crunching sound; she could even smell the apple. It reminded her of home, of their orchard in Wisconsin. Then she noticed a bucket full of juicy red apples just outside the stall.

Damien picked up a brush and began to groom his horse. She thought she was the only one who groomed her own horse. Her mother constantly said, "That's what servants are for," but Adele liked to do it. She had done it since she was a girl and she did not wish to give it up. It was the only thing she did that her mother disapproved of, though her mother had long ago stopped mentioning it.

Adele watched Damien for a moment. He had removed his riding jacket and wore a black waistcoat over a crisp white shirt. His hair looked windblown, spilling onto his collar as it had when he'd first burst into her room to rescue her from the kidnapper.

He had two looks, she realized—the rugged out-doorsman and the elegant London gentleman. She believed she liked the outdoorsman the best. It was more natural and untampered with. It was the look she found most fascinating.

Soon she was mesmerized by the sight of his big hand holding the brush, smoothly stroking the horse's shiny coat. Damien's muscular shoulder moved with such a lovely grace. The strength and breadth of his back was indeed worthy of admiration....

"I don't suppose you'd like to help," he said casually, and it took Adele a few seconds to realize that he was talking to her.

Blushing with embarrassment, she stepped out from behind the post. "It seems I've been discovered."

He glanced over his shoulder and grinned, and she melted. She had to put her hand on the post to keep from toppling over into the next stall.

Damien turned his attention back to the task of stroking his most fortunate horse, while Adele moved a little closer. "I thought you might like to know what happened with Dr. Lidden."

Damien froze mid-stroke. He stood still for a few seconds, then he lowered the brush to his side, turned and walked toward her. His boots swished across the hay and Adele felt the heat of his approach like a fast-moving fire, soon too hot to bear.

"And?" he said, stopping before her.

She smelled the natural scent of his body. It was so familiar. It assaulted her senses like a storm. "All is well," she replied shakily.

He took a deep breath and let it out. "Thank goodness."

"Yes," she repeated.

He stood before her, saying nothing. She didn't know what to say either. They had vowed to keep away from each other after their arrival at *Osulton Manor*. Yet here she was.

"And everything else is all right?" he asked. "You're comfortable here? You have everything you need?"

She nodded quickly.

"Good," he said.

Still he did not turn away. His horse nickered. Adele would nicker, too, if she were waiting for Damien to finish rubbing her down.

"I'm glad you came," he said, in a soft, husky voice. "I was thinking about you."

Feeling an onslaught of potent yearning, she gazed up at his dark eyes and strove to be sensible. She thought of his mistresses. She thought about his reputation and the fact that he was Harold's cousin, and she was engaged to Harold and did not want to jeopardize that, for she was happy with her choice.

Harold was a very nice man. He was the right choice for her. The temptation she felt around Damien was dangerous, and she had no business feeling impassioned in his presence. She would never want to marry *him*.

Why, then, could she not make these wayward feelings go away? Why could she not resist the wanton desire to see him, and the urge to stay here in the stables with him and do more than just talk?

Adele breathed faster. "I was thinking about you, too. I mean.... I wanted you to know that everything was fine."

They stood facing each other, saying nothing, and Adele thought her heart was going to give out. His eyes searched her face—from the top of her head to her lips, where he lingered a moment, then down the length of her body to her feet and back up again.

It felt strangely as if he had touched her in all those places. She felt weak and exposed before a man who possessed a great deal of experience and command when it came to women. It was no wonder he'd had so many lovers. She suspected most women would tumble into his arms quite happily when faced with this.

"So now I've told you," she said crisply and succinctly. "So, I should get back to the house."

He tilted his head, looking at her with disabling, spellbinding eyes. "Yes, you should."

Her lips parted. "All right then," she said, feeling utterly ridiculous. "I'll go."

She turned and left the stable, but felt his eyes watching her the entire way out.

Chapter 13

STILL IN HER NIGHTGOWN THE following morning, Adele left her bedchamber and went to her mother's room. She knocked softly, for it was still early, and entered. Her mother was asleep with her mouth open, snoring.

Adele approached the bed and whispered, "Mother?"

Always a light sleeper, Beatrice woke. She gazed drowsily at Adele, then lifted the heavy covers. "Adele, darling. Get in. It's chilly."

Adele climbed into the warm bed and lay next to her mother. It reminded her of the days in Wisconsin when the family used to sleep together in the one-room cabin. They'd had no servants to light a fire in the morning, so they often snuggled close.

Adele waited a few minutes before she spoke. "Can I ask you something?"

Beatrice opened her eyes. "Of course."

"You and Father always said I was the most well behaved of your three girls. I never got into trouble, and I'm trying to understand why I was so different from Sophia and Clara."

Her mother rested a hand on Adele's cheek. "You were different from the moment you were born. Even as a baby, you never complained when I put you to bed. You went to sleep. When you were a little girl, you were always happy and very independent. You never threw a tantrum or fought against anything."

"But I fought against Sophia and Clara. I tattled on them. I didn't like it when they broke the rules."

Her mother thought about that for a moment. "That happened in New York. You didn't do that so much in Wisconsin. You usually went your own way."

"I changed when we moved?"

"Well, you were growing up."

Adele thought about her life, how she'd always felt it was divided in two. First, she had been "Adele in Wisconsin," who had loved her pony and went riding alone in the woods. Then she had become "Adele in New York," who had loved her parents and wanted to please them, and often felt frustrated with her sisters, who did what they wanted when she could not.

Why couldn't she?

"Do you think I was born with this personality, to be good?"

"We are all born with a natural disposition."

"But can that disposition change?"

Her mother's brow furrowed. "Is something wrong, Adele? Are you not happy? Has your ordeal—"

"No, I am very happy, Mother. Please do not worry. I just want to understand the person I am supposed to be."

Beatrice smiled. "You are supposed to be you. And

you are perfect, Adele."

Perfect. There it was again. That word. It had never made her uncomfortable before. She usually took pride in it and enjoyed pleasing others. But now, since she'd been kidnapped, and since she'd let Damien kiss her and lie with her in the darkness, she felt as if she might be an impostor, and the walls around her were closing in, threatening to squeeze the very life out of her. She could barely breathe.

Over breakfast the next day, Adele smiled and took part in animated conversations about her nuptials. Her mother and Eustacia sat together at one end of the table, clucking like hens, while Violet sent amused, knowing glances Adele's way.

The family seamstress was mentioned, and Violet practically dropped her teacup into her saucer. "Oh no, Mother, you must consider a designer in London. Or perhaps that Worth fellow in Paris. Adele's marriage to Harold must be perfect, and to be perfect, she must have the very newest fashion. Her sister Sophia wore a wedding gown by Charles Worth, and she is a duchess, after all."

Eustacia's face lit up with interest, and Adele's mother beamed, nodding with pride. "Oh yes," she said. "It must absolutely be a Worth gown."

Adele glanced across the white-clothed table at her future sister-in-law, Violet, who looked very pleased with herself. Adele, on the other hand, heard only the word "perfect," and felt a great pressure squeezing around her chest.

After breakfast, Adele asked where Harold might

be, for she was looking forward to her tour of the house and gardens, and she didn't want to think about wedding plans anymore. They were becoming too complicated, and everyone seemed to be getting carried away with the details. Adele wanted only to begin her new life and get to know her fiancé better. She wanted to feel that this was her home, so she would finally be able to relax here. That's what mattered to her. Not the color of the bridesmaids' sashes.

She was told Harold would be in the conservatory. Or rather, the laboratory. She made her way there and entered. Her fiancé stepped out from behind a wall of bookcases. He saw her and jumped with fright.

"Oh, good gracious!" he said, resting a hand on his chest. "You surprised me, Adele." He smiled awkwardly. "What are you doing here?"

Adele approached him. He wore a white apron with a dark stain on the front. As she came closer, she noticed he smelled like sulphur.

"You promised to show me the house and gardens today. I'm especially looking forward to a tour of the stables. I heard you have some of the finest horses in England."

He gave her a flustered look. "I was just about to begin something here. You see, I'm working on the idea I discussed with your father regarding a new synthetic dye." He gestured toward a number of jars on the table. "I am in the process of producing something artificial that I believe will be more practical than any natural concoction. It's quite exciting, don't you think?"

Adele looked at the bottles. "Yes, it's very exciting."

"Your father believes it has business potential." An awkward silence arose and lingered. "Perhaps Damien could show you the stables," Harold suggested, sounding frazzled.

Adele's heart turned over in her chest. "I beg your pardon?"

"Damien?"

Adele froze. There was a movement at the back corner of the conservatory, close to the far windows, from behind the one potted plant that had managed to survive the renovation.

Hands behind his back, looking as if he had not wanted to be discovered, he stepped into view. "Good morning, Miss Wilson."

"Good morning," she replied, straightening her shoulders and feeling oddly defensive.

Harold smiled enthusiastically. "Yes! This is most opportune! Damien is the perfect person to show you the stables. It's his doing, you know," Harold said proudly, "acquiring the best horses. He's knowledgeable about that sort of thing. Damien, would you be so kind as to show my lovely betrothed to the stables?"

Adele wanted to sink through the floor. Damien didn't want to show her the stables. He had not even wanted to be discovered.

"Of course," he said, politely.

Adele put up her hand. "Please, I don't want to be a bother. I can wait, Harold. Truly. I wanted to see everything with *you*. Don't feel you have to entertain me. I don't want to intrude upon your experiments, and clearly, Lord Alcester was here talking to you before I interrupted and—"

"Don't be silly, my love!" Harold said. "Damien was bored anyway, weren't you, Damien? And he just told me that he wanted to go for a ride. Perhaps he could show you the estate as well. He knows these woods better than anyone, don't you, Damien? Always poking about outdoors."

Adele marveled at her fiancé's absolute trust in his cousin. Was Harold not aware of Damien's reputation with women? Or did he think Adele was incapable of swooning over a man's good looks? Obviously, the concept of passionate swooning had never occurred to him.

"Really," she said, backing away, "I don't mind waiting."

"No, no, don't leave!" Harold said with a rather desperate smile, taking a step forward to detain her. "In fact, I've been dreading taking you to the stables. I'm actually afraid of horses. I was kicked by one when I was twelve. Remember that, Damien? Nasty beasts, I daresay."

Harold was afraid of horses? He didn't like to ride? Adele had not known that. What else did she not know?

"Please, let Damien take you," Harold implored, "and I can show you the inside of the house later today."

Both Damien and Adele looked at each other. What could they say? To outwardly refuse to be together would suggest something untoward between them, and Adele certainly didn't want to admit to being uneasy around her fiancé's cousin. She should feel nothing but brotherly affection toward him.

Damien took a step forward.

"There now," Harold said cheerfully. "This will give me time to finish my experiment, and I will be very content knowing that you are in good hands, my dear."

Adele smiled nervously as Damien approached. Good hands, indeed.

It was as if they had never met before yesterday.

Damien escorted Adele to the stables and gave her a polite tour, describing where each horse had come from and when it had been purchased or, if not purchased, bred there on the estate.

She nodded, vastly pleased to be discussing horses, which was a subject near and dear to her heart. It made it easy to avoid discussing anything personal.

She recalled her sister Sophia's letters describing how the English could behave in such superficial ways—all in the name of propriety. Sophia had wrestled with the frustration of it all, never knowing what any of them were truly thinking. Adele suddenly understood what her sister had endured. Adele was now acting as if there were nothing between herself and Damien except the common link of Harold.

"Would you like to take a ride?" Damien asked, without making direct eye contact with her. A groom stood nearby, waiting for an official request.

"I believe I would," Adele replied, knowing that she should have said no, but she was desperate to escape this manicured palace and all the watching eyes.

The groom immediately set to work, saddling two horses. A short time later, she and Damien were riding side by side down the hill, trotting across the wide green lawns. They rode in silence for some time, and Adele smothered any urge to talk and bring up anything to do with the time they'd spent alone together.

Damien was certainly obliging the pretense that they had never met before yesterday. Perhaps it was best. Perhaps this was how it would be from now on. Out of respect for Harold, Damien would not be open in her presence. Yes, it was best.

They soon approached a lake and stopped to let the horses graze.

"Is that a teahouse on the island?" Adele asked, noticing a small, round building, painted white and surrounded by leafy oaks.

"Yes, but it's not an island, it's a peninsula," Damien replied. "We can get to it by riding to the other side of the lake."

"Can we?"

Too late, Adele realized she should have been blasé about the teahouse and everything else, but she could only keep up this pretense for so long before she was bound to slip.

"Or maybe I should wait for Harold," she quickly added.

Damien leaned forward and stroked his horse's neck, saying nothing for a few seconds while he gazed at her suggestively from under dark, long lashes.

"I doubt you'll get Harold down here any time soon," he finally said.

Adele gave him a sidelong glance.

He turned his eyes toward the calm lake and surveyed the landscape. What was he considering? Was he checking to make sure there was no one else about?

He glanced back at her, his dark eyes assessing.

There was something between them, she knew, even though they did not speak of it or, heaven forbid, touch each other. It was understood that it would remain unspoken. As long as they never openly acknowledged it, or acted upon it, they would be doing nothing wrong. They both knew where the line was drawn. The challenge, however, was in not crossing that line.

"You want to explore it now, don't you?" he asked, sensitive to her desires. His voice touched her like a feather and sent warmth through all her limbs.

When she didn't respond, he trotted off ahead. "Don't worry. I won't tell."

I won't tell. There were already far too many secrets where he was concerned. Along with far too many hidden, buried emotions.

Yet, against her better judgment, and for reasons Adele couldn't begin to understand, she could do nothing but follow Lord Alcester into the cool, shady forest.

Chapter 14

*T*HIS IS A MISTAKE, DAMIEN thought, as he led the way through the trees and around the lake. He should not have suggested they ride on. He should have started back toward the house. But he'd taken one look at Adele on her horse in the natural splendor of her feminine beauty, with her top hat perched at an enticing angle on her head, and he'd slid down the slippery slope of his less gentlemanly inclinations.

It was at that moment an instinct deeper than logic prevailed. It was the instinct responsible for his reputation for being able to successfully seduce any woman of his choosing.

He did not, however, choose just any woman. He had very particular tastes, and he always chose his lovers with careful, sound logic. Except for today, he thought irritably, when the opportunity to follow his more primitive desires had caused his body to respond promptly on cue with a most untimely arousal.

"I haven't thanked you for arranging for the doctor," Adele said, trotting up beside him. "I wasn't sure how to handle that. I'm glad you thought of it."

He had thought of a great many things over the past few days.

"Did you tell Harold you were going to take care of it?" she asked.

Damien steered his mount around a fallen branch. "No."

She considered his direct, flat response. "Why not?"

"The subject didn't come up."

The sound of their horses' hooves tapping over the soft earth filled the silence. "I did talk to him about it myself," she said, "after I had the doctor explain the situation to him. I wanted Harold to know that I had not been harmed."

"And what did Harold say?"

"He was relieved, of course, but I think he was a little uncomfortable talking about it."

Damien shifted in the saddle. He knew his cousin well, and he knew that Harold wasn't entirely comfortable around women, especially when it came to more intimate matters.

The truth was, Harold lacked experience, and Damien suspected he would be ill at ease on his wedding night. Painfully so. But it would be disloyal for Damien to express such an opinion to the woman Harold was going to marry. Instead, he would talk to Harold about it. He would prepare him for his wedding night and tell him what to do.

The thought of that caused a sudden tightness in Damien's gut. Could he do that? Tell Harold how to make love to Adele?

"I was surprised," she said, pulling him from his

thoughts, "when Harold suggested you show me the stables, given that we just spent so much time together."

"Harold trusts me."

"But how can he trust me?" she asked. "He doesn't know me as well as he knows you. It didn't even occur to him that I might be tempted by your reputed allure when it comes to women. Am I that predictable? Do I really come across as that pure?"

He glanced at her briefly, choosing not to answer.

"It's strange," she continued, "that even though we're engaged to be married, sometimes I'm not sure how Harold really feels about me. Do you think he would be jealous if he saw us now, riding alone to the teahouse?"

Recognizing Adele's need for reassurance where her fiancé was concerned, Damien found himself wishing for the first time that his cousin had more finesse. Adele deserved to be adored. If she felt adored by Harold, she would not need to ask Damien these questions.

At the same time, he disliked the idea of her being adored by Harold. Though he loved Harold.

"I'm sure he would be," Damien replied.

But in all honesty, Damien was not sure. Harold probably wasn't even giving it a second thought. He was more likely leaning over a beaker right now, concerned only with what was going on inside it, which frustrated Damien greatly.

He told himself it didn't mean Harold had no feelings for Adele. Harold was just being Harold.

"He'll eventually become more at ease around

you," Damien said. "I know the man he is beneath the surface and believe me when I say that he is a good man, the most honorable man I know. Give him time. You'll have your whole life to get to know him as well as I do."

She adjusted the reins in her gloved hands. "I have no doubt that he is a good man. You're right. I shouldn't try to rush things. I shouldn't expect to be intimate with someone I've only just met."

Yet she and Damien had only just met, and there was an astonishing level of intimacy between them. Though at the moment, they were both working hard to keep it at bay.

They rode around the lake and arrived at the path that led to the teahouse. "Will it be locked?" Adele asked.

"Yes, but I know where the key is. Harold and I used to come here when we were younger, before he discovered chemistry. We spent many hours fishing right over there." He pointed to the log they once sat on. "Harold's father used to enjoy the outdoors. He was always hosting shooting parties."

"What about your father and mother? Do you remember much about them?"

Damien drew his horse to a halt at the teahouse and swung down from the saddle, then went to help Adele. "My father was very much like Harold. Red hair and all. Eustacia was my father's sister."

"And your mother?"

"My mother...well, she had interests that didn't include me. I had no love for her, and to be honest, I don't remember that much about her. I never try to, because when I do, all I feel is resentment."

"You have no pleasant or happy memories of her at all?"

Adele's gloved hands came to rest on Damien's shoulders, and he took hold of her tiny waist. She leaped down, landing with a thud before him, her skirts billowing upon the air.

They stood motionless, staring at each other for a few seconds while he thought about Adele's question.

"I suppose I do. I remember her holding me and singing to me when I was very small."

But he didn't like to think about that. It hurt to remember his mother's tenderness. It gave him a knot in his stomach.

"Were you close to your father?" Adele asked. "You see, I come from a close family and it's difficult to imagine being a child and not feeling close to at least *someone.*"

He finally turned away from her and tethered the horses to a tree. "I suppose I was. We were very different, but we seemed to connect somehow. I suppose I knew he would do anything for me. I was loyal to him in return."

"Like you're loyal to Harold?"

The question made him uncomfortable. "Yes."

"When did you and Harold become so close?"

A memory flashed in his mind—an image of a day not long after his parents died, a month, perhaps. He had stumbled across some boys fighting at school, but it turned out to be boys beating on Harold. Damien had fought them off. He had felt useful that day, after weeks of shame and regret, blaming himself for his parents' deaths.

With nose bleeding and eyes tearing, Harold had looked up at Damien from where he'd sat on the ground, huddled against a brick wall, and said, "You're my best friend, Damien. You'll always be my best friend."

Damien stood outside the teahouse with Adele and told her all about that day, and he saw in her eyes that she understood. He told her other things about their childhood as well. He explained how Harold had always been able to see when Damien was missing his parents and had cheered him up with jokes or games. Damien gazed down at the ground, remembering so many little things....

The horses nickered, and both Damien and Adele went to pat them while they spoke more about the past. Then Damien retrieved the key to the teahouse from a jar nestled in a tree stump nearby and returned to unlock the door. He pushed it open and gestured with a hand for Adele to enter first.

She walked into the large, round room bathed in sunlight, her black boots tapping over the wide planks on the floor. She wandered leisurely around the perimeter, looking out the windows at the lake, then she moved to the center where a large table stood— also round—with twelve Chippendale chairs.

Damien removed his hat and closed the door behind him. "This was built in 1799, because of something Prince Edward, the Duke of Kent, said when he was a young man—that in a round building, the devil could never corner you."

"And do you believe that?" She turned her back

on him and strolled around, looking carefully at the small paintings of landscapes on the walls.

He let his gaze sweep appreciatively down the length of her curvaceous figure. "No. I believe he can corner you anywhere."

She nodded in agreement, looked around a bit more, then smiled at him.

"It's wonderful," she said. "I will come here often, I am sure of it, just to escape the...." She stopped whatever she was going to say and glanced up very briefly at Damien before turning toward the windows again.

He took a slow step forward. "Escape what, Adele?"

She faced him again and smiled sheepishly. "Oh, I don't know. The pristine perfection of it all. Everything is so clipped and manicured here, and I don't just mean the gardens, if you understand my meaning."

"I do."

"Personally, I prefer a setting more like this. Something small and cozy and surrounded by overgrown grasses. I love how the willow branches dip down into the water just over there, and how the leaves over here"—she pointed at the window—"block the view slightly. It's natural and unpredictable."

She met his gaze and smiled warmly, and he felt a stirring deep inside himself. She was beautiful, there was no question about that, and he was attracted to her in a physical way, which was not unusual. That could be dealt with. But there was so much more....

Feeling on edge, Damien dropped his gaze to his boots. He had prayed these feelings would disappear after he delivered Adele safely to Harold. He had prayed that he and Adele would both forget what had happened between them, but Damien could not. It was impossible. All he wanted to do now was pull her into his arms and do nothing but hold her. He wanted to take her to Essence House and show her the unkempt gardens and the cozy rooms that were full of mismatched pillows, and the stacks of books piled high on the floors because there was no room left in the bookcases, and no one had ever wanted to part with the books.

Damien knew Adele would love Essence House because she loved what was natural and unpretentious.

He feared suddenly that what he felt for Adele was more than just a fleeting lust for an attractive woman, and more than a simple desire for the forbidden. Now that they were back in the real world, it seemed to be much, much more.

Damien squeezed his hat in his hands and felt a dark shadow, like a storm cloud, settle over him and inside him. It was a shadow of impending doom, of shame and regret on the horizon. He couldn't move.

"What is your house like, Damien?" she asked, her expression bright with interest.

Not only could he not move, he couldn't speak, either. All he could do was stare blankly at her.

"Damien?" She sauntered closer. "Your house? It's called Essence House. Didn't you tell me that once? I looked the word 'essence' up in the dictionary this morning because I was thinking about it, and it means 'the real or ultimate nature of a thing, as opposed to its existence.' It means 'heart, soul, core, or root.'"

She continued to move closer in that carefree way,

and he wished she would stop. "In my imagination, your house is very different from *Osulton Manor*," she said. "The way I picture it, things aren't clipped. They are like this, aren't they?" She gestured toward the vista outside the windows. "Natural and overgrown and somewhat...messy?"

She laughed.

He didn't. He couldn't. "Yes, that's exactly what it looks like," he said flatly. "The truth is, I can't afford a gardener, and even if I could, I'd tell him not to touch a thing, because I love it exactly the way it is."

She stopped her carefree sauntering directly in front of him, only a foot away, close enough that he could see the flecks of gold in her eyes and the individual hairs in her delicate brows. He could smell the clean scent of her skin. Though it wasn't perfume he smelled. It was just her.

Her hands were clasped behind her back. She was swinging back and forth like a mischievous child, gazing up at him with impish eyes. She'd never looked at him like that before—so playfully and flirtatiously. It was the Adele he'd always known existed deeper down. The Adele she had never let loose. This Adele—the sensual one—awakened his sharply honed instincts and impulses.

"I'm glad you keep your garden natural," she said. "I wouldn't want to ever think of you with your wings clipped, so to speak. I like the idea of you being wild and soaring."

Damien fought to ignore the blood pounding through his veins. "Adele, you need to soar, too. Don't let them make you English."

Her smile faded, and her expression became serious all of a sudden.

Bloody hell. He didn't know where that had come from. She was engaged to Harold. He shouldn't have said that.

"I didn't mean that the way it sounded," he said, backtracking. "They're good people. They're my family."

She turned away from him and walked to the windows. Standing with her back to him, she said nothing. He set his hat down on the table, then moved around it and joined her, gazing down at her soft profile in the light reflecting off the calm lake.

"Why *would* you say that?" she asked, looking up at him. "Is it because of what Eustacia has been saying— that no one would guess I'm American? That I'm practically English already? Do I mold and bend into any shape, fade into any background, rather than be the real me? Or is it because everyone always assumes that I'm perfect, and you're the only one who knows I'm not?"

He wasn't sure what to say, which was out of his realm of experience. He *always* knew what to say to women. He knew what they wanted to hear, and he knew how to seduce the ones who wanted to be seduced.

But Adele—dear, sweet Adele—did not want to be seduced. She wanted truth. She was unsure of her future, and she wanted him to tell her everything was going to be all right.

"Yes, it's just because of that," he said.

She gazed out at the lake again. There was not

a hint of a breeze causing even the smallest waves. There were only random, circular ripples where the quiet fish bobbed to the surface.

"No, it's *not* just that," she insisted, and Damien's gut wrenched. Then she turned to him and began to speak quickly. "Harold is a wonderful man, I know that. I just wasn't expecting so much grandeur. I had no idea I would be living in a house like this. I don't know what I'm supposed to do. How will I know when to curtsy or not to curtsy, or how to be a proper hostess? I'm not prepared for this. How will I ever manage? Do you think I made a mistake coming here? Or did Harold make a mistake, believing in me?"

"You'll learn," he said. "You'll learn all of it, because you're smart. Harold wouldn't have proposed to you otherwise."

"But do I *want* to learn it? Maybe it's too much. I've always done what my parents wanted me to do, but sometimes I think they may have overestimated me. They always said I was the most sensible and dutiful of their daughters, and I suppose that's what I've always thought I was born to be—sensible, and to please others. I've been playing that role, but now I'm not so sure. I'm tired of this perfect life—the jewels and the shiny chandeliers and the overwhelming wealth. I don't want all those things, I just want...."

She gazed into his eyes, looking almost frantic. "Sometimes lately, I find myself not wanting to be sensible. I've never felt that way before. I've never been tempted to do anything that was different from what was expected of me. I was content to just do what people told me to do. But since the kidnapping,

I'm questioning that. And it scares me."

Her eyes were pleading. What did she want? Answers? Answers to what? Her place in the world? Her purpose? Her desires?

"There's a great deal in life you haven't experienced yet, Adele. That's all. You'll figure it all out in time."

"But I am going to become someone's wife very soon. I am choosing the direction of my whole future, the rest of my life. What if I discover that's not what I'm meant to be?" She stopped talking and bowed her head and cupped her forehead in her hand. "Oh, listen to me. How very silly I must sound. I have cold feet, that's all, and I've been listening to my sister too much."

"What does she say to you?" he asked.

The pleading look disappeared, and Adele's voice took on a calmer note. "She's always wanted me to go out and have an adventure before I settle down. But I already did that, didn't I?"

"Does she approve of your decision to marry Harold?"

Adele blinked a few times. "Oh yes. She likes him very much. Who wouldn't?"

"Of course," he replied.

Adele's gaze swept over Damien's face, from his eyes down to his lips, to his hair and back to his eyes again. He simply stood there, letting her look at him.

"I'm sorry," she said, "for being so emotional. It's not like me to act that way." She paused, staring at his face as if she were pondering something. Then at last she added, "Sometimes I feel like I'm a different person when I'm with you."

He gazed down at her wet, ruby lips, glistening in the sunlight beaming in the windows, and an unexpected shiver of need coursed through him. She was unlike any woman he'd ever known.

Perhaps it was because she opened up to him and told him things she didn't tell other people. Or perhaps it was her innocence and her goodness.

No, it couldn't be. The only thing he thought about when he looked at her was everything that defied innocence and goodness. What he felt for her was dark and sinful and wrong.

She gazed up into his eyes and said with a deep, resounding sadness, "Damien, sometimes I worry that I don't really know who I am."

"I know who you are," he softly replied.

He stepped forward, closing the last bit of space between them, and took in a deep breath. *At last,* he thought, feeling a blazing surge of anticipation in his veins. But with it came shame and remorse—even before he'd done anything.

She looked into his eyes and shook her head, and he understood what she was saying without ever really saying it. *This is wrong, please don't do it.* That's what her eyes told him.

It was wrong, he knew it was, but he couldn't stop himself. He folded her into his arms and held her, as he'd held her on the bed when she'd had the nightmare. Except then, he had done it because he had to. He had to keep her safe when he was bringing her home to Harold. He'd been acting as her protector.

Now he had no excuses. They had survived the ordeal and arrived at *Osulton Manor.* She was safe in every way but one. Because he should not be holding her. Harold should be holding her.

But still, Damien could not let go. His heart was pounding, racing out of control. He pulled back, took her face in his hands, and kissed the tip of her nose, then her forehead, then he lowered his mouth to hers—softly, wetly, so achingly that it hurt inside of him. Blood pounded in his brain. He swept his tongue into her mouth, and she made a little sound—a sweet, innocent whimper of pleasure and awakening.

Savoring the breathtaking sensation of her soft, luscious body pressed closely to his, and responding to the feel of her breasts crushed between them, Damien deepened the kiss.

Adele wrapped her arms around his neck, ran her fingers through the hair at his nape, and Damien's impulses, like fire under a splash of kerosene, flared with a gusty roar. He devoured her soft, supple lips with his own, and finally—*finally*—he let himself cherish her deep inside his broken heart.

Giving in to it all was like taking a cool drink of water, when he'd been almost dead from thirst. He couldn't stop guzzling. He wanted more and more and more.

He turned with Adele in his arms and slowly backed her up against the wall, his lips never leaving hers. Harold could have been watching from outside one of the windows, and Damien wouldn't have been able to stop this. That's how badly he wanted her—with desperation and a fierce, fiery need more powerful than anything he'd ever known.

He had lost himself. He was doomed. Yet still, he

couldn't stop, because the pleasure was so good, and the need to touch Adele and hold her was so great, he thought he might suffocate if he let go.

Bending slightly at the knees, he thrust upward with his hips. She raised a knee to open to him, while she drove forward in return, applying an exquisite, stimulating pressure upon his desires. It all came so naturally—this tantalizing, erotic dance that mimicked sex—even though they were fully clothed, upright against a wall.

Damien's senses reeled with lust. He wanted so much more than this. He wanted to bury himself inside her and feel the pleasure of everything she contained. He wanted to take her—in every way she could be taken—here and now on the cold, hard floor of this rotunda.

She sighed with contentment, and the deep, husky sound of her voice, full of raw, sexual need, sent his desires ramming hard against the crumbling wall of his self-control.

Feeling her hands cup the back of his head, he moved lower to kiss her neck, while he unfastened the top buttons at the collar of her bodice. *Adele....* He wanted to say her name, whisper it in her ear, but he didn't want to break the fragile spell, so he kept quiet.

She moaned again, running her hands through his hair and making a terrible mess of it, while Damien dropped reckless, openmouthed kisses across the moist, creamy skin just above her corset.

"Damien," she whispered, panting, as she tossed her head back. "Please, stop."

He heard the desperation in her voice, and realized

she was pleading with him again, only this time for something very different from before. She was asking him to back away because she didn't have the strength or the discipline to do so herself.

Damien labored to throttle his mounting desires. Quickly he stepped back and raked a shaky hand through his hair. All the breath sailed out of his lungs as if he'd been punched. It was a reaction to his sexual desires being suddenly and swiftly disrupted.

Adele stood against the wall. She gathered the top of her bodice in a tight fist and held it closed. Her cheeks were flushed. She looked shocked. Dismayed.

"I apologize," he whispered.

Adele's eyes filled with tears. "We shouldn't have done that."

"It was my fault entirely," he said.

"No, it was my fault, too. I wanted you, but I don't *want* to want you."

Her statement hurt, even though he knew it was the way things were. He didn't *want* to want her either.

"Please go away," she pleaded. "Go to London until this passes. It's wrong, Damien, and we both know it. Please just go away."

He stared at her shimmering beauty in the brightness of the room as she pleaded with him to do the right thing.

He nodded and walked out.

Damien strode to the house to leave a note for his aunt, to tell her that he was leaving. He passed his cousin Violet on the way up the front steps. "Damien," she said, "where are you going?"

He did not stop to talk. "To London."

"But what about tonight? We've been rehearsing a scene from *King Lear*."

"It will be stupendous, I'm sure." He entered the house and slammed the door behind him.

Violet remained on the steps, staring after her cousin, who seemed in a most hotheaded hurry. He is probably going to see that actress, she thought, lifting her parasol over her head and turning to continue down the steps on her way to the garden, where she'd heard Lord Whitby had gone walking.

Lord Whitby. Violet sighed heavily. He was so impossibly handsome she couldn't bear it. She'd once heard that opposites were attracted to each other. Perhaps it was true. She did love his golden hair. Thank heavens he hadn't come back from California engaged to one of those brash American heiresses. And thank heavens Harold *had* come home engaged to one.

Violet smiled. Fate was kind sometimes, was it not? Who would ever have thought Harold would manage such a thing, and secure Violet's own future in the process? And secure it soundly, because she had always been able to pull her brother's strings. Now it would be the family's purse strings she would pull.

She glanced over her shoulder to where she had just met Damien a moment earlier. He—on the other hand—had no strings to pull. He was no one's puppet. Lucky for her, the heiress still wanted to marry her trouble-free brother. And thank God Damien was leaving.

Violet stopped. She stood motionless on the grass. Was she being selfish by wanting Harold's marriage for her own advantage? She recalled what the vicar had said in church the week before: "We must put others before ourselves."

Perhaps she should try to be a better person, Violet thought fleetingly. She gazed upward as she considered it and pictured herself doing something charitable. Could she help the vicar when he went to collect bread for the poor?

Then she thought of the horrid, cheap cologne he wore. Violet wrinkled her nose and started walking again. No, she didn't need to work at being a better person. She had been blessed with a pretty face, and very soon a full bank account. Besides, the vicar was annoying. Everyone said he was a nice man, but he had a squeaky voice. She certainly didn't want to end up married to someone like him.

An hour later, after Adele returned her horse to the stable, she entered the house and walked quickly across the main hall to the stairs. She had just grabbed hold of the newel post when she heard someone at the top. Glancing up, she saw Damien.

Their eyes met, and they both halted where they were—she at the bottom and he at the top. She had not expected to see him. She had hoped he would be gone.

She considered backing off the step and standing up against the wall to make way for him to pass. Or perhaps she could keep her head down and dash up the stairs, passing him without a word.

After a few seconds, Damien started hesitantly down the steps again, his eyes never leaving hers. All she could do was stand there, frozen in her place.

He slowed when he reached the step she stood upon and stopped beside her. Her heart was pounding; she half expected him to tell *her* to leave *Osulton Manor*. She was the outsider, after all.

But he said nothing...nothing as he took her hand and led her off the step and into the quiet, private confines of the library.

Chapter 15

$\mathcal{D}$AMIEN OPENED THE LIBRARY DOOR, peered inside to ensure it was empty, then brought Adele in and closed the door behind him.

"We shouldn't be in here," she said, crossing the dark paneled room to stand in front of a window. "Not alone." She had to force herself to turn and face him with an appearance of confidence.

He had changed into city clothes—a crisp white shirt under a black jacket, and a long overcoat, open in front. Yet his wavy, black hair was in chaos, and despite the fine clothes, he had that wild, rugged look about him. His chest and shoulders were inconceivably thick and broad. He was a mountain. A beautiful windswept mountain.

When he finally spoke, his voice was deep and controlled. "I need to say something to you before I leave."

He is going to apologize and say it will never happen again. Then it will be over, and by nightfall, he will be in the arms of his mistress.

She clung to the image of his mistress. It strengthened her will.

He took a step toward her. "Are you absolutely sure you should marry Harold?"

Adele stared at him, dumbfounded. It was not what she'd expected him to say. And why was he asking her this? Did he mean to convince her she should *not* be sure? Was Damien willing to consider fighting for her himself?

She imagined becoming his bride instead of Harold's, and a part of her basked euphorically in the notion that it could happen, that she could be loved, truly loved, by her wild, black knight. There. She'd admitted it. A part of her was indeed dreaming of such an end to this situation.

But no. She clenched her fists suddenly. She should not fantasize about him that way. He was not the husbandly kind. He was currently in love with a scandalous actress, and he had no loyalty. He went from woman to woman. Adele should not imagine him as something he was not.

She reminded herself that he had unleashed her passions, certainly, but that wasn't necessarily a good thing. This change in herself was disconcerting and frightening. She didn't know what was on the other side of it, or how far it would take her. She didn't want to end up like Frances Fairbanks, promiscuous and not respectable and living for pleasure alone. Could that happen to Adele? Damien was a powerful temptation. He had enormous pull. Hence, he made her fear the possibility of tumbling into a dark abyss, a future full of regret. A life ruined, all because of a passionate, temporary madness.

"I'm sure," she replied firmly, embedding herself in her determination not to be carried away by it.

Damien slowly crossed the room, growing closer until he was standing directly in front of her. Adele realized she was holding her breath. She had to consciously force herself to let it out slowly.

"I've spent the past hour wondering if I should tell Harold what just occurred," he said.

Startled by the suggestion, Adele blinked up at him.

"Don't panic," he continued. "I would never hurt him for the sake of easing my own conscience. But I would hurt him to protect him." He began to pace around the room. "He lacks experience with women, Adele. He's innocent, and he's naive. What kind of wife will you be?"

The breath she'd been holding sailed out of her lungs in a single, thunderous heartbeat that shook her. So. He did not bring her in here to convince her to marry him. He brought her here because he doubted her decency.

Though a part of her was having doubts about it herself, her pride nevertheless bucked. "Damien, I value my integrity, and when I speak my marriage vows, I will not take them lightly."

"But when I kissed you, you kissed me back."

Adele raised her chin.

"Maybe you're not as perfect as you, and everyone else, thinks you are." He took another slow and careful step toward her. "That's what worries me. My mother was not faithful to my father, and their marriage ended very badly. I do not wish to see that happen to Harold."

He crowded her up against the wainscoting. She could smell him. She could see the rough texture of the stubble along his jaw. She could feel the size and the weight of him, as if he were on top of her, which in a way, he was.

"I will never be an unfaithful wife," she said.

Breathing hard now, she gazed at his lips, so full, so soft-looking. Despite everything, she remembered what they felt like, what his tongue felt like inside her mouth.

"But you've been an unfaithful fiancée."

Her eyes widened. He was right. She had been. But that didn't make it any easier to hear, coming from him.

She felt angry all of a sudden. Life had been so simple before she'd met him. Adele defiantly raised her chin. "How dare you reproach me when I had never sinned before I encountered you. If I have fallen from my pedestal, it was you who brought me down."

"Is that how you see me? As some kind of immoral snake?"

"Isn't that what you are? You bed scandalous women. You don't pay your debts."

Heated shock flashed in his eyes and she hated herself for saying these things. She didn't want to believe them, but it was easier this way.

"And you betrayed someone you cared about," she continued. "What happened between us was about temptation and weakness, and now you're comparing me to your mother, who was an adulteress. It's all despicable. I am sick over it. Everything between us has been immoral and I regret all of it."

Just saying the words was like a stake she was thrusting into her own heart. She had never been immoral before. She had always been good, and she hated to think that what they had shared had not been tender and loving. There was a part of her that still treasured what they had done. She had felt cared for and safe in Damien's arms, but she had to bury that part. She had to convince herself that it was dirty and shameful. That was the only way to survive this.

"You're too close, Damien," she said, fighting to stay focused.

Damien's eyes softened, and at long last, he stepped back. Adele grabbed hold of the windowsill beside her.

He stared at her for a long, excruciating moment. "Part of me wishes you were not so strong, Adele."

Anger and confusion welled up inside her and burst forth like water breaking through a dam. "Why? So that I would betray Harold and you could congratulate yourself for being right about all women being like your mother? That's why you haven't married before now, isn't it? You think all women are wicked and unfaithful, and you had to prove it with me. Harold told you I was saintly, and you didn't want to believe it. You didn't want to believe that *you* might be afraid to love someone, afraid to trust someone like Harold trusts me. You didn't want Harold to have what you couldn't have, because it made you jealous. Jealous of him for being able to love and trust someone. You are deficient and you know it, and you want to pull someone down with you, and that someone is me."

Shock and fury coiled together within her. She could barely fathom what she had just said to Damien. She'd never attacked anyone like that before—attacked his heart and soul in such a direct, cruel way.

But she'd needed to be cruel. She was angry with him. Angry with him for making her feel guilty and immoral, and for making her want him when he could not be had. She was angry with him because he was not willing to fight for her—to choose her over Harold. To let go of his own misguided belief that no woman could be trusted. He was using this—these accusations about her integrity—to release himself from what would be a painful undertaking.

He turned and walked to the door. "No. Because this would all be easier to bear if I could think badly of you. I want to, Adele. I want to hate you, but all I feel is guilt, because you're right. You are everything that's good in the world, and I did bring you down."

He did not look back. He simply walked out.

Adele collapsed onto a chair and struggled to catch her breath. *I did bring you down.*

Her heart throbbed painfully over all the hurtful words they'd just said to each other. Adele had told Damien he was deficient and immoral. She didn't want to think those terrible things about the man who had saved her life, the man who had kissed her and held her in his arms, but she had to. She had to think of his reputation and accept that he could never be her prince charming. That was a fantasy.

She waited for a few minutes until she was certain he was gone, then she hurried from the room.

Violet, however, did not hurry from the room. She

rose very slowly from the sofa she had been reclining upon—a sofa that faced the fireplace on the other side of the library.

She wanted to strangle Damien. Strangle him! Was there not one woman in England he could keep his hands off? Harold's perfect, virtuous fiancée, no less?

Violet ground her teeth together and cursed her cousin. *Damn, damn, damn him!* She would not let it happen. She would not let Harold lose the one and only woman who had ever managed to lure his attention away from his precious laboratory long enough to get him to propose. Violet had never thought she would see that day come, and if Harold lost Adele, it might be another complete lifetime before he looked up from his bloody experiments to take notice of another woman. And what were the chances the woman he noticed would be an heiress as wealthy as Adele?

Slim. Very slim.

Violet stood up and walked out, resolved that she would do something about this. She didn't know what yet, but she would figure out something, because she would not let that massive American fortune slip so easily from her grasp.

Damien knocked on Frances's dressing room door as he always did after a performance—twice, then twice again.

"Come in, darling," she called from inside.

He pushed the door open. The room smelled strongly of red roses that were lying about in bouquets. Sparkling costumes were draped over the backs of chairs, and decorative dyed feathers stood in tall vases.

He walked in and closed the door behind him with a quiet click. Frances swiveled around on the stool in front of her mirrored vanity. She wore only her chemise, corset, and stockings, along with her stage paint and heeled boots. She had taken the pins out of her thick, wavy red hair, and it spilled wildly onto her shoulders. She knew that was the way Damien preferred it. She did not know, however, that he would have preferred to see her without the paint.

Saying nothing, Damien slowly sauntered across the room, tugging at his neck cloth along the way.

He usually smiled at her when they went through these motions after a performance, but tonight, he had no smile for Frances. He wanted only one thing, and that was all. He felt no need to charm. But she was not the type of woman who required it.

She slowly stood and meandered teasingly toward the red chintz sofa against the far wall, and sat down, leaning back. Damien came to a full stop in front of her and looked into her eyes while he finished untying his neck cloth. He left it dangling around his collar.

She looked up at him for a moment, reading him, then she sat forward on the edge of the sofa cushion. "Someone's in the mood for something very naughty this evening." She then proceeded to unfasten his trousers.

Damien closed his eyes, waiting to feel the desire flow through him as it usually did—a desire that he wanted and needed to feel tonight—but to his surprise and annoyance, a spontaneous reflex brought his hands up to gently take hold of her wrists. Before he knew what he was doing, he had taken a well-defined step backward, and Frances was looking up at him with an expression of bewilderment.

"Is something wrong?" she asked.

For a moment, he had no answer, then at last he said, "Forgive me Frances, I'm sorry."

She shook her head, not quite able to understand. He wasn't sure he understood it himself. He didn't understand anything about himself lately.

"Sorry for what?"

He turned away and fastened his trousers. "I shouldn't have come here."

"Why ever not?"

"Because I would only be using you," he said flatly.

"I've never minded before."

Frances. She was no ordinary woman.

Damien faced her again. "We've always been friends, and you've known that, but something has changed. Things are different now."

Her eyes narrowed with anger. "What's different? It's not because of the bracelet, is it? I certainly didn't mean to become possessive, Damien."

"I know that."

"Then what's the problem? Are we not friends anymore?"

He hated this. "I believe the time has come for us to be friends *only,* instead of what we have been to each other in the past."

"But why?"

There was no point dragging this out. She deserved the truth—at least part of it. The rest he would keep to himself, until he could figure out how to deal with it. "Because it's time I found a wife."

Her jaw jutted forward. "That doesn't mean we have to stop seeing each other."

"I'm afraid it does." Because no woman would have him if he was still connected to Frances, and he needed someone to have him. He needed a wife of his own. The sooner the better.

Frances's head snapped back as if she'd been hit in the face with a ball. "I'd tarnish your reputation, you mean."

He offered no reply.

"I have news for you, Damien. Your reputation was tarnished long before I invited you into my bed." Her eyes flashed briefly with fury before she turned without warning and picked up a pink perfume bottle from her vanity, and hurled it across the room at him, striking his wrist bone. As luck would have it, the bottle was open, and the lilac scent poured all over him.

He was still recovering when a tall, glass paper-weight of a nude woman came whirling through the air and smashed into his face.

"Bloody hell!" He cupped his eye and bent forward.

"You deserve it, you bastard!" she screeched.

Damien straightened. He did deserve it, he knew it, so he was willing to let it go. But when a vase— much larger and undoubtedly heavier than both the perfume bottle and the paperweight combined—was launched at him, his generosity reached its limit. He deflected the vase, and instantly moved to restrain Frances.

He wrapped his arms around her from behind, took a few hits, but finally managed to calm her down enough to feel somewhat confident that she wasn't going to throw any more glass objects at him.

"I hope you rot in hell," she ground out, breathing hard.

"I'm sure I will."

He held her like that for a moment or two, feeling deeply ashamed. He had always been honest with Frances. They both knew what their relationship was about, but tonight he had come here to use her to relieve his own tensions and to suffocate his angst and confusion over another woman—a woman who was engaged to his cousin.

He had sunk very low.

Eventually, Frances's breathing slowed and her body began to relax in his arms. After a moment, she said, "I hate you."

"I know."

"You're a bastard."

"I know that, too." He rested his head on her shoulder, and let out a deep, miserable sigh.

She sighed, too. "Your eye is bleeding."

She stepped out of his arms and put her hands on his face to examine the gash at the top of his cheekbone.

"Look at this," she said, shaking her head. "You make me crazy, Damien. No man has ever made me crazy before." Her voice softened. "That's what I hate most about this."

Blood was dripping down the side of his cheek. He wiped it on the back of his hand.

"Maybe I'll be better off," she said, going to fetch a

cold cloth. "Maybe we both will."

Chapter 16

TWO DAYS LATER, ADELE SAT in her bedchamber at *Osulton Manor*, staring absently out the window at the Chauncey Maze. Clara knocked softly and walked in.

"Seger and I will be leaving soon," she said. "They're loading everything onto the coach now."

Adele stood. The thought of her sister leaving sent a sudden, intense wave of emotion through her, and she had to stifle the urge to cry—as she often had to do lately, whenever she thought about her family leaving her here alone, or never seeing America again. It was not Adele's habit to cry. She was usually a master of stoicism in the face of adversity.

She managed to put on a brave face for her sister, because she didn't want to lay all that on Clara's shoulders. It helped when she reminded herself that she would be traveling to London soon to visit her oldest sister, Sophia.

"I'm sure you'll be glad to get home," Adele said. "You've been away for a long time now."

Clara moved fully into the room and took Adele's hands in hers. "I will, but I will also leave here feeling very worried about you. Are you sure you'll be all right? You don't seem like the same sister I knew back in New York—the sister who always had everything well in hand. You've seemed sad, Adele."

Sad. Yes, Adele had indeed been that, which made no sense because she was surrounded by happy people, and she'd gotten what she'd always wanted—a wonderful fiancé her parents approved of.

After Damien left, Harold had finally taken her on a tour of the house. In addition, Eustacia had taken her and her mother on a carriage tour of the estate and into the village, and Adele had spent many pleasant hours with Harold's grandmother, getting to know the elderly woman and enjoying her intelligent conversation. Adele had participated in each evening's activities, singing and playing instruments in the drawing room. Everything had been quite perfectly lovely.

"Does it have anything to do with Lord Alcester leaving?" Clara asked, hitting the mark as she always did.

Adele finally realized that she could not continue to keep this problem to herself. Clara knew. She had always known. She had simply not pushed.

"Yes," Adele replied at last.

Clara's eyes warmed with compassion. "I know that you think you have to hold everything together and be the perfect daughter and the perfect fiancée, but you don't have to be perfect. Nobody is. Come and sit down."

They sat on the edge of the bed.

"Tell me everything," Clara said, "and I'll see if I can help."

Adele nodded. "All right. Though I'm not sure where to begin...at the beginning, I suppose. It started the first night, when he came to rescue me in the kidnapper's cottage." She recalled her first glimpse of him. "He broke into my room, strong and forceful and extraordinary looking, and when the kidnapper tried to shoot me, he saved my life. I was grateful, but at the same time wary of him, because everything about him was frightening. He'd just killed a man. Then later, I remember wishing that it had been Harold who had come, because somehow I knew that Damien and I would experience things together that we should not experience."

Adele described the conversations they'd had and the trouble she'd had sleeping. She told Clara about Damien sharing her bed after she'd had too much wine.

"He could have taken full advantage of the situation, but he didn't do anything I didn't want him to do. And he knows me, Clara. He sees inside the real me, and he has made me see inside myself, too. And it happened after three short days. When I'm with him, I say things and feel things that I've never felt before. I open up to him completely, and because of that, I find myself doubting my relationship with Harold."

"You don't think Harold knows the real you?" Clara asked.

Adele lowered her gaze. "I don't think he really sees me, not the inner me. He talks, but he doesn't listen.

I feel rather invisible when I'm with him. I feel like a shell of a person, whose only purpose is to nod and smile and agree with his opinions. Which is basically the person I was in New York."

"You're not that person now?"

Adele shook her head. "Ever since I met Damien, I've been questioning who I am, and I think I understand it now. I wasn't happy after we left Wisconsin. Our way of life in the city was so strange to me, and I was no longer free to roam in the woods by myself. I didn't know what to do with myself, so I just did what people told me to do. I clung to rules and tried not to think about my life before. I couldn't bear the longing for the country. And when Mother introduced me to Harold, I was content to marry him because I had begun to forget the person I was before. But then I met Damien and I became attracted to the wildness in him, and his lack of care about society's rules. He makes me remember who I was before New York. He makes me feel free."

Clara nodded. "But what does that mean for your future?"

"I'm not sure yet," Adele replied. "One thing I do know is that I need to live in a place that makes me happy. New York wasn't right. I felt displaced and frustrated. I couldn't be myself there."

"Will *Osulton Manor* be the right sort of place?"

Adele considered it. "Possibly. I love the countryside. I could become very attached to this part of England."

"But you need to become attached to more than just the place, Adele. You must also become attached to your husband."

Adele looked down at her hands on her lap. "I hope that I will be able to feel that way."

"Hope is not a plan," Clara said. "What about Damien? How will you feel about being his cousin by marriage?"

Adele shook her head. "I don't know. We said some terrible things to each other before he left. He compared me to his adulterous mother, and I told him that what we'd done was immoral. I believe he was intentionally trying to push me away because he is very protective of Harold, and I was trying to do the same, so I don't know if we could ever get past that. What exists between us does not feel right. It feels very wrong."

Clara squeezed Adele's hand.

"Harold is obviously the better man," Adele said. "He's decent and honorable, but I'm not sure that we are very compatible. I need to find out. I need to see if we can catch up to the level of intimacy that I had with Damien."

"Maybe you will never catch up," Clara suggested.

Adele sighed hopelessly. "Please don't say that. I don't want everything to fall apart. Everyone would be so hurt and disappointed. I've promised myself to Harold, who is a good man. I've made a commitment, and I take my promises seriously. I can't break his heart, and certainly not for a man I could never trust."

"Because of his reputation?"

"Yes, and the things he said to me in the library. I'm not sure he's capable of being a good husband. He had a difficult childhood with tragic circumstances surrounding the deaths of his parents. He doesn't know what a happy marriage is. He has never been able to commit to one woman. He's jaded."

"You should listen to your heart, Adele—the organ that sees better than the eye. That's an old Yiddish proverb," she added. "You say you don't want to give up on Harold, but maybe you shouldn't give up on Damien, either."

Adele sighed heavily. "I would rather forget him. I believe he's with his mistress now—the actress. I know it shouldn't bother me, but to think of them together is like a knife in my heart. I want to get over this foolish infatuation. If you can help me with that, I will be eternally grateful."

Clara thought about it. "All right, here's what I suggest. Give yourself some time. Even a week can make a difference. I know I said that I wanted you to have a great romance, but I also know from experience that these things can indeed be fleeting, especially where an unsuitable man is concerned.

"Now that Damien is gone, what you feel for him might simply pass, and you might realize you prefer Harold after all. If it does, everything will be very easy. If it doesn't, you can deal with it then. You'll be coming to London soon, and you can take the opportunity to see how Damien behaves. If he does something to earn your respect, you might discover that there could be more between you. Promise me you'll come to me if you still want him after a week away from him. I've been through this, Adele. I know what you're feeling."

Adele hugged her sister. "Thank you. I will follow your advice."

The London balls and assemblies that were held over the next few days did not find Damien in attendance, as a black eye on account of an angry mistress was not becoming of a gentleman in search of a wife. Nor was he inclined to flirt when he was irritable most of the time because of his creditors and his London house tenants, who had taken it upon themselves to upgrade the stove in the kitchen and send him the bill.

He was irritable for other reasons, too. He was ashamed of the way he had lost all control in the teahouse with Adele, who, before she'd met him, had never done anything she needed to regret. He was ashamed of the way he had treated her in the library afterward, questioning her integrity, when Damien was the one at fault. He was the one who had kissed *her.* He had been the one to suggest they ride alone to the teahouse, even after she said she would prefer to return with Harold another day. He had indeed dragged her down.

She must despise him now. She had every right to. Perhaps it was best.

He was also ashamed of betraying Harold's unwavering trust—Harold, his closest friend since childhood. He was ashamed for treating Frances badly as well. All in all, he was not proud of himself on any count.

He spent many hours thinking about his future. He did not wish to continue along this low and sordid path. If he was ever going to return to *Osulton Manor* and remain a part of the only family he had, he would need a wife of his own to prevent him from coveting Harold's. He needed to live a respectable life. But this was not a new wish. He had always wanted to rise above the disgrace that was part of his childhood, and therefore a part of him. He wanted a proper marriage—a marriage different from what his parents had—and it had become more than clear lately that he could no longer put it off. Essence House needed funds. It needed its lord and master, and for other more heartfelt reasons, he needed a woman in his life. A woman he could love and trust.

The following week proved slightly less trying. Damien's eye had begun to heal, his tenants paid their rent, and he was able to pay his creditors something to at least keep them from knocking on his door every other hour.

Regarding his regrets, he was still trying to forgive himself, which was not something he was particularly good at, but at least he was making an effort.

Consequently, he danced, he chatted, he flattered, and he charmed. He met many young women of good breeding, and many wealthy ones on a desperate social climb in an upward direction into the aristocracy. Some were American. Others were English, daughters of businessmen who had recently earned a substantial income, and looked upon an eligible viscount as a most beneficial stepping stone.

So, he kept busy and appreciated the many pretty faces that were new to the London Season. He had a goal, after all—to find a bride and bring her home to Essence House. And for Damien, a goal was always effective to keep his mind and body focused and disciplined. He thought very little about Adele.

Except on the rare occasions when he let down his guard, often when he was drifting into sleep. It was during those moments he thought of her and felt a very deep and mournful longing.

Chapter 17

*F*OR EIGHT DAYS STRAIGHT, ADELE did as Clara suggested. She went on with her life as a guest at Osulton, and she waited. She waited for Damien to fade from her memory. She waited for Harold to do something wonderful and stir her passions. And she waited for the guilt over her intimacies with Damien to subside.

The guilt never did subside. Neither did the two other things happen. She'd said good-bye to Damien eight days earlier and she was still missing him and longing for him, despite all the hurtful things they'd said to each other. She watched the end of the road and fantasized about a black horse galloping up the hill with a dark knight on his back—a handsome, dark knight with wind in his hair, coming to rescue her again, from all her doubts and questions.

That didn't happen either.

On the ninth day when she woke up in the morning and gazed longingly out the window, she realized she had become utterly pathetic. Surely Damien wasn't pining away over her. He was the kind of man who could sweep one woman from his heart quite effortlessly—not that any one woman had ever truly occupied his heart for any significant length of time—and move on to the next. He was probably with his mistress at that very moment, in her bed, kissing her and holding her and laughing with her. Adele had pictured him with the beautiful actress more than once that past week, and each time, she'd been overcome with jealousy, even though she didn't even know what the woman looked like.

Adele needed to get over this foolish heartsickness. She sat up and told herself that she didn't need to be rescued, especially by a man like Damien Renshaw. She was in control of her emotions, and her life at the current moment was as close to perfect as it could be. She was engaged to a respectable and decent English nobleman, her family was proud of her, and she was surely the envy of most women in America, and probably England, too. She had been welcomed with open arms into her fiancé's family, and she would one day give birth to the next Earl of Osulton. Everything about her life was a dream come true. She must absolutely forget Damien.

Adele promptly rang for her maid because this was a new day. She was ready to get dressed.

That very afternoon, however, in the closed coach on the way to a neighbor's house for tea, Damien's name came up in conversation, and Adele felt her resolve flying out the window.

"Did you know that Damien had a black eye?" Violet said quietly, when Eustacia's head tipped to the side and she began to snore over the rumble of the rattling coach.

Adele's stomach lurched as the coach went over a bump.

"Supposedly," Violet said, "it was his mistress who gave it to him. That actress—the Fairbanks woman." She shook her head at the sordidness of it all.

"What happened?" Adele asked, quite unable to resist asking.

Violet leaned in closer, seeming to enjoy the juicy details. "She cut him with a glass. Or threw it at him more likely. I'm not sure why, but I do know that they have a very turbulent relationship. It's not the first black eye Damien's received, I assure you, but he doesn't seem to mind. It doesn't stop him from seeing her, and others like her." She looked intently into Adele's eyes. "What do you think it is about women like her? Why are they so good at luring men like Damien into their beds? Maybe it's the risk and the danger. Or maybe if they're passionate in one way, they're passionate in others, if you understand my meaning. It's all a great mystery, isn't it?"

"Yes, it is."

The coach leaped over another bump, tossing Violet and Adele almost up off the seat cushion. Adele considered her relationship with Damien.

Was that what she had been to him? Something risky and dangerous because she belonged to his cousin?

"I suppose Damien is ripe for the picking for a woman who craves sin," Violet continued. "Have you heard the story about his parents?"

"Some of it," Adele said. "I know his mother had

an affair."

"Yes, that's true, but there's more to it than that." Violet leaned closer and whispered. "Damien's father was so brokenhearted, he killed himself over her betrayal."

Adele stiffened in shock. "Damien's father?"

"Yes. Witnesses say he went looking for a fight in the worst part of London and provoked the other man. It was the very day they buried Damien's mother." Violet sighed. "Poor man. He was kind and decent like Harold. He even looked like him. He gave his heart to his wife, and she crushed it. She married him for his title and his money, then right away went out and spent as much of it as she could, mostly on her lovers."

"I had no idea," Adele replied.

"Well, from what I've heard, Damien is following in his mother's footsteps and hunting the streets of London as we speak, looking for a rich wife. He needs money quite desperately. Perhaps that's why Frances threw the glass at him."

He's looking for a rich wife? Adele had not known about that. She had told Clara that Damien knew her in a way that Harold did not, and she had felt as if she knew him, too. Intimately. But she had not known this.

She felt very naive all of a sudden. Then her mind darted about at the ramifications. Was that why he kissed her in the teahouse? Did he think he could steal her away from Harold and get his hands on her marriage settlement? Had he hoped to make her believe that they shared a special bond, only to seduce her into leaving Harold?

No, she didn't want to believe that. Yet the doubts and suspicions were coming at her from all angles. Where Damien was concerned, nothing was ever straightforward. Everything about him—the things she'd heard, the way he treated her—made her feel wary. He constantly said he was loyal to Harold, yet he had kissed her. Obviously, he was not as loyal as he claimed.

But neither was she.

"Well, none of it is any great secret," Violet continued. "I'm sure you would have heard all the scandalous talk eventually." She leaned closer to Adele—who was now feeling sick from thinking about all this—and touched her knee. "I beg your pardon for revealing so many horrid things, but I thought it would be best if you heard it from one of us, and I hope you will not judge Harold by the way Damien lives and treats women. Damien and Harold couldn't be more different. You chose the right man, Adele, I assure you, and I am so glad that you are as decent as Harold. You would never do to him what Damien's mother did to his father." She gazed out the window.

The coach hit another bump, and Eustacia stirred in her seat. "Have we arrived?" she asked, looking around in a daze.

Violet patted her mother's knee. "No, Mother, we have quite a distance to go yet."

London
One week later

Adele peered out of the coach window and saw her sister Sophia, standing on the steps of her grand Mayfair mansion. Beside Sophia was her husband, James, the ninth Duke of Wentworth, widely known as one of the wealthiest men in London. With them were James's sister, Lady Lily, and his younger brother, Lord Martin.

Adele and her mother stepped out of the coach, and Sophia came dashing down to greet them. "You're here! Finally!" she shouted, throwing her arms around both their necks.

James smiled and descended the steps. "Madam," he said, bowing over Beatrice's plump, gloved hand and gazing with amusement at the absurdity of her purple hat. "A pleasure, as always. And Adele, how good of you to come. Sophia has spoken of nothing else these past few days."

Adele smiled, while Beatrice blushed and giggled. "Oh, James, you are too charming for words."

He gestured toward Martin and Lily on the stairs. "Do you remember my brother and sister?"

"Of course," Beatrice replied. She gathered her skirts in both hands and hurried up to meet them halfway. She threw her arms around Lily's shoulders and hugged her tightly. "My darling girl, it's such a delight to see you again. You look beautiful. And you, Martin, grow more handsome with every passing day."

Sophia grinned flirtatiously at her husband. To

Adele, the passion they shared was clear as day.

Adele wanted desperately to share a similar bond with Harold. That was what would save her, she was certain of it. Thankfully, he was on his way to London with Eustacia and Violet, and they would spend time together at a few balls for which they had already received invitations.

Adele looked into her sister's eyes—the eyes of a happily married woman and the proud mother of two beautiful boys—and decided firmly that she, too, wanted a close, happy marriage. She did not wish to spoil her chances for that by losing sight of the secure future that was within her reach.

Perhaps, she thought at last, it was time to flirt with her fiancé, and try a little harder to fall in love with him.

Chapter 18

"*I* BELIEVE THERE MUST BE AT least two hundred people here," Harold said, resting his hand on Adele's waist to step into a waltz, and glancing around the brightly lit ballroom. "You know I have a knack for estimating numbers of things? Go ahead, Adele. Start counting the people. I'll wager an error of no more than ten."

Adele glanced around also, realizing it had not even occurred to her to estimate the number of people in the room, nor did she feel like counting them. She was more interested in appreciating the music and the magnificent movement of some of the more skillful dancers. There were also the musicians to watch. They were exceedingly talented, especially the violinists, who controlled their bows with such precision.

"I'm sure you're right," she replied, determined to avoid the chore of actually counting them. "Two hundred to be sure."

Harold smiled. "Yes, two hundred. I wonder how many hors d'oeuvres they prepared? They would need at least five per person."

He proceeded to calculate the total.

"You are a wonderful dancer, Harold," Adele said, attempting to distract him with what she hoped was a suggestive grin. "I like being close to you like this."

His eyebrows lifted. "Really? Even when it's so warm? It's rather stuffy, don't you think? All these people dancing.... It creates an uncomfortable degree of heat. But the warm air rises. We should be thankful for that." He looked up at the high ceiling. "Imagine how hot it is up there. I wish I could send up a thermometer. I could hoist it up by throwing a wire over that chandelier."

Adele looked up, too, then tried to tempt his attention back to her. "Perhaps after this," she said with a teasing lilt to her voice, "we could go for a walk in the garden. In the moonlight."

"I doubt we'd be able to see the moon through the fog, but it will be cooler out there away from this heat, so, yes, it is a splendid idea. I'll ask my mother to join us."

Adele blinked up at him. "I was hoping...perhaps... that we could go alone."

Who would have thought that flirting would make her feel like such a dunderhead? Was she truly that inept? Or was Harold not attracted to her?

"Alone?" he said. "Well, I suppose we could, but Mother looks rather lonely over there. Look."

Adele glanced to where Eustacia stood by a table of tarts. True, she did look as if she were waiting for someone to come and strike up a conversation with her, but one would think that when a gentleman was invited for a private walk in a moonlit garden with a lady—his fiancée!—he would somehow arrange for some *other* person to entertain his mother.

The waltz ended, and Harold stopped abruptly, waving for Adele to follow him to the tart table.

"Come, my dear!" he said cheerfully. "Those are raspberry tarts, and Mother is about to finish them off."

Adele followed him off the floor. It appeared that flirting with her fiancé was going to prove more difficult than she had initially imagined.

Later in the evening, Adele and her mother joined Eustacia and Violet near the entrance to the ballroom, where they met Sophia and Lily.

"What a delightful gathering," Beatrice said. "But you haven't been dancing nearly enough, Lily. Why aren't you out on the floor? You are young and full of energy. Unlike Eustacia and me."

The two older women exchanged complaints about their sore feet, while Lily looked about uncomfortably. The fact was, she had danced very little. She could not have enjoyed having it pointed out.

Just then, Lord Whitby approached, looking handsome in his black and white formal attire. "Ladies," he said with a bow. "You all look radiant this evening."

Violet raised an arched eyebrow and smirked. "Lord Whitby—charming as usual."

His appealing, blue-eyed gaze drifted languidly to Violet's face. The corner of her mouth curled up, and they gazed at each other for a few heated seconds.

Adele wondered why she couldn't manage to

achieve that sort of exchange with Harold. Everyone else seemed capable of it. What was she doing wrong?

"May I inquire about your card, Lady Violet?" Whitby asked, his smoldering gaze never veering from hers.

"You most certainly may." She inclined her head enticingly.

The next thing Adele knew, Eustacia was penciling in his name for later in the evening, and he was walking off, leaving the entire group of them flicking open their fans to cool themselves.

Adele looked around at everyone uncertainly. She had much to learn. Or maybe it was Harold who had something to learn. Perhaps it was he who needed to be awakened—as Lord Whitby undoubtedly was.

Adele glanced at Lily, who was staring after Lord Whitby. He had not inquired about her dance card. In fact, he had not barely noticed her. He had been too busy responding to Violet's brazen flirtations. Adele glanced discreetly down at Lily's card. There were no names written in for any more dances that evening. Lily's shoulders rose and fell with a sigh, and she consulted her timepiece.

Adele was dressing for Sophia's At Home—the one day during the week when the duchess was always available to receive callers—when a knock sounded at her door. "Come in."

The door opened slowly, and Lady Lily walked in. Her dark hair was pulled into a loose bun on top of her head, and she wore a simple gown of gray silk. Pale skinned, with a tiny nose and full lips, she was an extraordinarily pretty girl. Adele often thought Lily would look striking in brighter colors, but for some reason, she preferred not to stand out.

Lily stood for a few seconds, glancing around nervously before she finally spoke. "Adele, may I ask you a question?"

"Of course. Please sit down."

Lily sat on the sofa, and Adele joined her.

"Last night," Lily said, Lady Osulton mentioned her nephew, Lord Alcester. Do you know him very well?"

Adele stiffened, wondering where this was going. "I met him at my fiancé's home when I arrived there. I know him a little."

"The reason I'm asking is because I met him a few nights ago at a ball, and I danced with him. From what I understand, he is looking for a bride this Season."

The room seemed to become very warm all of a sudden. Adele shifted in her seat. "Oh?"

"Yes, and, well...it's no secret that he has a reputation, but I wondered if you could tell me anything about him, since you know him personally."

Adele stared blankly at Lily. "What would you like to know?"

"Are the rumors true? The ones about his mother, and the ones about his former mistress, the actress? They say he used to go to her dressing room after all her performances, and that he was the first man to ever break her famous, unbreakable heart."

"He broke her heart?" Adele asked.

Lily spoke quietly. "Yes, didn't you hear? Some

people are saying that he wishes to redeem himself. He broke off his relationship with Miss Fairbanks two weeks ago, the very day he returned to London after being away at *Osulton Manor*. And meeting you and your mother, I believe. He told Frances he didn't love her anymore, and she had to cancel her performance the following night because she couldn't stop crying. He hasn't seen her since." Lily lowered her gaze again. "Well, that's what the gossips say, anyway. Who knows how much of it is true?"

The very day he returned to London? That was the day he had kissed Adele in the teahouse. Was that why he had told Frances he didn't love her anymore?

The thought that Damien was no longer making love to his mistress made Adele far, far happier than it should. She had to mentally shake herself, however, and force herself to remember all the reasons that she needed to forget him—like the fact that he was on the hunt for a rich wife.

"I-I don't know anything about Miss Fairbanks," Adele said. "Regarding the other matter you mentioned—about his mother—I have heard that she led a scandalous life, but obviously, you've heard that, too."

"Yes, but may I ask, do you believe him to be redeemable? Do you think he is seriously looking to settle down and live decently?"

Adele felt her blood rushing to her head. "Are you in love with him, Lily?"

Lily squeezed her hands together in her lap again. "I don't know him well enough to be in love with him. But he certainly is the most handsome man I've danced with in a very long time. I would like to fall in love with *someone*. But of course, that someone has to be respectable and trustworthy."

Adele suddenly envisioned Lily dancing with Damien. Smiling up at him. Lily loved to ride. She preferred the country over the superficial glitter of the Season. She was very beautiful. Her brother was rich and would no doubt provide a very generous dowry. She was a perfect match for Damien.

"Would you like me to speak to James or Sophia about him?" Adele asked, secretly hoping that Lily would say no.

Her eyes brightened. "What I was really hoping was that you could tell me what your fiancé Lord Osulton and his sister Violet think of him. They would know him better than anyone, I should guess."

Remembering the conversation that she'd had with Violet in the carriage, Adele strove to remain objective about the information Lily was seeking. "I am afraid that Violet has not described her cousin in the most flattering terms. She told me that he was looking rather desperately for a wealthy bride this Season. But in my family, we believe that each person must make up his or her own mind about people and not judge them by what others say. Perhaps Lord Alcester does want to redeem himself. My advice would be to get to know him yourself and follow your instincts."

There. That was objective. Well done, Adele.

Lily's expression changed, as if she were disappointed in Adele's response. She gazed out the window behind the sofa. "I'm afraid I don't completely trust my instincts, so I've surrendered to the conclusion that I must listen to what others say and allow myself to be guided by those I trust." She stood up to leave.

Adele wished she knew why Lily was so withdrawn around men, why she didn't trust her instincts. Adele knew that Lily's father had been a cruel man. Perhaps that was the reason?

"Don't be discouraged by Violet's opinions," Adele heard herself saying firmly, with no small amount of surprise. "Lord Alcester might very well wish to change the way he has lived his life. I would recommend that you keep an open mind."

Lily smiled down at Adele, but the smile seemed weighed down with a slight melancholy. "Thank you, Adele. You are very kind, and I daresay very sensible."

Adele hardly felt sensible lately. She couldn't even manage to fall in love with her own fiancé. She set her elbow on the armrest and bit down on her thumbnail. She was beginning to think she should just give up on this whole engagement and return to New York and resign herself to spinsterhood for the rest of her life. Wouldn't that be a relief?

While Lily was sitting in Adele's bedchamber asking questions about Damien, her brother, the Duke of Wentworth, was asking similar questions on the other side of town.

"Tell me something," James said to Whitby as they sat in front of the fireplace at his club. "You met Alcester recently when you were at *Osulton Manor.* What did you make of him?"

Whitby raised his eyebrows and sat forward, intrigued by the question. "Why do you ask?"

"For one thing, Lily danced with him the other

night."

Whitby leaned back again and downed the last of his brandy. "That's all? They just danced?"

James inclined his head. "Odd question."

Whitby slowly blinked. "You know that she's like a sister to me, James. The simple fact that you are asking made me wonder."

"Ah. Well, I am indeed wondering a few things myself, mostly because I witnessed some wagering yesterday. Bets are being placed on whether or not Alcester will return to Miss Fairbanks's dressing room after he slips a ring on the finger of a rich wife."

Whitby laughed. "You don't say. Which way did the bets go?"

"Most wager that Alcester will be supporting the arts again very soon."

Whitby nodded, seeming not the least bit surprised. "So, you think he's after Lily's dowry?"

"It's possible."

Whitby waved a finger at James and smirked playfully. "You brought this on yourself, you know, marrying an heiress and making yourself one of the richest men in England."

"I'm quite aware of that. Fortunately, Lily has a good head on her shoulders."

"Yes." Whitby gazed down into his glass. "She does indeed. What do you want to know?"

James crossed one leg over the other. "I want to know if you think the man is trustworthy. I won't fault him for looking for money. I was looking for it myself when I married Sophia. But I do need to know if he intends to behave as a gentleman after he gets it."

"I really don't know, James. I spoke to him only a few times."

"But you've been getting to know his cousin Violet. What's she like?"

Whitby grinned. "Enchanting."

James narrowed his eyes knowingly. "She's rich. At least she will be, once Harold and Adele join hands at St. Georges. Has she ever spoken of Alcester?"

"No."

"Are you going to propose to her?"

Whitby considered the question. "I don't know. Maybe."

With a resigned sigh, James smiled. "And I was so sure you'd come home from America with a Yankee bride on your arm and American dollars in your bank account."

Whitby set his empty glass on the table beside his chair. "In the end, it will still be American dollars. Straight from Adele to Lord Osulton to his sister, Violet. No offense, James."

James regarded his old friend directly. "None taken. It's the way of the world these days. I'll see you at the Wilkshire ball tonight, assuming you're going, of course."

"I am."

"Very good." He stood up to leave. "It should prove to be a lively affair."

Chapter 19

THAT EVENING AT THE WILKSHIRE ball, all agreed
that Adele's gown was the most spectacular—the
pinnacle of high fashion. It was a satin, cream-colored
gown by Worth, with purple velvet roses woven into the
fabric, and an off-the-shoulder neckline, ornamented
with lace and velvet trimming. The form-fitting bodice displayed her tiny waistline to full advantage, and
the entire ensemble, studded with pearls and gem-
stones, complemented her thick, upswept golden hair.

On any other occasion, she would not have cared
a whit about her appearance, but she had wanted to
look her best that night. She had wanted to stand out
among the other London beauties, and she could not
pretend there was no explanation for it.

She had not been at the ball long when she spotted
Damien on the opposite side of the room. Earlier that
evening, before dressing, she had promised herself she
would not overreact at the sight of him, but she hadn't
seen him for more than two weeks, and now that he
was within view, she was, quite frankly, paralyzed.

He wore a black suit with white waistcoat and white bow tie, and his wild mane of hair was slicked back. He wandered around the perimeter of the room with grace and charisma, talking and laughing with other gentlemen, attracting the gaze of every woman who looked his way.

It was impossible not to stare, Adele realized miserably. He was breathtaking in every way a man could be—handsome, charming, and most importantly, he was her beautiful black knight. He had saved her life and become her protector. She had touched him and kissed him and been held by him, and despite the fact that their last conversation had broken her heart, she had spent countless hours conjuring him in her thoughts. She could not even try to let this opportunity to steal a look at him pass her by.

Just then, he turned, and their gazes locked and held from clear across the room. He started toward her. Adele sucked in a breath. She turned her back on him, and with a sudden tremor of panic, glanced at her mother and the others. Eustacia was laughing and talking. Violet was looking around the room with a hopeful, searching gaze. Lily was listening politely to whatever Eustacia was talking about. No one seemed to know that Adele was screaming inside.

She felt him approach behind her. The others glanced at him and smiled, and their circle opened for him. Adele had no choice but to turn and face him and say hello. He inclined his head in return, then he immediately directed his attention to someone else.

"Lady Lily," he said with an appealing, heart-stopping smile, "how wonderful to see you again." He made small talk for a moment, then said, "Perhaps I may have the honor of a spot on your card?"

Naturally, the honor was granted, and he bowed politely and went away.

Adele calmly sipped her champagne and nodded at the conversation that had now resumed, while she struggled to come to terms with the fact that she would like to spit. She hated herself for it, because she knew she had no hold over Damien. She was engaged to Harold, and they had both agreed that what happened between them should be forgotten.

Yet she felt jealous. Jealous of Lily, whom she liked very much.

None of her emotions made any sense to her. Evidently she was not as composed about this as she'd thought she could be.

She remembered Clara's advice—that if her feelings didn't go away after a week, there might be a problem. Well, there was most definitely a problem.

At that moment, Harold appeared beside her with a bright smile. "Ladies! What a crush this is! Three hundred people at least! I just counted them, and there are still others coming in!"

Adele—still feeling heat in her cheeks and knowing her face was flushed—turned to her fiancé. She needed to talk to him. She could not go on like this. She needed to resolve her future. "Harold, it is indeed a crush. Will you take me outside for a walk on the veranda?"

"Oh." His smile became strained, and he glanced around at the other ladies, looking as if he didn't want to be rude. Adele wished he could have sensed that she needed to be alone with him right now, and had made that his first concern, instead of worrying what others might think.

Damien would not have given the others a second thought. He would have looked into her eyes, and he would have known.

"All right," Harold reluctantly agreed, his smile fading further as he offered his arm.

Adele walked with him onto the flagstone veranda and moved to the far end, where a large oak tree stood close to the house and served as a cozy canopy.

"There now," Harold said. "Feel the cool air. You'll be refreshed and ready to go back inside before you know it."

Adele closed her eyes and turned her face upward toward the dark sky, inhaling deeply and letting it out. "Yes, it is indeed refreshing."

After a few more deep, cleansing breaths, she began to feel better. She slowly opened her eyes. Harold smiled, then he seemed to take a moment to admire her lips.

"You're a very pretty girl, Adele," he said.

All at once, hope and euphoria coursed through her, because she had been waiting so long for some sign of affection from Harold, and he had finally found it in himself to express it. Grasping at what felt like the last shred of hope for a happy future with him, Adele turned to see if there were any others on the veranda. There weren't. She and Harold were alone. She gazed at him in the evening light and took his gloved hand in hers. Then she took a tentative step closer to him, needing to test the waters of her future, and rose slowly up on her toes to touch her lips to his. The breeze whispered gently through the tall oak beside them.

"Adele!" Harold put his hands on her shoulders and pushed her back down. Her heels clicked on the flagstones. "What are you doing?" he whispered heatedly.

Adele opened her eyes. "I wanted to kiss you," she explained. "We've never really kissed before."

"Yes, we have!"

"Not on the lips." While a part of her felt humiliated and mortified having to explain the subtle degrees of a kiss, another part of her wanted to shake Harold. Shake him violently and tell him to wake up.

"We're in a public place, Adele. It's hardly the right time."

Staring up at her fiancé in the dim light, she realized with a sad, sinking feeling, that there would probably never be a right time. Harold was not in love with her, nor was she in love with him.

"And perhaps this is acceptable behavior in America," Harold continued, "but we are not in America, and young ladies do not kiss gentlemen at balls. You're in England now, and you're going to have to change a number of things about yourself."

Adele stared blankly at him. There was no point trying to talk herself into this any longer. She could not marry him.

"Good heavens, Adele. You need to get some color back into your cheeks. You'll feel better if you dance." He reached for her dance card and pencil. "I'll write Damien's name in. He's free for the next few."

She pulled her wrist away. "No, Harold, really, I

don't need—"

"Yes, you do, Adele." He grabbed for the card again. He was not trying to be difficult, she realized. He actually thought he was being helpful.

But how could he not see that she didn't want to dance with other men right now, especially his cousin, whom she had spent three intimate days and nights with?

"You just need a lively dance," Harold said.

"That is not what I need!" she shouted, this time losing her patience completely and yanking her hand away.

He stared at her for a moment, perplexed. She was perplexed as well by the total lack of emotional understanding between them, and by her own outburst. She was not doing the proper, polite thing. Nor was she doing what someone else wanted and expected her to do. This was completely out of character for her.

And it was shockingly satisfying.

Harold straightened his shoulders and smiled again. "Perhaps you just need to rest your feet."

Rest her feet. Adele labored to control her frustration. They really did not know each other at all.

They returned to the ballroom in silence, and he delivered her to her mother and Eustacia. Adele noticed suddenly that Lily was not with them. She turned her eyes toward the couples who were dancing.

There they were. Lily and Damien, waltzing around the room—spinning and swirling. They made a handsome couple with their matching dark hair, both of them immensely attractive in their own right. They appeared to be having a wonderful time with each other.

Adele tried not to stare but glanced their way discreetly whenever she could. Each time she looked at them, she was sobered by a heavy sadness that hung over her like a cloud. She should be the one out there on the floor with Damien, talking and laughing. Wasn't she the one who had shared an intimate bond with him? Or was she the world's worst fool to believe that? Perhaps he made all women feel that way.

The dance ended, and Damien escorted Lily back to Eustacia. Lily's cheeks were flushed, and she was glowing with bright smiles and laughter. Damien stayed for a few moments, standing beside Adele, talking to Eustacia and Harold.

The intensity of his presence beside her, even though he wasn't touching her or talking to her directly, made her passions catch fire. She realized with sorrow that she had not felt so vibrant and alive since he had left her, more than two weeks ago. She might as well have been asleep all that time.

She shifted her weight and accidentally brushed her arm lightly against Damien's for a mere fraction of a second. The contact was like a drug.... Intoxicating. Debilitating.

She shifted her weight back again. The conversation sustained its ebb and flow, and Damien did not seem to notice the brief contact. Adele, on the other hand, had to take a moment to recover from it.

She knew in that moment that she was doomed. As much as she had tried to talk herself out of her feelings—because of Damien's reputation and the rumors that he was only looking for money—and despite the fact that he was loyal to Harold and claimed he would never betray that loyalty, she wanted him. Passionately. With every ounce of her soul. And she was hurt by the attentions he paid to Lily, even when Adele knew it made no sense because she had no claim on his affections.

She took a deep, steadying breath and glanced across at Harold, whose eyes were wide with excitement and interest as he listened to Beatrice talk about American cowboys.

Adele felt sick. Her emotions had defied the sensible plans she had made, and she was going to have to change those plans and disappoint many people. She could not marry Harold. She wanted very much to board a ship and go home.

"Miss Wilson, perhaps I may have the honor of a dance?" Damien asked, turning toward her.

Adele's gaze shot to his face.

"Oh yes, do go and dance!" Eustacia said. "You look so bored, Adele!"

"Indeed, you do, my dear," Harold agreed. "Damien, take her for two dances, will you?"

Adele felt her heart begin to pound. She glanced at her mother, who, unlike the others, was not smiling.

Damien held out his gloved hand. She met his gaze and realized she couldn't stop herself from going with him if she tried. Here was an opportunity to spend the next few minutes in his strong, capable arms, dancing with him, looking into the depths of his dark eyes. It was an opportunity to satisfy her longings, however briefly that satisfaction would last.

At this point, what did it matter? She was going to let her family down anyway, and Harold's family, too. Why not steal one last moment of rapture before she—sensible, dependable Adele Wilson—made the deliberate and conscious choice to leap, for the first time in her life, into the deep chasm of everyone's disappointment?

Chapter 20

"**I**S EVERYTHING ALL RIGHT?" DAMIEN asked, sounding genuinely concerned as he led Adele onto the dance floor.

He held out his hand and Adele stepped into position. The waltz began. "I'm perfectly fine, thank you."

"Did you pull that answer out of your sleeve, Adele? *I'm perfectly fine.* Honestly. I know you're angry with me about what happened that last day at Osulton, and I wish you would just tell me that you hate me, or anything. Stop being so polite. So bloody *English*. God, one would never believe you were an American."

"I beg your pardon?" she said. "I'm every inch an American, and just tonight, Harold said I had to stop acting so much like one! That's two conflicting expectations about how I should behave, and quite frankly, Damien, I'm done being what everyone else thinks I should be."

Damien gazed down at her for a moment. "Well.

That was a load off your cart."

Adele's eyebrows pulled together into a frown. She huffed. Then all her muscles relaxed. He had done it again. He had lifted the lid on her boiling emotions and let out the steam. How did he always know when she needed that?

"Yes, it was a load off," she replied.

He twirled her around the floor, leading her smoothly and skillfully toward the outer edges of the room. His voice softened. "Let us begin again, Adele. Please. How have you been?"

She followed him through a sideways turn. "I've had better days."

"I assume you're torturing yourself over what happened between us."

It was remarkable how quickly he dove straight into the heart of a matter.

"Of course. What about you?"

"Naturally. Harold is my cousin. But I've also been torturing myself over the way I treated you in the library before I left. You were right to send me packing. You should have tossed a glass of water in my face while you were at it. I deserved it because I did drag you down with me. I am a scoundrel."

They danced across the width of the room. "So, you no longer believe I am the angelic creature Harold proposed to? Do you still think he is in danger?"

Damien paused before answering, then he spoke softly. "Maybe you were never so angelic to begin with."

Adele bristled. She didn't know how to take such a remark. All she knew was that she refused to let him make her feel ashamed. "You *are* a scoundrel, Damien."

He shut his eyes and shook his head. "I didn't mean to insult you. What I meant to say is that you are a woman with passions, Adele, like any other woman, and you should not have been made out to be a saint. That is an impossibly high standard to live up to."

Her heart was racing. She was in pain, heaven help her, and it was because of him, because he touched the depths of her heart, even when she did not want him to. She was so angry with him. Why did he have to do this to her? He should not have asked her to dance. He should have kept his distance.

"But women with passions and desires," she said, "are eventually unfaithful. Isn't that what you think? And because I've shown you those passions, I've fallen from grace in your eyes, have I not?"

"In a way," he replied. "But perhaps that was a good thing."

His reply only fueled Adele's antagonism toward him. She wished he did not have the power to hurt her like this, but he did. And the fact that he thought badly of her shouldn't matter. She hated that it did. Hated it. She also hated that she could not keep herself from becoming defensive. She could not let him go on thinking badly of her, because she was not a bad person.

"I told you before that I will never be an unfaithful wife," she said. "When I speak my marriage vows, I will be true to them."

He offered no reply.

"You don't believe me," she said with barely controlled shock and hostility. She shook her head. "This is outrageous. I wish this dance would end."

"I didn't ask you to dance to fight with you," he said.

They waltzed around the room very fast. Adele recalled suddenly how he and Lily had looked when they were dancing together earlier. They had been smiling and laughing. Damien was not laughing now. He was looking over Adele's shoulder, his expression dark and serious.

She tried to push her anger off to the side. "Are you going to propose to Lily?" she asked, when they reached the far corner of the dance floor.

"Probably."

Adele worked hard to keep her composure. "I suppose I shouldn't be surprised."

He considered her statement for a moment, then looked over her shoulder again. "I take it you've heard that I have an urgent need for money."

"Everyone has heard it."

The waltz finally came to an end, and the dance floor began to clear. Damien and Adele remained in the center of the room, however.

"Harold told us to dance twice," he said.

The room hummed with conversation while the guests found their partners. Then other couples moved onto the floor. Music started up again. Adele found herself unable to do anything but step back into Damien's arms.

They began to dance, and he returned to the subject of Lily and his need for money. "You think that as soon as I get my hands on Lily's dowry, I'll go back to

Frances and break Lily's heart."

Adele spoke plainly. "I am concerned for her."

"Like I was concerned for Harold?"

Adele narrowed her eyes at him. "We keep coming back to that, don't we? It seems we don't respect or trust each other very much. Is it possible we could ever get along? We've witnessed each other's disgrace, and when we see each other, we will always be reminded of our weaknesses. There will always be resentment and mistrust."

They danced in silence for a few measures. "We're fighting again," Damien said. "Future cousins shouldn't fight."

But they would not be cousins. Adele was going to return to America, just as soon as she tumbled off the pedestal everyone seemed to think she sat upon. Everyone except Damien.

He stopped dancing suddenly and stepped away from her. "You don't think that's why I kissed *you,* do you? Because of your money?"

She considered her answer carefully while other dancers waltzed by them. "I admit it crossed my mind, considering what the gossips say."

He did not reply right away. Then he took her into his arms again and resumed the dance. "I will be honest with you. The gossip is correct on one point. I do need money. I'm completely broke, and the creditors have been banging at my door for months. I informed my steward that I would do my best to find a wealthy bride before the end of the Season, and I intend to do just that. There. That's the ugly truth. But rest assured, I did not kiss *you* because I wanted your father's settlement. I could not even fathom stealing you away from Harold, even that day in the teahouse when I lost all control, and I still cannot. I kissed you because I couldn't resist you. It was as basic and fundamental as that."

"Because you are a scoundrel," she said flatly.

His voice softened. "Yes. Because I am a scoundrel. But I do regret what happened."

"I regret it, too." She hoped that saying it might help her to commit to it.

The music ended, and their dance was over. She stepped out of Damien's arms, but he did not return her to her mother right away.

"I hope," he said quietly, "that we will be able to move past this. You're going to be Harold's wife soon, and I'm going to be someone's husband. It's my deepest wish that we will forget everything that happened between us, Adele, and go on to have a normal, uncomplicated acquaintance as cousins by marriage."

She could see in his eyes that he was sincere. He wanted to put this unpleasantness behind them.

For a fleeting moment, she wanted desperately to tell him that she could not marry Harold, that she wished he would get down on his knee right there and plead with her to become his wife instead. She could take a step toward him and whisper it in his ear...*I'm not going to marry Harold.* Then they could join hands and run out of there, as fast as they could, past all the watching eyes, not caring about the gossip, and escape, just the two of them, to his house in the country.

Oh, how a part of her wanted that. If only he

knew....

But, of course, she could not give in to such a temptation. This man was a self-proclaimed scoundrel who wanted to marry someone—anyone—for money, and he had the power to make Adele lose all common sense and reason. He could crush her heart into a thousand tiny pieces when all was said and done, when he returned to his mistress, as she knew he would.

Besides, she owed it to Harold to tell him the truth before she told anyone else. She could not take the coward's way out and run away from that responsibility. So, she kept her decision to herself. Damien would learn of it soon enough.

Chapter 21

*D*AMIEN STOOD ALONE IN THE corner of the ball-room reflecting on everything he had just said to Adele. He felt almost dizzy.

It was over. He had apologized. He had told her he intended to move on, which he fully intended to do. He would find a wife, and he would love that woman, whoever she might be. He would not give in to temptation again.

Reaching for a glass of champagne on a silver tray held by a footman, Damien turned when Lord Whitby appeared beside him. "Alcester, good to see you."

Damien noted that Whitby was not alone. He was accompanied by his friend the Duke of Wentworth—a highly respected and sometimes feared peer of the realm, who also happened to be Adele's brother-in-law, as well as lady Lily's brother.

Damien cursed to himself. It was turning out to be a hell of a night.

They each came to stand on either side of Damien, surrounding him, as it were.

Whitby raised a glass to the duke. "James, I don't believe you've met Viscount Alcester."

There were not many men tall enough to meet Damien's gaze on an equal level. The duke was one of the few who could.

"No, I regret I have not had the pleasure."

Damien cordially inclined his head. The duke responded in kind.

They, all three of them, stood side by side for a moment or two, watching the floor. Then Whitby said, "Pleasant night for dancing, isn't it?"

"Indeed," the duke replied.

Another moment of silence ensued. Whitby finished his drink. "I believe I see an old acquaintance. Will you excuse me?"

He walked off, leaving Damien alone with Wentworth.

Damien's instincts were finely tuned when it came to men who were of a mind to protect sisters or daughters from men like himself. Thus, he knew that Whitby had left them alone intentionally. It was an arranged opportunity for questioning.

He turned toward Wentworth, and said simply, "Well."

The duke took his time studying Damien's eyes with shrewd diligence. He appeared utterly relaxed. He was in no hurry to reply. Then at last, he spoke. "It seems we share a few acquaintances. Adele Wilson, for one. My wife's sister."

"Ah." Damien was surprised. He had rather been expecting the duke to hone in on Damien's intentions where Lady Lily was concerned. Perhaps that would come next. "Yes. Osulton and I are cousins."

"Lord Osulton, Adele's fiancé. I've met him once or twice over the years. He has a keen interest in science, does he not?"

"He does."

"And you. Where do your interests lie, Alcester? Not in science, I presume."

Damien could feel the inquisition beginning. "No, not in science. At least not on an experimental level."

"I thought not."

Damien turned his eyes to the dance floor again and took a deep swig of his champagne.

"I suppose," the duke said coolly, "that it's high time I expressed some gratitude to you."

Surprised, Damien turned to him again. "Gratitude?"

"Yes. For your.... How shall I put it? Your errand. My wife, Sophia, was greatly relieved to see her sister again."

Damien stared into Wentworth's cool gaze. "I didn't think anyone outside of *Osulton Manor* was aware of that particular errand."

There was a small hint of a smile in Wentworth's expression. "My mother-in-law finds it a challenge to keep secrets from her daughters."

Damien nodded, understanding. "I've spent some time with Mrs. Wilson. She's an interesting woman. She and my aunt have struck up quite a friendship."

"And I would wager they are like two peas in a pod."

"They talk of nothing but wedding bouquets and bridal sashes."

"Ah, the romance of impending nuptials," the duke said. "Nothing stirs a mother's soup like an offspring's wedding."

Damien smiled, amused and a little surprised that this was not unfolding as he had expected it would.

The dance came to an end, and the room mixed and shifted. Damien and the duke remained where they were, however, until the orchestra began again.

"I understand you have a preference for the outdoors," the duke said. "Your skill as a horseman is quite renowned."

"I enjoy riding."

"As do I. I prefer the country. Fresh air, trees and birds."

Damien merely nodded.

"My sister-in-law also prefers the outdoors. Adele, I mean. She, too, loves to ride. Sophia once told me that when Adele was a girl, she sold her hair to keep her horse. That was, of course, before Mr. Wilson introduced himself to Wall Street."

Damien glanced briefly at Wentworth and nodded again. Wentworth held no drink. He stood with his hands clasped behind his back, watching Damien's face. "But you know about that," he said with a faint smile.

Damien, somewhat unnerved, faced forward again.

For a long while, they stood together, saying nothing, until Damien felt the duke's intense gaze turn to him once more. "You've met my sister, as well. Lily."

"Yes."

"I saw you dancing earlier."

Damien was beginning to feel as if the duke had

eyes in the back of his head.

"She's a lovely young woman," Damien said. "You must be proud."

"I am indeed."

Damien felt the duke's probing gaze upon his profile, then at last he looked away. "I must return to my wife. She's expecting me for the next set."

Raising his glass to the duke, Damien said, "It was a pleasure, Wentworth."

"Likewise. Good evening, Alcester." With that, he took his leave.

Damien also turned and walked out. He was more than ready to leave, for he had just been sharply and perceptively evaluated by a man who seemed to know far too much. Damien might as well have spilled his guts onto the floor.

Shortly after the duke walked away from Damien, Violet approached Lily.

"Are you having a good time?" she asked, checking inside her sparkling, beaded reticule to see if she had brought a fresh pair of gloves. She had. She snapped it shut and smiled. "I saw you dancing with my cousin."

"Lord Alcester? He's a very good dancer."

Violet grinned mischievously and raised an eyebrow. "A good dancer? That's not what most women would say about Damien."

Lily gazed uneasily at Violet. "No?"

Violet chuckled. "No. Most would use the word 'handsome,' or 'virile.'" She nudged Lily. "Don't tell me you haven't fallen for him. He's the catch of the Season."

Lily merely smiled.

"He likes you," Violet said. "I could tell by the way he was looking at you. But you're so pretty, how could any man not fall in love with you? What do you think of him?"

"Your cousin?"

"Yes, of course, my cousin!"

Lily swallowed uncomfortably. "I think he's very nice."

"Yes, he is." Violet linked her arm through Lily's. "Oh, darling, how I would love for us to be like sisters. If you married Damien, we would be. Damien knows Whitby. They seem to have become quite friendly lately. What a grand foursome we would make. We could go places together and—oh, it would be just stupendous."

Lily gazed at Violet with surprise. "You're going to marry Whitby?"

"Well, nothing's official yet, but it will be soon, I'm certain. He's magnificent, don't you think?"

Lily gazed across the room to where Whitby was standing. She knew exactly where he was. She did not give her opinion.

"He's close to the duke, I understand," Violet said.

"Yes. He and James have known each other since they were boys."

Violet took in what looked like an exceptionally fulfilling breath. "Whitby and the Duke of Wentworth. I will enjoy being welcomed into your circle, Lily. We will have such fun together."

"Yes, I'm sure we will." Lily gazed across the room at Whitby again, who was helping the aging, gray-haired Countess of Greenwood rise from her chair. Lily rested her hand on her belly. She felt slightly ill. But she had always known this day would come—the day Whitby would propose to someone.

She decided in that moment that this would be her last ball of the Season. She was not enjoying herself. Not at all. She wanted to go home to Yorkshire, to the country. She couldn't be here for this. She would leave London first thing in the morning.

That night, Adele lay in bed staring at the ceiling, thinking of her future. She could not marry Harold. That much was obvious. Which meant she was going to have to break the news to her sisters and her mother, then she would have to explain her decision to Harold. None of it would be easy, but it had to be done, so she would do it, and she would be brave in the aftermath.

Tomorrow, she decided with firm resolve. She would tell everyone tomorrow.

But what then? She rolled over onto her side and gathered her pillow in her arms. She did not think she could remain in London. She did not want to hear about Damien proposing to Lady Lily. She did not want to think about him kissing her or touching her the way he had touched Adele in the teahouse. Nor could she bear the possibility that she might learn too late that she had been wrong about him, and then watch while he turned out to be a perfect husband.

So, she would go home to America. She would start again, careful this time not to put herself in the position of trying to please everyone but herself.

She would not make that mistake again. She would carve out a life of her own and think about what *she* wanted. If she was lucky enough to marry, it would be for love, nothing less. She would find a man she could feel passion for, as well as trust and respect.

Or perhaps she would consider a career of some sort. Something to do with horses. What would her father think of that?

Adele closed her eyes and thought about what she would say to everyone the next day.

She suspected her mother was going to need some very strong smelling salts.

Chapter 22

ADELE WAS SITTING WITH SOPHIA in the Wentworth House drawing room when Clara, wearing a dark brown, slim-fitting walking-out dress with a matching hat, was shown in. She pulled off her gloves, sat down on the sofa and took hold of Adele's hands. "What is it, darling? I came the moment I read your note."

"She has something she wishes to discuss with us," Sophia said as she poured tea for Clara.

Adele decided she didn't want to waste time. She wanted to come straight to the point. "I'm not quite sure how to tell you this, because I know it will come as a shock, and I hope you won't be angry with me, but I wish to break off my engagement to Harold."

Both her sisters fell silent. Then Clara spoke quietly. "Is it because of what we talked about at *Osulton Manor*?"

"What did you talk about?" Sophia asked.

Clara began to explain. "You remember that Lord Alcester rescued Adele from the kidnapper and delivered her safely to Harold?"

"Yes."

"Well, she and the viscount spent three days and nights traveling together, and—"

Sophia held up a hand. "You don't need to explain, Clara. I understand." She turned to Adele. "You care for Lord Alcester? Why didn't you tell me sooner?"

Adele gazed apologetically at her eldest sister. "I was going to, but there never seemed to be a good time, and I kept hoping that it would pass. But it didn't, and it doesn't matter now. I don't want Damien. That's not why I can't marry Harold. I would have made this decision even if I had never been kidnapped and rescued by Damien. At least I hope I would have made it."

Sophia glanced uneasily at Clara. "Good heavens, I've been encouraging Lily to consider Lord Alcester. I wouldn't if I had known."

Adele shook her head. "If he is inclined to propose to Lily, that is perfectly fine. It's their business, not mine. I just want to go home."

"But Lily left London this morning," Sophia told her. "She didn't say why, but we all know she doesn't enjoy the marriage mart."

Adele was surprised. Lily had said she wanted to fall in love.

Clara spoke up. "But if Damien has no hold on your feelings, Adele, why don't you want to marry Harold?"

"Because I don't love him. It's as simple as that."

"But you thought you did at one time," Clara said.

"Yes, but that was before—" She stopped herself.

"Before you met Damien," Clara finished for her.

Adele stood and paced around the room. "Yes, before I met Damien. But that doesn't mean I want to marry him. He just helped me see that I wasn't the person I thought I was." She stopped in front of the window. "Mother is going to think he was a very bad influence."

Sophia blew out a breath. "To be sure."

They were all quiet for a moment, digesting the news, then Clara said, "When will you tell Harold?"

"Today," Adele replied. "I'll hate hurting him, of course, but I think this is best dealt with in a decisive manner. Then I will go home as soon as possible. I want to find a purpose in my life, or a dream of my own to work toward. I'm tired of drifting in the direction of other people's pointing fingers."

Sophia rose to her feet. "I think that sounds wonderful, Adele."

Adele smiled. "So…will you help me explain it to Mother?"

Her sisters pulled wary faces.

"Of course we will," Clara said.

"Most definitely," Sophia added, "because I anticipate you're going to need all the help you can get."

Two hours later—after no shortage of sobs and arguments, and general, all-around misery from Adele's mother—Adele stood on the front steps of Osulton House in Belgravia with her two sisters, tapping the large brass door knocker and trying to keep her nerves steady.

Harold, may I have a moment alone with you? she

rehearsed in her mind. Or perhaps she would need to speak to Eustacia first. *Eustacia, would you be so kind as to give me a moment alone with your son?*

Her whole body churned with dread. She hoped Eustacia would not react the same way her mother had, toppling backward onto the sofa with her mouth open wide. Eustacia and her mother were similar creatures, however....

Adele turned to Clara. "Do you have the smelling salts?"

Clara patted her reticule. "Do you even need to ask?"

Just then, the door opened, and Henderson, the butler, appeared with his usual stony expression. He took one look at Sophia and Clara, however, and made a bow. "Your Grace. Lady Rawdon." He then turned his attention to Adele. "And Miss Wilson. Good afternoon."

Adele squeezed her reticule in her hand. "Is Lord Osulton at home?"

"I'm afraid he is not. The family left for the country not more than an hour ago."

Adele's eyes narrowed questioningly. "Whatever for?"

He inclined his head. "I regret to inform you that Lord Osulton's grandmother is ill."

Adele tensed. "Is it serious?"

"I believe it is, Miss Wilson."

Adele turned to Clara and Sophia. "This is terrible. Poor Harold. I must go, too. I am still his fiancée after all. Surely Mother will take me."

Adele started back to the coach with speed and

determination in her gait—something Clara and Sophia had never seen in her before.

"Thank you," Sophia said to the butler, before she and Clara had to scramble to keep up with their baby sister on her way down the steps.

Part Three

Wisdom

Chapter 23

*I*T WAS PAST NOON THE following day when Adele and Beatrice were greeted at the door of *Osulton Manor* and invited inside. The house was somber. Adele and Beatrice were shown into the drawing room. Eustacia was standing alone at the window.

"Oh, my dears," she said, turning to welcome them. "How good of you to come. We left in such a hurry, we had to leave it to Henderson to explain where we had gone."

Beatrice embraced her. "We came as soon as we heard."

"Is she any better?" Adele asked.

Eustacia held a handkerchief to her nose. "The physician doesn't think so. He said it wouldn't be more than a few days. A week at most." She shuddered with a sob, and hugged Beatrice again. "Oh, my dear, dear mother. What will I do without her?"

Beatrice led Eustacia to the sofa, and Eustacia lifted her puffy, watery gaze. "Adele, go and see my mother now. Harold is with her. It will mean so much to him that you came."

Adele bent to squeeze Eustacia's hand and met her mother's worried eyes. Beatrice had made no secret of the fact that she had hoped this visit would change Adele's mind about Harold. Adele did not know what would transpire. Perhaps it would change her mind. Perhaps it would not. She only wished for clarity and an absolute certainty in her decision, whatever it turned out to be.

She made her way through the house to the east wing where the dowager's rooms were located and knocked upon the door. No one answered, so she quietly entered.

The dowager's sitting room looked the same as always. It was cluttered with old pillows and interesting knickknacks—evidence of a lifetime of collecting special treasures. Adele passed through to the double doors that led to the dowager's bedchamber but hesitated. She must prepare herself. Harold was surely going to be distraught. She would do her best to comfort him, and she would hold off on the news about her decision to end their engagement. Now would not be the time to deliver a second blow.

The doors were slightly ajar, so she peered through the narrow opening. She could see only the foot of the bed, but she heard a quiet weeping.

Oh, poor Harold.

Adele closed her eyes and bowed her head. She gently pushed the door open, but it was not Harold she saw. The person sitting next to the bed, with his head resting on the dowager's hand, was Damien.

Adele pressed her hand to her heart.

He must have sensed her presence because he turned and looked at her. His eyes were colored by a dark, despairing anguish, along with a measure of shock from seeing her when he had not expected it.

Adele swallowed over a sudden painful lump in her throat. Damien—the black knight who could raise his sword and conquer any enemy, and the scoundrel who could, at his whim, seduce any woman.... He was weeping.

Adele stood motionless while they regarded each other warily. Then Damien rose from his chair and crossed toward her. He stood for a moment, staring into her eyes, then he pulled her gently, tenderly into his arms. Adele shuddered with surprise at the contact, not realizing how desperately she had wanted to touch him and hold him, despite all her reasons not to.

He embraced her for several seconds, then buried his face in the crook of her neck. She allowed it, because she could not forget all the times he had helped and comforted her when she was distraught. But when he laid a trail of kisses across her cheek and took her face in his hands and gazed down at her lips, Adele realized she was not allowing this as a gift of comfort. It was an excuse to take from him what she wanted for herself. Closeness. Intimacy.

Elated just to be in his arms, jubilant simply to see him, she ignored the little voice in her brain that reminded her that anyone could walk in and find them this way, gazing into each other's eyes like lovers. Or that the dowager could open her eyes and see what sin they were committing, what betrayal, when

Adele was still engaged to Harold.

But in all honesty, and to Adele's utter shame and bewilderment, none of that mattered. Not at this moment when Damien was holding her and telling her with his body that he still cared for her. All she wanted to do was ease his woes and mend his heart.

Damien closed his eyes and shook his head. "I shouldn't be touching you like this."

"Please, don't apologize."

He said nothing for a few seconds, then his voice was a mere whisper when he spoke. "What are you doing here?"

"I heard about your grandmother." They glanced with concern at the bed where she lay. "How is she?" Adele asked softly.

"Not good. All her life, she's had a spark in her eye. But not today."

"What did the doctor say?"

Damien explained the prognosis—that at her age, this illness would take everything she had, and leave her with nothing. Her breathing was already shallow and erratic, which suggested the worst.

"Has she been conscious?" Adele asked.

"Not this afternoon. I've been sitting here, talking to her for over an hour, trying to get her to wake up, but—"

Adele reached for his hand and clasped it tightly in hers.

"We were able to talk earlier this morning," Damien said. "She had a great many things to say."

Adele waited patiently for him to continue, but for the longest time he simply stared at the rug, then he glanced uncertainly at her.

"I'm listening," Adele said.

He glanced back at the bed. "She told me something I didn't know. That my father kept a secret from me and the rest of the world." Damien faced Adele again. "There is something I never told you about the way my parents died."

Adele remembered what Violet had told her....

"Damien, you don't have to hide it," she said. "I already know. Violet told me something after you left for London. She said your father killed himself."

His brow furrowed. "You knew that?"

"Yes, but I don't know how it happened, exactly. I only know what would be considered gossip, I suppose."

He swallowed hard. "Well, I don't think anyone knows how much of it I consider to be my fault. Except for my grandmother."

Adele reached for his hand. "Oh, Damien. What happened?"

He sent a glance her way—a glance that told her he appreciated her sympathy and understanding, and that it was difficult for him talk about this part of his past. "I was only nine when I found out my mother was having an affair," he admitted quietly. "I was angry with her, and I didn't have the sense or experience in life to handle it tactfully, so I told my father. He was devastated, and he went after my mother with a pistol."

"Good heavens."

"I mounted my horse and followed him to the house where her lover lived, but I didn't get there in time. My father had found them together. He meant to shoot them both, I believe."

Adele braced herself for the worst. "Did he murder her, Damien?"

"No. He threatened to, but then he ran out. My mother tried to go after him, and that's when I came along. She took my horse from me, but she fell along the way, galloping across the park, and that's how she died. I was the one who found her because I was running after her."

Feeling a deep pain in her heart, Adele spoke in a hushed tone. "I'm so sorry."

"I ran home to tell my father, and that was even worse than what I had told him before. Then, on the day they buried my mother, he went into Whitechapel and got himself stabbed. Purposefully, it's believed. I blamed myself, of course, for causing all that destruction."

Adele swallowed hard at the shock of all this. "But you were just a boy. It wasn't your fault. And you were only the messenger."

"Not a very tactful one."

Adele put her arms around his neck and hugged him. He squeezed her tightly in return.

"But this morning," he said, "my grandmother told me that my father suffered from what she called an unsteady constitution, and that he had tried to take his own life more than once. Even before he met and married my mother."

Adele laid her hand on Damien's cheek.

"For years she's been trying to convince me that what happened to my parents was not my fault,"

Damien said, "but I never believed it. She didn't want to tell me about my father's past attempts to end his life because she feared I might think I inherited that trait, and that I might give in to it."

They both gazed at his grandmother for a moment. "How do you feel about all this now?" Adele asked.

"I believe that I need to forgive the nine-year-old boy who didn't know any better. But I don't believe I will ever be able to let go of the guilt. I will always feel remorse when I remember how I told my father. I did not try to spare his feelings. I didn't even think of that. I was only angry at my mother and wanted to see her punished. I said terrible things about her."

Adele digested all this with understanding. "You were only nine, Damien. You didn't have the maturity to understand what was happening. It's only natural that you were angry. And you're right. You do need to forgive the nine-year-old boy you were then. Your regrets are the regrets of a man who knows how he would handle the situation today. And you most certainly would handle it differently. I know you would. I've seen the way you've handled everything that has happened between us, and how you have treated Harold."

Damien kissed Adele's hand. "You are very kind," he said.

Adele swallowed over the lump in her throat and fought to keep tears from her eyes.

"Let's not talk about that anymore," he said. "It's good to see you."

Adele watched his face, so beautiful in the gray light filtering in through the windows. His dark eyes were closed. He looked calm as he kissed the back of her hand, then held it to his cheek.

"It's been a trying day. Just give me this moment." He kissed her hand again.

Adele trembled. She couldn't have told him to stop if she'd wanted to. All she could do was revel in the sensation of his soft, warm lips upon her skin.

"You can have as many moments as you wish," she whispered, wanting to be selfish and greedy for once in her life, and barely recognizing the husky timbre of her voice. "I'm tired of fighting it."

He stopped and lifted his gaze and seemed to be waiting for an explanation.

She didn't know if she should tell him about her decision not to marry Harold. She was afraid of what Damien might think. Would he see this as another careless, thoughtless act from an inconstant woman who could not be faithful to the cousin he loved? Or would he be pleased? Pleased that she was finally following her heart?

She continued to watch his expression, then felt her own eyes grow heavy with yearning. She was in love with this man. She couldn't deny it, and the truth was flailing inside her, kicking and screaming to get out....

"I'm not going to marry Harold," she said at last, and the weight of the whole world lifted from her shoulders. There. It was out. Damien knew. "I'm going to tell him as soon as I can."

Shock glimmered in Damien's eyes. "May I ask why?"

"Because I don't love him, and it wouldn't be fair to either one of us." A hot quivering began in Adele's belly, and she glanced at the bed, wondering fleetingly if the dowager was awake, if she could hear them.

Just then, the outer door of the sitting room opened. Both she and Damien stepped apart in time to see Eustacia and Beatrice push through the double doors to the bedchamber.

Eustacia stopped when she saw them. "Damien. I didn't realize you were here."

Adele glanced at her mother, who regarded her with disapproval.

Eustacia crossed to the bed. "Hello, Mother," she said softly, but the dowager did not stir.

Damien turned his back on all of them and walked to the window. He gazed out at the gray sky. Adele's body was still trembling because of what she'd just told Damien.

She didn't know what consequences would arise from her confession. Her mother was not happy with her decision. That much she knew. What would Eustacia think? And Harold? And what would Damien want after all was said and done? She couldn't deny that she was still dreaming of a happy ending with her handsome black knight. Even now, her body was warm with desire and anticipation after what had just occurred between them. She wanted more of him—more conversation, more touching. She hoped her cheeks were not flushed.

Beatrice moved to stand on the other side of the bed and turned her eyes to Adele. "I wonder where Harold is?"

Adele heard the reprimand in her mother's voice, for she had always considered Damien a threat, even though Adele had never openly revealed her feelings.

Quite unexpectedly, the dowager stirred. "Did someone mention Harold?"

Eustacia leaned over the bed. "Yes, Mother. Adele is here."

"Adele?"

"Yes, that's right. She's engaged to Harold. Remember?"

"Oh yes," the dowager said sleepily. "Harold was here earlier, but he went to the teahouse."

The teahouse. As soon as the words passed the dowager's lips, Damien's gaze shot to meet Adele's. The teahouse was their place together, and Harold had gone there for some reason.

"Perhaps I'll take a walk and find him," Adele said.

"Yes, you should," her mother replied, as if she sensed an urgency in the present situation.

"He would like that, Adele," Eustacia said. "He is quite worried about his grandmother. He'll be pleased to see you."

Adele nodded, and walked out.

After Beatrice and Eustacia left the room, Damien approached the bed. "Harold is not in the teahouse, Grandmama. You know he never goes there. Why did you tell Adele that?"

Her white hair was splayed out all around her, and she slowly, weakly turned her head on the pillow. "Because I thought you needed to be alone with her. You should go there."

"You heard our conversation?"

"Of course," she said, her voice shaky and without

vigor. "And I saw your lack of discretion just now, holding her in your arms like the wicked scoundrel that you are. Perhaps that's why I'm feeling better all of a sudden." She tried to sit up. "I think I might be able to take some soup."

Amused as he so often was with his grandmother—and more than a little relieved to see the return of her fighting spirit—Damien gently eased her back down. "Don't try to get up, Grandmama. You're ill."

He tucked the covers in all around her.

"I was quite surprised," she added, "when Adele admitted she didn't want to marry Harold. I almost laughed, but I didn't want to interrupt."

He chuckled softly.

"What are you going to do about it?" his grandmother asked.

Damien sat down and rested his elbows on his knees. "I don't know. Harold will be devastated when she tells him."

"Devastated is not the word," his grandmother replied. "He will be disappointed, without doubt, and his nose will be out of joint, but that doesn't mean you have to suffer along with him."

"But it is almost certainly my fault that Adele is changing her mind. I kissed her. I talked to her about things that were entirely too personal. I corrupted her."

His grandmother took a moment to gather her strength before she answered, managing somehow to rise up on an elbow. "You corrupted her with your charm, you devil. You awakened her to passion. You could hardly help it, but she'll be all the better for it."

"I'll never forgive myself."

His grandmother lay back down again. "Now that is something I will not hear. You have tortured yourself long enough over other events that were not your doing, and I will not go to my grave believing that you intend to continue torturing yourself about something new."

She began to cough suddenly, and Damien helped her sit up for a moment.

"But there is something," she said, when he laid her back down, "that I must tell you, Damien. I am ashamed of myself, and I cannot go to my grave if—"

"You're not going to your grave, Grandmama."

"Yes, I am. If not today, it will be some other day, because that is life. Everything that lives, dies eventually."

Damien kissed her frail hand. "Have you not told me enough today?"

She shook her head. "Not nearly enough. There's something you need to know about your mother."

Damien felt all his muscles grow tense. "What is it?"

She coughed again, then managed to say, "Your mother didn't marry your father for his title to satisfy her own ambitions. She had been most cruelly forced into it by her father."

Damien narrowed his eyes at his grandmother. "But after she died, everyone said—"

"I know what everyone said, and that is what I am most ashamed of. I could have squashed those rumors, but I remained silent."

"Why?"

A tear spilled from her eye. "Because I was angry with her for how she betrayed my son. I was heartbroken over his death and I needed to blame someone. But she was very unhappy in the marriage. She loved that other man. She always did. She could never give him up. Looking back on it now, I think she should have run off with him instead of doing what her family wanted her to do."

"'That other man,' you say. There was only the one?"

"Only one. And I believe she tried her best to love your father, but it was not a good match."

"Why are you telling me this now?"

"Partly to ease my own conscience," she replied. "I should have told you before and I should have been more understanding about your mother's situation. All she ever wanted was love. Instead, I nursed my anger for too many years."

Damien held his grandmother's hand. "But she committed adultery."

"Yes, and she suffered for it, and then she died for it. I don't want you to suffer, Damien. Learn from your parents' mistakes and marry for love. That is where you will find the honor that has eluded you all your life. And remember that not all marriages end in heartbreak. Not if there is love."

Damien nodded and bowed his head.

"Adele is doing the right thing," his grandmother added. "A loveless marriage brings disaster for everyone. She should not marry Harold if she doesn't love him." She squeezed Damien's hand. "Tell me the truth now. Do *you* love her?"

"I might," he whispered.

"Liar. There is no 'might' about it. I saw you holding her just now. And aside from being a great beauty and the object of your desire, that young American is intelligent and sensible. She has honor. And you have a great deal in common. Any fool could see you are meant for each other. I'm surprised Harold didn't see it and bring her home for you instead of himself. But that is Harold, isn't it? Never really seeing what is outside of a beaker. He's got his head in a glass box, that boy.

"If you want to help him, pull him out and slap him across the face. Wake him up. We've all been protecting him long enough, because he is so much like your father and we've all been frightened to death that he will turn out the same. And you... You've been trying to make amends for what happened to your father. That is why you've hovered over Harold all your life, and you know it. But he is a grown man, and his happiness is not your responsibility. To protect him now, and to let Adele slip away, would only force the past to repeat itself. Marry for love, Damien. No matter the cost."

Damien listened to his grandmother with surprise and confusion. She was telling him to betray Harold.

But Damien was not even sure Adele would ever want him as a husband, even if he did what his grandmother was suggesting. Especially if he did. Adele was unshakably honorable, and she would have reservations about dashing into the arms of her fiancé's cousin so soon after she'd jilted him.

On top of that, Damien knew she did not respect

him. She knew about his search for a rich wife, and about Frances and the other women before her, and Adele did not believe he was capable of being faithful. She'd even said they didn't trust or respect each other, and they reminded each other of their weaknesses. He wasn't sure she could ever let go of those impressions, even if he did everything in his power to convince her otherwise.

Yet his grandmother was right. Anyone with eyes could see that they were made for each other. They shared the same interests, and Adele was at least attracted to him in the physical sense. She had proven it in bed with him and in the teahouse, and again today when she'd admitted she was tired of fighting her passions.

He wondered if he should go down to the lake and talk to her. Perhaps he could at least determine what might be possible after she ended her engagement to Harold.

Damien smiled at his grandmother and kissed her hand, then rose from his chair, and left to fetch his horse.

Chapter 24

*A*DELE REACHED THE LITTLE ROUND teahouse on the lake and stepped past the overgrown grasses that lined the path to the door. There was no horse tethered anywhere nearby. She approached the door and knocked but no one answered, so she circled around to a window, cupped her hands to the cool glass, and peered inside. The teahouse was empty. All she heard were the soothing sounds of the woods—oak leaves whispering in the soft breeze, English sparrows chirping, and the gentle cooing of wood pigeons. Harold must have come and gone.

Adele closed her eyes and breathed in the fresh scent of the lake. The forest beckoned to her in its usual way, so she decided to take advantage of the solitude. She wandered along the mossy bank of the lake and found a fallen tree to sit upon.

A short while later, she heard a horse nicker and the soft tapping of hooves over grass. Adele rose to her feet just as a horse and rider appeared from around a bend in the path. It was not Harold, however. It was

Damien, and her heart leapt.

What a sight he was—darkly handsome and striking on his big black horse.

"Harold's not here," she explained. "I couldn't find him."

Damien walked his horse closer, came to a stop, and dismounted. He stood a few feet away, his expression serious. "I didn't think you would."

Bewildered, she sat down again.

Damien led his horse to a tree and tethered him. "I doubt Harold was here at all today. He hasn't thought of this place in years."

"But your grandmother said—"

"My grandmother can sometimes be a busybody," he informed her, walking toward her, bending under a low-hanging branch. Twigs snapped under his footfalls. "And I'm sure it gave her great pleasure to manipulate the goings-on in the household this morning. I think it helped revive her. She asked for soup."

"That's wonderful news."

Damien joined Adele on the fallen log. He plucked a long piece of green grass and wrapped it around his finger. "I should tell you that she saw us together in her room earlier when we thought she was asleep. She heard everything we said to each other."

"Oh dear."

"It's not the end of the world," Damien added. "She already knew how I felt about you. Don't ask me how." He tossed the rolled-up blade of grass into the water.

Adele felt strangely numb with apprehension—a

simmering fear that events would unfold too quickly, in a way she could not control. "Did she hear me say that I wasn't going to marry Harold?"

"Yes."

Adele covered her face with her hands. "I didn't want anyone to know about that yet, not when she is so ill. The last thing I wanted was to come here and upset everyone."

"Grandmother wasn't upset," he said. "She has become forgiving in her old age, I've just discovered, and she can certainly keep a secret."

For a while, they sat together looking at the lake and listening to the ducks quacking. Then Damien turned to her. "What will you do, Adele, after you tell Harold the truth?"

"I will go home to America," she replied without hesitation. "I want to start over and take time to think about what I want out of life, not what my parents want for me, or anyone else. I want to be free."

His voice was calm and serene like the lake. "You would not consider staying here and starting your new life in England?"

"No," she said quickly, because she was afraid to hope for things she was not sure of, and she was not sure of Damien. "This is not my home."

"But you were willing to make it your home with Harold."

"That was the old me," she said. "The new me knows that I do not want to live like this." She gestured in the direction of the house.

"In a giant palace with strict rules and clipped gardens, you mean."

"Yes. I have always felt that I had to be perfect—clipped and manicured—and perhaps that's why I am uncomfortable in a setting like this. I want to go back to the way it was before we had money and became so concerned with manners and appearances. As strange as it sounds, I long for a more natural chaos."

"But what if the home you could have was a smaller country manor? A house covered in ivy that no one has been able to control for years. A house with an overgrown garden and a collection of dusty books that is hideously disorganized? What if that house had an impressive stable with horses, and fields and meadows with fences to jump when you go riding? And what if the servants were simple country people, who had always been encouraged to laugh with their master?"

Adele's stomach began to flutter with a strange mixture of excitement and consternation. "What are you asking, Damien?"

"In my own roundabout way," he explained, "I suppose I am asking very carefully about possibilities, and I want to know if the reason you changed your mind about marrying Harold has anything to do with me."

She turned her face away from him and stared across the still water. "Oh, Damien. Surely you know…it has everything to do with you. I would never have known what I was missing if I hadn't met you. You introduced me to the person I truly am, deep down. You helped me discover my passions, and you taught me that I have a soul of my own, and that I can follow my heart and change the path of my life."

"I am glad. I would hate to think of you like a bird

in a cage—a bird who never knew what it felt like to spread her wings and fly."

Adele looked up at the clouds. "I'm still not quite sure I know what that will feel like, but I am going to find out."

She felt Damien's eyes on her profile. "I admire you, Adele, for your spirit and your goodness."

"My 'goodness'? I thought you believed I was not as good as everyone presumed me to be."

"You are as good as anyone can possibly be, because no one is perfect. Perfection is not real, but you, Adele, are very real."

They were quiet for a moment while they watched a duck fly in and land on the water's surface with an audible *swish*.

"Adele," Damien said, "would you ever consider marrying *me*?"

Nothing could have prepared Adele for the shock of hearing the question she had longed for so desperately. But even while excitement and joy exploded in her heart, she continued to cling to her good sense. Though she had decided to be free, she could never completely let go of "sensible Adele." She would not make any rash decisions.

"I promise I would never put you in a cage," he added.

Adele managed somehow to find her voice. "Damien, you know I am attracted to you, but that doesn't mean we should marry. Think of how we have argued."

"But what if I've decided that you are the only woman for me? Is there no chance I could win you?"

Adele stared out at the lake. She had to consider that question very carefully. "A few days ago, Lily was the one you wanted. Not long before that, you were making love to Frances Fairbanks."

"I was with Frances before I met you, not after. That's over now. And I was only considering Lily because I believed you were going to marry Harold."

She sighed. "I know you are in need of money. You told me so yourself, so you must understand my reservations and my need for caution. How could I be sure that you aren't simply seizing an opportunity that has suddenly presented itself because your cousin is no longer in the picture?"

"That is not the case."

"But how can I be sure? You've had nothing but casual mistresses your entire life, and the world seems to think you will return to that way of living as soon as you find a wealthy bride. You have never been inclined to settle down until now, when you are forced to because of your financial problems. I admit we have much in common, but marriage is more than a sharing of similar interests. It is a sharing of values, and that is where we differ."

An intensity filled his voice. "Perhaps we don't differ as much as you think. All my life I have grieved over my parents' failure as a married couple, and I vowed I would never let that happen to me. I want a real marriage to a woman with honor—a woman I can love and trust. I have not been able to find that woman before now."

She could not believe this was happening. Whether his motives were pure or tainted, he was fighting for her, like the conquering hero that she'd always imagined him to be.

Adele squeezed her hands together on her lap, searching for control. Though she loved that fairy tale quality about him at this time, she could not let herself be blinded by it. She could not close her eyes to other things—the qualities that had real importance in the world.

"But you don't trust me," she said. "You have questioned my integrity on numerous occasions, and if I were to run off with you, I would be doing the very thing you believe all women do—betray their husbands. Or fiancé, in this case."

His eyes brimmed with gentle understanding. "I feel differently about that now. I believe I am beginning to forgive my mother for what she did. Just now, when I was riding down here, I remembered certain things about her—the way she smiled and the way she used to kiss the top of my head when I was small. For the first time, I felt hopeful. I know now that what my mother did was more complicated than it appeared on the surface, as is everything in life, I suppose."

Adele gazed down at the mossy ground. "I'm happy to hear that, Damien. Truly I am. But what about Harold? I thought you were forever loyal to him. He does not even know that I wish to end our engagement, yet here you are, ready to swoop down like a vulture and steal me away before it is even done." Her voice had gained fervor on the last few words.

"I am not indifferent about that," he said. "I will have a difficult time explaining myself to him."

"I should think so. I can't imagine my own dilemma

if I wanted a man my sister loved and planned to marry." She stopped what she was saying and kicked at the grass with the toe of her shoe. "But to be fair, I don't think Harold truly loves me."

"He believes he does, because he has not experienced much of life. He spends all his time in a room with glass walls, looking out, but never venturing out. He makes choices based on duty and intellect, rather than emotion. Intellectually, you were a good choice."

"Because I am wealthy," Adele said.

"Not just that, Adele. You are charming and lovely and decent. He recognized those qualities in you, as I have, and he admires them. So, he will be disappointed, even if it is not a passionate love he expresses."

Adele shifted on the rough log. "But I know your propensity for guilt. Would you be able to live with yourself if you hurt Harold, when the strongest dynamic of your relationship has always been your desire to protect him?"

Damien spoke with conviction. "Today my grandmother suggested that I have spent my life trying to protect Harold because he is so much like my father, and I've been trying to make up for what happened. She insisted that I recognize that Harold is a grown man, and that it is not my responsibility to ensure he is always happy. She even suggested it might do him good to suffer a little, because we have all treated him like something breakable, fearing he would turn out like my father. She was guilty of it herself, she said, and I am sure you've noticed that Eustacia is always doting on him, telling him he can do no wrong."

Adele considered that as she stood. "But must you hurt him in order to help him escape his sheltered life? What a convenient time to change your perspective, when there is an heiress to be had."

She walked away from him and stopped at a large oak where she rested her hand on the rough bark. She heard Damien rise and follow to where she stood, but she kept her back to him.

"No," he said firmly. "I will not allow you to say that, or even think it. I am in love with you, Adele, and your wealth has nothing to do with it. I would marry you with or without your settlement."

Adele stiffened. Her heart had not stopped pounding this entire time. She struggled for a clear comprehension of her thoughts and feelings. A part of her reveled in hearing him say he was in love with her. *In love with her!* And he would marry her without her settlement?

Though she kept her back to him, she could feel his presence behind her. How she longed to turn around and touch him, but another part of her could not ignore all the reasons why she must be careful.

When she did not respond, he did not retreat. He strengthened his position. "Whether I am making excuses for my lack of loyalty to Harold or not," Damien said, "I don't know, and I don't care. In the end it doesn't matter. The fact is, I want you, and my desire for you has eclipsed my loyalty to my cousin. If I must choose, I will be disloyal to him, and I will choose you. There, I have said it."

I will choose you.

Adele was breathing hard now. His words had hit their mark. Her defenses began to collapse and surrender. At long last, she turned.

Damien—tall and dark before her—gazed down at her with the look of a warrior who was exhausted after battle but still every inch the conqueror.

She did not know what to do. She loved him, she knew she did. She had felt connected to him from the first day they met, and she had been denying it all this time because she did not feel he could be faithful to one woman for the rest of his life.

But he had tried to convince her that he could. She had seen him weeping over his grandmother's bed. He had fought this attraction from the very first day, and fought it hard, because he had not wanted to hurt or betray a member of his family.

Perhaps there was more to him than what she had let herself see. Perhaps she had focused on the wrong things.

He moved a little closer. "Please don't say no, Adele. Think about it at least. Promise that you will consider it. Even if you are not ready now, perhaps in time…."

An almost tangible, tension-filled need settled in the air between them as Adele gazed up at Damien's lips. She wanted him. Certainly, her body wanted him, and she wanted to be held by him, but she could not allow herself to become a slave to her physical passions. She must think more intelligently than that.

Nevertheless, when he cupped her chin in his hand—his brilliant gaze holding her captive—and lowered his mouth to hers, she was lost. His kiss was tentative at first, as if he were testing the waters of her consent. The sensual pull of his allure was unstoppable, and Adele stepped into his arms with tremendous urgency and deepened the kiss.

His response was immediate. He swept her up off her feet, as if she weighed no more than a feather, and carried her along the mossy bank of the lake, farther away from the rotunda and into the greenery. Adele kissed him while he carried her through a grove of poplars, then he bent low to enter the private, quiet shelter of a weeping willow, whose graceful branches touched the ground.

He knelt on one knee and laid her on the soft grass, then came down to lie upon her. Again, she slid her hands around his neck and pulled him close for what felt like a soul-reaching kiss.

Her body began to burn, and any lingering resistance toward this forbidden pleasure crumbled, for she was no longer bound by her sense of commitment to Harold. She wanted Damien selfishly and wantonly, and she wanted out of the cage.

His lips moved across her cheeks and down her neck, and she arched her back on the grass. She slid her hands under his jacket collar and over his shoulders, squirming as she tried to push his jacket off. She wanted to feel his skin.

Damien sat back on his heels and ripped the garment off, tossing it to the ground beside them, then he tugged at his neckcloth and came down upon her again. This time, she welcomed him fully with her body, sliding her hands up under his shirt and wrapping her legs around him.

"If you tell me to stop, I will," he whispered huskily. "All you have to do is say it."

She nodded to let him know she understood, but

she had no intention of stopping him. Not this time. She was tired of resisting what she wanted for herself. Leaning to the side on one elbow, Damien began to unbutton her bodice. Seconds later he was pressing it open and rubbing his hand over the top of her stiff corset.

"May I have your permission to remove this?" he asked.

"Yes, please, Damien."

He worked the fastenings and the corset came loose beneath his masterful hands, and the cool air touched Adele's skin, hot and damp beneath her light, cotton chemise. She closed her eyes and marveled in awe. She was outdoors with Damien and finally able to breathe. She became lost in the moment, drowning in her desires, and cared nothing about consequences.

Soon, her body relaxed as he stroked her and loved her, and she felt wondrously free and wanton. The last of her inhibitions fell away as he whispered in her ear, "You have my heart, Adele."

It was not like her to act without careful consideration, but she was no longer the old Adele. She now knew the meaning of impetuousness, of fevered, out-of-control acts of passion.

"And you have mine," she replied.

It was all he had been waiting for. She was dimly aware of his hand working the buttons of his trousers. A breeze blew the willow branches all around them, and the leaves whispered. Adele opened her eyes to look up at Damien in the dim, afternoon light, and he was never more handsome than he was in the moment when he entered her.

The pressure caused some discomfort, but it also caused a need. Despite the pain of the penetration, Adele pushed back in response and soon felt the rupture of her maidenhead. Almost instantly, the pain diminished with the realization that Damien was inside of her. She was able to lie back and revel in the fulfillment of her dreams as pleasure coursed through her body like an electric current. She whispered words of delight in Damien's ear.

She had longed for a sense of freedom in her soul, and this was it. This was what it felt like to soar.

Rolling to her side on the grass, Adele snuggled close to Damien as they wallowed in the lingering joys of their lovemaking.

"When will you tell Harold?" Damien asked.

Adele's mind went blank. She had not wanted to think about that yet. She was enjoying this freedom too much. She wanted to exist only in the moment, without concern for the future or difficult decisions.

"I'm not sure," she replied, "but it must be my decision, and mine alone. I do not want to be guided, yet again, by what others tell me I should or must do."

He wet his lips. "I don't mean to tell you what to do. I only want you to know that I am here for you, Adele, not to lead you, but to stand beside you."

How was it possible that he always knew the right things to say? Sometimes he filled her with such bliss, she could barely believe she wasn't dreaming.

"What about Harold?" she asked. "I don't relish the thought of destroying your relationship with him. He's like a brother to you."

"I hope that he will want me to be happy, the way I have always wanted him to be happy."

"Perhaps he will forgive you," she replied, "but I suspect he will hate me forever."

Damien stroked her cheek. "It wouldn't matter. What I said before still stands. If I must choose, I choose you, no matter the cost. You are my future. I hope you will choose me over all else as well."

She snuggled closer, happy to be in his arms, even though she was still in turmoil. She was not yet sure she should leap so quickly from one man to another. A few days ago, when she had decided to end her engagement to Harold, she had imagined living on her own, even embarking on a career of some sort. But now, was she being too quick to throw all that aside? To rush into a marriage with a man whose integrity she had always questioned?

She knew she adored him; that wasn't the problem. She only wished to do what was right and what was wise—for her. Unfortunately, at the moment, she wasn't sure of the wisest course of action. She was afraid she had been carried away by her passions.

Just then, a twig snapped and there was a rustling in the woods. They both went silent and turned toward the sound.

"What was that?" Adele whispered, reaching for her drawers.

"I don't know. Get dressed," he whispered, rising to his feet.

He fastened his breeches and pulled on his jacket. He was still buttoning it when he pushed through the curtain of willow leaves and disappeared.

Chapter 25

Adele watched Damien through the branches as he moved about the woods in silence, like a panther searching for prey.

She frantically pulled on her corset and bodice and got to her feet. The willow leaves separated again, and Damien reappeared.

"Well?" she asked.

"I didn't see anyone. It could have been an animal."

"Your horse?"

"Perhaps." He gazed over his shoulder. "Though it seemed to come from the other direction."

He bent to pick up his neckcloth. "We should head back to the house."

Adele agreed and they left the shelter of the willow tree and walked along the path, hand in hand. When they reached the teahouse, Adele said, "I should try to find Harold right away and speak to him."

Damien nodded. "I'll wait here for a while, so we don't return at the same time. We don't want to raise any suspicions before you've had a chance to explain everything."

She rose up on her toes and kissed him on the cheek. "I'll find you when it's done. We still have a great deal to talk about, Damien. I fear this may be happening too fast."

"Not for me," he replied. "I have never been more certain about anything. I know that I want to spend my life with you."

She hesitated, then she nodded and started walking.

Damien called out to her. "Adele."

She stopped and turned. He was standing beside a rose bush. His hair was a wild mess, his clothes looked ragged and worn. She glanced down at his feet. There was mud on his boots.

He took a step forward. "I don't recall if I said it to you or not...."

"Said what?" she asked.

He paused, and when he spoke, his voice was smooth like velvet. "That I love you."

A leaf drifted down through the air and landed on Adele's head. She felt only a gentle breeze through her hair, and a simple, joyful contentment inside herself. "I love you, too."

Then, feeling buoyant and full of cautious hope, she made off for the house.

Adele went straight to the conservatory—or rather the laboratory—to search for Harold. She did not find him there.

Next, she went to the dowager's rooms and was pleased to discover the woman was sitting up, drinking soup with Eustacia at her side. Adele stayed for a short time to visit, but since it was Harold she wanted to see, she left them and went to knock on his bed-chamber door.

No one answered at first, but then he called out, "Enter!"

She pushed the door open. He was sitting on the edge of his bed, and when he saw that it was Adele, he stood quickly and straightened his neck cloth, appearing flustered. "What are you doing here?"

She was slightly confused by the question. "Did no one tell you that my mother and I arrived this morning? To see your grandmother?"

"Well, yes," he said awkwardly. "Mother told me, of course. I meant, what are you doing knocking on my bedchamber door? It's hardly proper, Adele."

She forced a smile, remembering how uncomfortable Harold could be about bending or breaking rules.

"I apologize," she said, "but I would like to speak with you privately. Could we talk in the library?"

He pasted on his customary, cheerful smile. "Certainly."

She hesitated because she thought he might accompany her, but he seemed to want her to go on her own and wait for him there.

As she turned to leave, she stole a quick glance around at the furnishings, and realized it was probably the only time she would ever see the inside of this room.

After Adele closed Harold's bedchamber door and the sound of her footsteps disappeared down the hall, Harold let out a breath of relief and sat back down on his bed.

Violet got up off the floor and smoothed out her skirt. "Upon my word, I'm getting tired of this."

"What do you mean?" Harold asked.

"Oh, nothing," she said irritably. "It's just that this is not the first time I've had to duck down and hide in a room when that woman enters it."

Harold accepted her explanation without asking for further clarification.

"Will you be all right?" Violet asked her brother, gazing at him with genuine sympathy, for he was truly no match for Damien. Not in a woman's eyes.

Harold nodded. "Yes. I don't care anymore. I don't care if he hates me. There was a time when we were close, but now...I don't think I can ever forgive him for this."

Violet touched Harold's shoulder. "He doesn't deserve your forgiveness. He knew how much you loved her. He should have to grovel for your forgiveness for the rest of his life."

"I *did* love her," Harold insisted, "and he should most definitely have to grovel for my forgiveness. But it wouldn't do him any good." He gazed up at Violet with a bitter glimmer in his eye. "Because we are finished, he and I."

Harold kept Adele waiting in the library for at least ten minutes before he entered, looking uncharacteristically serious. "I apologize," he said, closing the door behind him. "I had something to attend to."

"It's quite all right."

They both sat down and looked at each other for

a few awkward seconds. There had been many awkward silences between them, which was exactly why Adele had to end this engagement and explain her change-of-heart as kindly and gently as possible.

She sat forward on the edge of the chair, laced her fingers together on her lap, and said, "Harold, I—"

He held up a hand. "Please stop, Adele. I know what you are going to say."

"You do?"

"Yes." He wet his lips, and his cheeks reddened. Slightly unnerved, Adele waited for him to continue.

"I saw you today," he said. "I saw you under the tree. I know what happened."

Adele went numb. She sat in silence, staring at him, as a wave of horror washed over her. She covered her mouth with a hand. "Oh, Harold...." Her voice shook when she spoke. "What were you doing there?"

"Mother told me that you had gone there looking for me. Naturally, I went to find you."

She shifted agonizingly in the chair. "Harold, I'm so sorry. I wanted to tell you. That's why I went down there in the first place. To talk to you because I thought you were there."

"But Damien got there before I did."

She paused. "Yes."

Harold stood and paced to the window. "You cannot know how shocked and devastated I was to see—" He stopped himself.

Adele was mortified.

"Damien..." Harold said with grim loathing. "My own cousin. We were the best of friends, ever since we were boys. He was like a brother to me."

"He still is," Adele said, hoping to prevent a complete dissolution of their friendship. She could not bear to think it would be severed because of her.

"No," he replied.

Adele stood and went to him. "He tried to fight it, Harold. He tried very hard, and so did I. It just happened, that's all. Neither of us ever wanted to hurt you."

She touched his shoulder, but he shook her hand away. "You had already decided you didn't want to marry me?" Harold asked. "That's why you went looking for me?"

"Yes."

"Because you wanted to marry Damien instead?"

She hesitated before she answered. "No. I was just going to go home to America on my own. I didn't know what I wanted."

He glared down at her. It was the first time she'd ever seen anger and pain in his eyes. He was always so cheerful and happy. "Did he propose to you?"

"Yes."

He bowed his head and shook it. "Damien," he said, through a jaw that was clenched tight with fury. "He had no right."

"Harold...."

He turned from the window and paced angrily around the room. "And you.... How could you let him seduce you like that? What were you thinking?"

"I can't really explain it."

"No, I should think not. But you must realize how foolish you were. He has forced himself upon you, Adele."

"No, it wasn't like that. He never forced me."

"I mean he forced the situation to go as he wanted it. He wants your money, and he did what he does best in order to get it."

She shook her head.

"You don't believe that? You think he's in love with you?" Harold continued to pace. "I suppose I should not be surprised. He knows what women like to hear."

Adele bristled at that.

"Do you have any idea what's been going on in his life lately?" Harold asked. "Do you know about the creditors? About Frances Fairbanks?"

"Everyone knows about her."

"But they don't know she's with child."

A sudden jolt caused all thoughts and responses to wedge in Adele's brain. She stared at Harold, not quite able to accept what he was saying.

"She wants Damien to marry her, of course, but she has no money, so he is not inclined to propose. He does, however, possess some miniscule fragment of integrity in his own misdirected way, because he is determined to support her and the child. Hence, the urgency for a quick alliance with an heiress."

Adele swallowed hard, biting back the hurt she felt. *He was going to have a baby with Frances?* He had never said anything. He had led her to believe their relationship was over.

"Do you know this for certain?" Adele asked. "Or is it just drawing room gossip?"

"Damien told me himself, and ridiculously, I was the one who convinced him that he should find himself a fiancée as soon possible. How's that for a stab in the back? He set his sights on *you*."

Adele felt sick. She had to sit down.

"Do you believe me now, that he is not to be trusted? Do you understand why I am so furious with him, for acting in such a devious, underhanded manner, and taking advantage of you so deplorably? My own cousin!"

"I don't know what I believe at the moment," Adele said.

Harold stopped pacing and met her gaze. "I will still marry you, Adele, if you wish it. It is Damien I am most angry with, and I hold myself partly responsible for this. I-I should have taken better care." He approached and took her chin in his slender hand and looked down at her with a sympathetic expression. "I am of the opinion that you were taken in, but only because you are so good and innocent, and you do not see the bad in other people."

Her dander perked up its head. "That's not true, Harold. Everyone thinks I am perfect, but I am not, and I was not 'taken in.'"

He dropped his hand to his side. "If what happened between you and Damien results in a child, I will accept that child. He would be my second cousin, after all. I would only hope that it would be a girl."

Adele squeezed her eyes shut. "Harold, please don't speak of this sort of thing. I'm sorry, but I cannot marry you, and I would feel the same even if I had never met Damien. You and I, we don't love each other. And we have very little in common."

"You respect me, do you not? Violet told me you

said I was the most decent man you knew."

"That is true."

"Well, that is something to build on."

"It is, but...I don't want to build on it. I don't want to marry you, Harold, and nothing will change my mind."

"Will you marry Damien? Despite what I've told you?"

"I already said I don't know." She held a hand over her stomach to try and quell the terrible churning.

"If you do," Harold said callously, "I assure you, you will live to regret it."

With nothing left to say on that matter, Adele moved toward the door, but stopped and turned. "I'm very sorry about all this, Harold. I will leave Osulton today, just as soon as I can pack my things. I will ask you to say good-bye to your mother and your grandmother for me. Please tell them that I had come to care for them very much, and I never wanted to hurt any of you."

With that, she walked out.

Harold sank into a chair, covered his face with both hands, and ground out a string of expletives.

Three hours later, Damien stormed into the conservatory, where Harold was setting up for an experiment.

Damien stopped on the opposite side of the laboratory table and slammed a letter down with a smack. The table jumped, and a carefully arranged collection of glass bottles wobbled, noisily clanking into each other. Harold bent forward and grabbed for them, hugging them together to prevent them from falling.

Damien leaned forward on his fists. "What in God's name did you say to her?"

Chapter 26

*H*AROLD'S FACE PULLED INTO A frown and he straightened, making sure, however, that the bottles were steady before he let them go. "You have a lot of nerve coming in here and demanding answers from *me.*"

Damien straightened also. They were eye to eye on opposite sides of the table. Pent-up rage, in each of them, crackled in the air between them.

"I asked you a question," Damien said.

Harold glanced down at the letter. He picked it up and read it. As Damien watched his cousin, he recited the letter in his own mind, for he had read it so many times, he'd memorized it:

> *Dear Damien,*
>
> *I am leaving Osulton Manor today. Please do not try and follow me. I was carried away by my passions today and I do not believe it would be wise for us to marry. I know about Frances, so I must protect my heart in this matter.*

*I must also inform you that I spoke to Harold
and ended our engagement. He did not take it
well, as he had been the noise in the woods.*
Adele

"What did she mean," Damien said, "that she must protect her heart? What did you tell her about Frances?"

"What do you think I told her? The truth, of course. Despite your improper intimacy with her, she did not deserve to be kept in the dark about your urgent need for a rich wife, or about your creditors or Frances. I would not allow her to be taken advantage of in that way."

"She knows about all that. I never lied to her."

"This is outrageous!" Harold said. "I should not be the one explaining myself. You should be!" Harold walked around the table. "You seduced and ruined my fiancée!"

Damien stared into his cousin's furious eyes and managed to collect himself. He fought off the shock and anguish over Adele's hasty departure and her decision that she would never marry him and realized that Harold had his own reasons to be angry. And he was right. Damien had indeed done the unthinkable.

"Perhaps we should take this outside," he suggested, knowing there was much to be worked out, and this room constructed of glass was not the place.

Harold ripped off his apron and threw it on the floor. "Damn right we should." In a most uncharacteristic manner, he forcefully led the way out.

Violet took the news that Adele had left *Osulton Manor* with neither grace nor understanding. She glared hotly at her mother in the drawing room and balled her hands into fists.

"My brother is an incompetent cretin! If she is gone, it is his fault for not knowing how to treat a woman! He is hopeless! No one will ever marry him!"

She collapsed into a fit of tears on the sofa, not the least bit comforted by her mother stroking her back.

"Now we shall be beggars!" Violet sobbed. "Harold spends all our money on his silly experiments, and I will have to marry beneath me, because all the best men in London want those rich American girls with their big dowries!" She dropped her head into her hands. "And Whitby! Now I will never have him!"

"There, there, Violet, it's not so bad. You still have your beauty to recommend you."

She peered up at her mother as if she had sprouted horns and wiped the flood of tears from her cheeks. "She is gone, Mother! *Gone!* She left Harold, and we will not get her settlement!"

Violet dropped her head into her arms again, and sobbed, "Oh, why does everything always have to happen to *me!*"

Damien followed Harold out to the large veranda at the back of the house. They both walked quickly with long strides to the stairs that led down to the rectangular pond. The wind had picked up. The green hedges of the maze were blowing, and low-hanging clouds were racing and changing shape across the gray sky. The pond was dancing with shadowy ripples.

Damien descended the stairs. Harold waited for him at the bottom, on the clipped green grass. They faced each other squarely.

"All our lives," Harold said, "you have been the favorite. You were the strong one—fighting off bullies for me at school. You were the generous one—teaching me to play sports, even going so far as to stay behind in a race to run beside me and encourage me. I remember all those things, Damien, and I always believed it was because you were my friend. That is why I trusted you to bring Adele home to me."

"Harold, I—"

"I'm not done. You did not help me. All you ever did was make me feel like I wasn't strong enough to do anything on my own, and if it weren't for you—watching over me all the time like I was a weakling—maybe I would have gone to get Adele myself."

Damien stared at his cousin. "I *was* your friend, Harold."

"No, you were not. You just wanted to show off to everyone and pound your chest."

Damien shook his head. "You make it sound like I was the one with all the blessings. Dammit, Harold, no one ever thought I was the better man. You were the one who could do no wrong. You've always had everything—parents who loved each other and loved you, a perfect palace to live in with a mother who still takes care of everything. You don't have money problems. You are happy all the time because you have nothing to worry about except the results of your experiments. I was orphaned at the age of nine with the burden of guilt for my parents' death, left with debts you could not even fathom.... So forgive me for learning how to be tough."

Harold's eyebrows lifted. "You are suggesting that you have cause to resent me? I've never heard anything so ridiculous in my life! No one can resist your charm. Grandmother has always favored you, and don't pretend not to know it. You flatter her and flirt with her like she was a debutante, and she would do anything for you. You have her wrapped around your devious little finger."

"For what *devious* purpose, may I ask?" Damien replied, trying to grasp his cousin's logic. "She has nothing to leave any of us in her will. It all went to my father's debts. She has only the pleasure of her last days, and I will not apologize for caring about her enough to enjoy making her feel good."

"Like you made Adele feel good?" His tone suggested the worst.

Damien labored to control his anger. "You will forgive me for saying that that is something you, as her fiancé, failed to do. You were too busy mixing potions."

"That is low, Damien. I loved her."

Damien laughed. "Did you now? Tell me another one!"

"I did! You don't know what I feel!"

"I know you had no time for her. I know you didn't care enough to worry that she had been ravaged by her kidnapper. You didn't even want to hear what happened to her, because it was not pleasant for you. I also know that you wanted her for her father's interest in your chemical inventions. You were hoping to make the history books."

Damien and Harold stood motionless, staring at each other like two wolves, each waiting for the other to attack.

"Let's see who's the strong one today!" Harold grunted as he lunged forward and slammed his shoulder into Damien's gut.

Damien staggered back. "I won't fight you, Harold!"

"You damn well better, or I'll knock you off your feet! And it's about bloody time I did!"

They fell over onto the grass. Damien went down on his back, and Harold straddled him.

He threw a punch, catching Damien in the jaw. Pain shot through his whole head. He tried to grab Harold's arms, but Harold was thrashing—slapping uncontrollably at him.

"I won't fight you, Harold!" he said a second time, finally wrapping his hands around his cousin's slender wrists to restrain him. He had to use all his strength. Harold was still trying to slap at him.

Damien's voice was low and grinding when he spoke. "I could flatten you in a second, cousin. I suggest you stop now, before I'm forced to defend myself."

Harold slowly, eventually gave up the fight. He bowed his head in defeat and rolled off Damien. They both lay on their backs in the grass, looking up at the sky.

"Damn you," Harold said. "I hope you rot in hell."

"You're not the first person to say that."

Harold turned his head toward Damien. His voice

was cold and unfeeling. "Every one of your mistresses, I presume."

"Every damn one."

Harold looked back up at the sky. "Well, if I can't have Adele, I'm glad she's gone. You would have made her miserable."

Damien shook his head. "How can you say that? Did you ever stop to think that I might have truly loved her? Surely you must have. You know me, Harold, better than anyone. You must have known I would not steal a woman from you, my closest friend, without a very good reason. I would not hurt you for a temporary flirtation. Or for money."

Harold was not moved by Damien's pronouncement. "She told me you proposed."

"I did. I wanted to spend my life with her, and it killed me to think of her marrying you, but I weathered it because I couldn't bear to hurt you. But eventually I was worn down. The love I felt for her chipped away at my strength and resolve, and I had to choose between her and you. I just couldn't let her go. I loved her too much."

"Even though you would betray me in the process," Harold replied.

Damien sighed. "I hoped you would understand. And forgive me."

Damien sat up and gazed toward the pond. Harold sat up, too. For a long while, they sat in silence as the wind blew all around them, until Damien turned to his cousin.

"I'm sorry for making you feel weak when we were children," he said quietly, looking him in the eye.

"That was never my intention. I admit I was overly protective of you, but only because I blamed myself for my parents' deaths, and I felt happiest when I was helping you. I didn't want you to end up like my father. I wanted to make sure you were always happy and comfortable. You were all I had."

Harold simply stared at Damien.

"And I still cling to the hope," Damien said, "that you will understand what happened between Adele and me, and forgive me, because she is gone now, and I am...." His voice trembled. "I am devastated."

Harold went pale. "You're devastated?"

"Yes. I loved her, so much, I was willing to throw away everything to be with her."

Harold's eyes narrowed. "But...I thought you wanted her money."

"No. No! Did Adele say that?"

"No," Harold replied, "but considering the circumstances...."

Damien leaned on one arm. "What circumstances, Harold? I must be stupid today, because I am missing things."

Harold shifted to sit on his heels. "I know about Frances."

"What, exactly, do you know? Is this what Adele's was referring to in her letter?"

Harold paused, then he whispered, even though there was no one within earshot to hear them. "I know about the baby."

Damien felt his forehead crease. "What baby?"

"Your baby. I know you want to provide for the child."

The child? Damien's head began to spin. "I beg your pardon? A baby with Frances? This is bloody news to me."

"You didn't know?"

Damien almost laughed. "You say it like I'm the last to know, but it's not true, Harold. I know it's not."

"How do you know?"

"If you want me to be blunt, I know because the last time I made love to her, she started her courses that very night."

Harold's mouth dropped open. The wind was blowing even harder now. "You're sure?"

"Yes, I'm sure. I always kept careful track of these things. Who said otherwise?"

After a few seconds, Harold faced the other direction. He seemed to be considering something. "Violet."

Damien rose irritably to his feet. "Violet said that?"

"Yes," Harold said, rising also. "But there's something else you should know. I...I told Adele that *you* told me about Frances and the baby. I lied about that because Violet suggested it would be better if it wasn't just drawing room gossip. I'm sorry, Damien. I believed there was a baby. Violet said it was true, and I was so angry with you."

Damien rested his hands on his hips and bowed his head.

"And Damien," Harold said, "I wasn't the one who saw you in the woods today. It was Violet." Harold dropped his head into his hands. "I guess I'm not such a decent fellow after all, am I? I'm a bit of a liar, in fact. And not only that, I'm about the worst fool in the world. I was manipulated by my spoiled brat of a sister."

Violet was still sobbing when Damien and Harold walked into the drawing room, on the war path. Eustacia looked up—shocked by the sudden, rather passionate intrusion. "What in heaven's name is going on?" she asked, wrapping her arm protectively around Violet.

Eyes red and puffy, cheeks stained with tears, Violet sat up. She wiped the back of her hand across her cheek and frowned at Damien. "You bastard."

"Violet! Your language!" Eustacia shouted.

Violet did not take her eyes off Damien. Her lips pursed into a thin line. "Why couldn't you just leave her alone? Why *her?* You could have any woman you wanted, and you had to go and spoil Harold's chances for happiness!"

Damien approached her. His eyes were dark and hooded, his voice quiet and dangerous. "You have some explaining to do, cousin."

She shuddered with a weepy intake of breath. "What are you talking about?"

"You told Harold that Frances Fairbanks was having my child."

Eustacia gasped and put a hand over her mouth. "Good heavens!"

Violet shifted nervously on the sofa. "I did not."

"Yes, you did," Harold said.

"No, I didn't!"

"Yes, you did!"

"No, I—"

Damien held up a hand. "You lied, Violet, and Adele has made decisions with inaccurate information. You will fix the problem."

"But I didn't have anything to do with it!"

Harold stepped up. "It is just like you, Violet, to blame someone else. Remember when you broke the blue vase in the gallery, and you said you didn't know who did it? I saw you do it, you selfish brat, and I saw you deny it. That was last year! You were old enough to know better." He turned to Eustacia, pointing his finger. "Mother, *she* did it. She was practicing tossing her shawl over her shoulder."

Harold turned to Damien. He gazed at him for a long, drawn-out minute. His voice grew calmer. His shoulders relaxed. "If she won't tell Adele the truth, Damien, I will tell her."

"Harold...." Damien said, interrupting.

"No, let me finish. I'm sorry. I should have been able to see that you and Adele were better suited to each other, and that you cared for her. I should have been more aware of what was going on around me."

"Harold, I'm so sorry."

"You don't need to be. You're a good man. I should have known you would never seduce Adele just for her money. I will tell Adele that I was wrong to doubt you. I will tell her that I am sorry for not loving her the way she deserved to be loved, and I will tell her that you love her, and that I know it's true because you told me, and I believe you because you are the most decent fellow I know."

Damien gazed with disbelief at his cousin. "I would be obliged," he said.

Harold nodded. "She and her mother were heading to her sister's house in London. Perhaps we should go now."

Damien and Harold left the drawing room. As they made their way down the main stairs, Harold posed the question: "Do you think Whitby will still propose to Violet if she doesn't have money from Adele's settlement?"

Damien inclined his head. "I have no idea what's in Whitby's mind. I suppose it remains to be seen." Then he went quickly to summon the coach.

Chapter 27

Wentworth House
London

THAT NIGHT, SOPHIA QUIETLY PUSHED open the door of her husband's study and peered inside. "Are you busy?"

He leaned back in his chair and smiled at her. "Not at all. Come here." James held out his arm.

Sophia went to him and sat down on his lap. "I wanted to tell you that Adele and Mother have arrived."

"Is Adele all right?" James asked.

"I don't think so. She told me about what she said to Harold when she broke the news to him, and he didn't take it well. But she is more upset over what happened with Damien. Oh, James, I believe she is deeply in love with him. She hasn't told me everything, I don't think, but she did tell me that he proposed."

"Did he now?"

"You're not surprised?"

He shook his head. "I recognized a certain look in his eye when I spoke to him about Adele at a ball one night."

Sophia rested her head on his shoulder. "Well, she refused him, and she is determined not to change her mind. She just wants to go home."

"To America?" James's dark brows drew together. "Why? It is my opinion that Alcester has been misunderstood by many people who think—"

"Frances Fairbanks is with child," Sophia told him. "It's Damien's, but he won't marry her because she has no money. It appears that the relationship is not over."

James lifted Sophia off his lap and stood. "Where in the world did Adele hear that?"

Sophia shrugged. "I don't know. Harold, I think."

He shook his head. "If it's true, I'll eat my valet's boot."

"What do you know, James?"

"I know that the manager of the theater where she appears is a great supporter of hers, giving her all the best parts, and it's a well-known fact that two gentlemen of substantial means have been providing for her rather extravagant means of living, and I assure you, they all collect their rewards. So, there is no way she could ever prove the child was Alcester's, if there even is a child."

"Oh, James, that is positively sordid."

"Yes. Alcester was wise to break it off with her. Besides that, I've made it my business to learn everything there is to know about Damien Renshaw, and by all accounts, he is a decent fellow."

"Why didn't you say anything?"

"I assumed it would all work itself out, that Adele would see the light. But this lie that is circulating is unfair. Would you like me to look into it?"

"Oh James, yes. Would you?"

He touched her cheek with the back of his hand. "If it will ease your mind, Sophia, I will go straight to the source. I will speak to Miss Fairbanks myself."

Chapter 28

THE NEXT MORNING, THE BUTLER of Wentworth House entered the drawing room and announced Lord Osulton and Lord Alcester. Sophia, Beatrice, and Adele all stood up. Adele placed a hand on her stomach to try and mollify the sudden nervous butterflies.

Sophia greeted her guests and invited them to sit down. "Would you like some tea, gentlemen?" she offered.

"That would be very nice, thank you," Harold replied while Damien never took his eyes off Adele.

Sophia stood up and walked to the velvet bell pull, but Damien stood before she had a chance to put her hand on it. "Forgive me, madam, but may I request a moment alone with your sister?" He bowed deferentially toward Beatrice. "A moment with your daughter, Mrs. Wilson?"

Beatrice rolled her shoulders. "I should think not."

Sophia winced. "Mother...."

Damien would not be deterred. "I know you have not always approved of me, Mrs. Wilson, but let me assure you, my intentions toward your daughter are honorable. A moment is all I ask."

Beatrice gazed pleadingly at Harold. "Lord Osulton?"

He stood also and bowed. "His intentions are honorable, Mrs. Wilson."

Beatrice stammered with bewilderment. More than a little surprised herself, Adele met Harold's gaze. What had happened between them? What had changed Harold's opinion of Damien? The last time she had spoken to him, he considered his cousin a scoundrel and a fortune hunter. Had he learned what James had told her?

Sophia crossed the room and stopped before her mother, who was still sitting. "Come, Mother. We will wait outside the door."

Beatrice rose reluctantly. Harold went with them and closed the door behind them.

Adele watched Damien move to stand in front of the mantel piece. "In your letter," he said, "you asked me not to follow you, but I couldn't let you go on believing something about me that is simply not true. I have not fathered another woman's child. That was a lie."

Her heart pounded, as it often did when Damien was nearby. Slowly, she stood and made her way around the table in the center of the room, to cross toward him. "I know."

He inclined his head to the side. "You do?"

"Yes."

"How?"

She sighed. "My brother-in-law the duke seems

to have a high opinion of you. He has been making inquiries. I am pleased to say that he spoke to Frances himself last night. She knew nothing of a baby and was surprised such a thing was even suggested."

Damien exhaled.

Adele stopped before him, close enough to put her hands on his chest if she wanted to. She did want to, but for the time being she resisted the urge.

"What happened?" she asked. "Why did Harold lie to me about Frances? And why is he here this afternoon, vouching for your honor in front of my mother?"

Damien turned his hat over in his hands. "He didn't know he was lying to you. Violet made up the story about Frances and encouraged him to tell you that I had admitted to being the father of the child. Violet wanted you to marry Harold, so that she herself would have a large dowry to settle upon the man of her choice."

"Lord Whitby?" Adele asked.

"Most likely."

"She admitted to that?"

"Not really, but she's always had a problem admitting to her misdemeanors. Harold is going to address that when he gets home."

Adele felt her eyebrows lift in surprise. "I am pleased to hear it."

"Adele...." Damien took a small step forward. His voice was strangely hushed. "I came here to tell you something else. Something you must hear from my own lips. Something I hope you will believe." He stood before her, his dark eyes gleaming, his chest rising and falling with shallow breaths. "I know that you have many reservations about me, and after all that has happened, for good reason. But I vow by all that is holy that when I become a husband, I will never be unfaithful to my wife."

She eyed him soberly. Despite her foray into her own wild passions, she had come this far, never completely letting go of her prudent nature. She would not simply tumble into Damien's arms now after one small promise of fidelity. Nor would she base her decision on the opinion of her brother-in-law—that Damien was not what people thought he was. She was going to use her own mind and form her own opinion.

In that light, she needed more from Damien. If she had learned anything from her experiences over the past month, it was to think of what she wanted in life, and to ask for it, to settle for nothing less. She knew she wanted Damien, but she would be absolutely certain of him first, before she gave him her whole heart.

"People have been placing bets," she said, "that you'll go back to Frances, or someone like her, after you've married an heiress for her money. Did you know that?"

He pressed his lips together with disdain. "People should mind their own business. I gave you my word that I am not after your money. I don't care about it and I will prove it. We can make do without it, Adele."

She sighed. "Damien, you enjoy women. You have never been able to commit to just one."

"But have I not explained well enough why I formed

temporary relationships with women like Frances?"

She glanced at the door, hoping no one was about to barge back in, because she wanted desperately to hear what he was going to say.

"Because contrary to what others think of me," he said, "I take marriage very seriously. I admit that I have not been a monk. All my life, I have craved some form of intimacy with women—perhaps because of what I missed in my childhood, losing a mother—but I was careful to choose women who were open and honest about wanting relationships without commitment, because I never wanted to risk being forced to marry a woman I did not love. I did not wish to be miserable like my parents and destroy a family because of it—especially if there were children involved. I always intended to be in love with the woman I married and be confident in my decision to marry her. And it would help if she loved me in return."

"But you had concerns about me," Adele reminded him. "You said it yourself—that I was not faithful to my fiancé. As I became more open and aware of my passions, you became more threatened by memories of your parents. You *did* think I was like your mother, and it broke my heart that you believed I was dishonorable, even though it was true in certain ways. The fact is, I couldn't go through life feeling as if my husband did not trust or respect me completely."

"I didn't know the truth about my mother, Adele, and I was self-righteous. I was angry with her because she was not perfect, but she had a difficult burden to bear. I know that now. I must forgive her for her weakness, because I have suddenly found myself in a similar situation—in love with a woman who was forbidden to me. And you...." He took a step closer and laid a hand on her cheek. "You are not perfect, Adele. I know that. At first I thought you were, which is why I was enamored with you in the beginning. But then I saw the passion in you, and yes, I mourned the loss of my perfect, pure Adele, and I felt guilty for being the cause of that, but I needed you to break out of that perfect shell in order for us to be together, and you did.

"So now, I cannot idolize you anymore. You have flaws. You made a commitment to my cousin, and you fell in love with another man and broke that commitment. But that man was me, and hurting Harold was the right thing to do. So, when I look at you now, I know that you are as close to perfect as any real person can be. I do trust you, Adele. Completely."

Adele stared, speechless, stunned by his vehemence and honesty. She remembered the morning she woke next to him at the inn, the final day of their travels. She had felt happy, safe, and content next to him. Everything had felt right. There was no other word for it.

All at once, she wanted more than anything to wake up beside him again and feel that same sense of contentment—that all was right with the world—every day for the rest of her life. It was where her heart was meant to be. With him. In his home. At Essence House.

It was time to admit the truth to herself. She *loved* him. She loved Damien Renshaw, with every inch of her soul, and she believed in him. Wholly and absolutely. It was time to trust her heart. To follow it, and to go after what she wanted.

"From the first moment I met you," she said shakily, "I was drawn to you, and it brings me some relief to finally know that I was not so wrong after all to care for you the way I did. I believe my heart had seen you better than my eyes."

She watched the strain in his face fade away. He wet his lips, looking hopeful and joyful, though still tentative.

"There was more to you," she continued, "than what could be seen or heard about through other people's misguided opinions. What I have learned about you this morning—that in your own strange way, you have always wanted love and fidelity—I like very much."

He gripped both her hands in his. She had never seen him look so vulnerable before. Her knight. Her black lion, who feared nothing.

"Is that all, Adele? You *like* what you have heard? Can there ever be more? Because I must have more."

"There is already more," she replied, feeling an overwhelming urge to laugh out loud. "Much more. I love you quite hopelessly, Damien Renshaw, and I have loved you for what seems like forever."

His lips fell upon hers suddenly, without reservation or composure. He swept her up into his arms until her feet lifted clear off the ground, and Adele shook with bursts of laughter. Or were they sobs of joy?

He kissed her deeply as if the intimacy could erase all the agony and frustration of the past month— when they had both been certain they could never have each other.

Well, they *would* have each other. Utterly and completely for the rest of their lives.

Damien pulled back and dropped to one knee. He held one of her hands in his and kissed it tenderly before he lifted his gaze to look up at her face, into her eyes.

"Adele Wilson, I love you. I want to be with you forever. I want to have children and grandchildren with you, I want to laugh with you, go for long walks in the woods with you, make love to you, and I want to make you the happiest woman on earth, if I can. You are the only woman in the world for me, and I cannot imagine my life without you. Will you marry me?"

She squeezed both his hands and pulled him to his feet. "Yes, Damien. Yes, to everything."

He pressed his lips to hers again, with passion and love and the promise of forever. Then he rested his forehead upon hers and smiled down at her. "You have made me so happy. I've never been this happy before. Not once in my life."

"There is more to come," she promised. "I will make you happy again, every day if I can. I am a better person for knowing you. I am happier with myself. When I look in the mirror, I no longer see a stranger. I know the things I want. I know I want a simple life with you in your messy, unpretentious house." She grinned.

"Then messy and unpretentious is what you shall have. I am most pleased to be marrying a woman who will not make me get my hair cut."

Her eyes widened in horror. "Cut it? I should think not!"

He smiled. "It's a fright in the mornings."

"It's beautiful."

Damien pulled her into his arms again and kissed her hand. Then he reached into his pocket and pulled out a red candy stick. Adele's lips parted in surprise as she took hold of it.

"Damien...."

"I've been wanting to give you this and so much more ever since that first night you told me about wanting something you didn't think you could have. So here it is. You can have what you want, Adele. I will devote my life to making sure you know it."

Adele took his face in her hands and kissed him passionately on the mouth. "Will Harold be all right with this?" she asked. "Will Eustacia and your grandmother ever forgive us?"

"I believe they will," he replied, "because Harold is a true friend. We will move past this, and he will survive."

She smiled. "He will be my friend, too, Damien. He always was."

"There will only be one problem," Damien said, glancing off to the side.

She cringed with a pang of apprehension. "What is that?"

"We will all have to continue to put up with Violet. God give us strength."

Adele laughed, and pulled him close for another kiss.

Epilogue

Wentworth Castle, Yorkshire
Two months later

*J*T WAS JUST BEGINNING TO rain when Lily walked quickly back from the stables following her early morning gallop across the moors. She wore a black riding habit and top hat, but her shiny new boots—crunching over the white rocks in the courtyard—were pinching her feet. She looked forward to getting out of them and finding her old ones before someone gave them away.

She entered the house and was just pulling off her gloves when a footman approached with a letter on a silver salver. "For you," he said.

She picked up the letter and glanced at it. It was from Sophia. She stuffed her gloves into her pockets and tore at the seal. Lily slowly climbed the stairs while she read....

> *Dear Lily,*
> *The Season is finally over, and James and I and*

the boys will be coming home soon. Martin will follow a day or two later.

I can hardly wait to see you and Marion, and the boys are looking forward to returning to the country where they can run about and play with the ponies. They have especially been missing the little gray one.

You will be pleased to hear that Adele is very happy in her new home at Essence House. It was exactly as she had imagined it would be, and she told me she felt as if she was born to live there. I am so happy for her. She sends her love.

(In case you are wondering, my father insisted on giving them a very generous wedding gift, even though they protested it strongly. But you know my father. When he wants to do something, he does it. Adele has grown to be very much like him, I daresay.)

Please tell Marion that I found a lovely hat for her yesterday, and I believe it will go well with her blue day dress with the navy velvet trim. I will bring it when I come.

I hope all is well at home, and I will see you in a few days.

Love,

Sophia

P.S. You may also be interested to know that Lord Whitby left London early this Season and returned to his country house. James said he was trying to avoid Miss Violet Scott, who evidently was making rather a spectacle of herself, following

*him everywhere. What a shame. She was very
pretty. Though I don't think she is quite Whitby's
type.*

   See you soon,
   S.

Lily stopped at the top of the stairs and read the
postscript again. A single tear ran down her cheek.
It was not sadness, but relief that she felt—a most
delightful, invigorating wave of relief.

Author's Note

The heroine of this book, Adele Wilson, is the youngest of three fictional sisters who leave old New York to go husband hunting in London in the late-Victorian period. While these sisters are entirely fictional, I based each of them on a number of real-life American heiresses, as well as some fictional characters from the works of some nineteenth and twentieth-century novelists.

The most obvious models for this trilogy are the Jerome sisters—Jennie, Clara, and Leonie, who according to the book *To Marry an English Lord,* by Gail MacColl and Carol McD. Wallace, came to be known as "the Beautiful, the Good, and the Witty." My own three fictional sisters I would similarly describe as "the Beautiful, the Adventurous, and the Good."

Jennie Jerome married Lord Randolph Churchill, second son of the seventh Duke of Marlborough, and they became parents to a baby boy who would later lead the nation—Winston Churchill. You can read about Jennie and Randolph in the book, *Jennie: The*

Life of Lady Randolph Churchill, by Ralph Martin. Jennie's two sisters also married Englishmen.

Another real-life American heiress was Consuelo Vanderbilt, who married the ninth Duke of Marlborough in 1895. She is perhaps the most prominent example of an American heiress abroad, partly because she wrote a book about her life—*The Glitter and the Gold.* In it, she describes the hardships and heartbreaks she faced as a young woman who was expected to do her duty to her family by marrying into the British aristocracy. Sophia, the oldest Wilson sister, in my book *To Marry the Duke,* is the closest to Consuelo, as she also marries a duke and experiences much loneliness as an outsider.

In this series, Adele's mother, Beatrice Wilson, is loosely based on Consuelo's mother, Alva Vanderbilt, who aggressively fought the social divisions between the old New Yorkers and the *nouveaux riches*. In March 1883, Alva held a costume ball in honor of her friend Lady Mandeville, a fellow American who had married an English lord in 1876. Alva invited a thousand guests, and all were anxious to see the extravagant mansion Alva and her husband had just built on Fifth Avenue. She neglected to invite the old New York matriarch, Mrs. Astor, however, because according to protocol, Mrs. Astor—being the social superior, who had not acknowledged the Vanderbilts previously—had to call on Alva first. Mrs. Astor finally did have a card delivered to Alva and was subsequently invited to the Vanderbilt ball.

My fictional heroine Adele describes the Knickerbockers in New York when she's in the cottage with Damien. If you're interested in reading about Old New York, try *The Age of Innocence,* by Edith Wharton. Wharton was born into an old New York family, but spent much of her life abroad in Europe. In addition to *The Age of Innocence,* she wrote about American heiresses in London in another of her novels, *The Buccaneers,* which is one of my favorite books and inspired me to write this series.

Edith Wharton became good friends with Henry James, who was also born in New York and chose to live much of his life abroad. He, too, wrote a number of great books about Americans mixing with Europeans. My favorite of his novels is *Washington Square,* set in old New York. This—and the society Edith Wharton writes about in *The Age of Innocence*—is the socially exacting world Adele is so anxious to leave behind.

I hope you enjoyed this trilogy about the Wilson sisters. If you did, you may want to read my spinoff series (Can This Be Love Trilogy) which begins with *Love According to Lily.* The novel was originally published by Avon/Harper Collins in 2005 and received a Reviewers Choice Award from *Romantic Times* for Best Historical Romance of 2005, and also the Bookbuyer's Best Award from Greater Detroit RWA. Read on for an excerpt from that novel and my complete booklist.

If you would like to stay informed about my future releases, or learn about my monthly autographed book giveaway, please visit my website at www.juliannemaclean.com and sign up for my email newsletter. I would love to send news to you!

Lastly, if you would like to know when an ebook edition from my backlist goes on sale for 99 cents (or is occasionally offered for free), please go to my author profile on Bookbub and click the "follow" button. You'll be sent an email whenever there's a flash sale.

I am also on Facebook and Twitter where I chat with readers every day.

–*Julianne*

Excerpt from
Love According to Lily

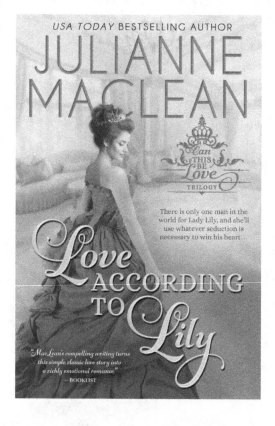

Excerpt Copyright Julianne MacLean
Publishing Inc. 2020

There is only one man in the world for Lady Lily, and she'll use whatever seduction is necessary to win his heart....

"MacLean's compelling writing turns this simple, classic love story into a richly emotional romance."
—*Booklist*

"It takes a talented author to segue from a light-hearted tale of seduction to an emotionally powerful romance that plays on your heartstrings...a very special, powerful read." —*Romantic Times Book Reviews*

Being raised in a strict, humorless household did nothing to dampen Lady Lily Langdon's wildly romantic nature—nor cool her lifelong affection for Edward Wallis, Earl of Whitby, her elder brother's oldest, dearest friend. But Edward cannot see the lovely woman she's become for the young schoolgirl she once was. So with lessons in flirtation from her American sister-in-law, Duchess Sophia, Lily means to open Edward's eyes and win his heart.

But just when her seduction begins to take hold, a shocking twist of fate forces Edward to take stock of the reckless life he has lived. Flirtation with his best friend's younger sister is the last thing he wants, but Lily cannot give up the dream of rapture that surely awaits her, if only she can prove to the handsome, haunted earl that it is never too late to fall in love.

Prologue

Wentworth Castle, Yorkshire
Summer 1872

*I*T WAS AT THE YOUTHFUL age of twenty-one that Edward Peter Wallis, Earl of Whitby, raised a coffee cup to his lips and made the conscious decision that he did not want to die. Or rather, he did not want to grow old—for being young was far more entertaining.

"Here comes your little sister, dashing up the hill," Whitby said to his friend James, the Duke of Wentworth, who sat across from him at the breakfast table.

They'd had the table brought outside onto the sunny stone veranda, having decided they needed fresh air to ward off the disagreeable effects of their excessive consumption of brandy the night before. Although now it seemed a rather idiotic idea, as the sun was casting a blinding reflection off the sterling silver coffeepot in the center of the table, making it necessary to squint. And squinting was never advisable when one was nursing a pounding headache.

"Look at her run," Whitby said, lounging back in his chair as he watched Lily, her blue-and-white skirts flying everywhere. "You don't suppose she's going to ask me to play hide-and-seek, do you? Good Lord."

"Maybe tag," James replied irritably, resting his forehead on a finger.

Whitby was still wearing the same clothes he'd worn the night before, and his face was prickly with stubble. He felt grimy and quite honestly disgusting, yet he couldn't help smiling at Lily, who was racing toward him with a fresh smile on her face, her bright dress clean and crisp. She had just turned nine.

He leaned toward James. "When do you think she'll be old enough to realize we're still half pickled when she comes running up the hill to our breakfast table? I swear it goes completely unnoticed by her innocent eyes when we stagger our way to find her behind the rosebushes or wherever she takes herself off to hide." He lowered his voice to a near whisper. "And she giggles, James. She doesn't know we find her because we can *hear* her." He chuckled and took another sip of his coffee.

"Speak for yourself, Whitby. You may still be pickled, but I am sober enough to feel the throbbing in my brain, and if Lily asks me to chase her...."

"You'll tell her to go play with her dolls."

Lily came to a slow stop on the veranda, breathing hard and smiling. She wore her shiny black hair in two braids with blue ribbons that matched the broad ribbon sash on her dress. "Lord Whitby! I knew you'd be here this morning!"

"And how did you know, Lily?" he asked, leaning forward in his chair and resting his elbows on his knees, ignoring the pounding in his head. "Did a little bird tell you? Or perhaps it was that spider on your shoulder." He pointed.

Lily jumped and brushed at herself. "Where?"

Whitby laughed, though it hurt to do so.

Lily shook her head at him. "You are a tease, Lord Whitby. And you need to take a bath. You both do. You smell like cigar smoke."

Whitby raised an eyebrow at James. "From the mouths of babes."

"I'm not a baby," she said. "And for that, you shall have to be the seeker. Close your eyes."

Amused—and as always, quite unable to refuse darling Lily anything—Whitby did as he was told and closed his eyes.

Lily's boots tapped quickly along the flat stones toward the left. "Come and find me!" she called out a few seconds later.

The thought of getting up out of the chair gave Whitby pause. He didn't really want to move. "Damn, James, why don't you go." Whitby tipped his head onto the back of the chair. "She's *your* sister."

"But she asked *you,*" James said.

"She always asks me."

"That's because I never play with her. You have much to learn about discouraging unwelcome female attentions, my friend."

Knowing he'd never convince James to play with Lily, Whitby forced himself to stand, though it cost him much. "There is no such thing as unwelcome female attentions, James. Even if they *are* from a nine-year-old."

Whitby heaved a deep sigh and grudgingly crossed the veranda. "Here I come!" he called out.

He descended the steps and immediately saw the bright, white hem of Lily's dress behind the birdbath, which was nowhere near wide enough to hide her. Yet she thought she was invisible.

Smiling and chuckling, he shook his head. "Perhaps you're behind the azaleas!" He walked softly toward the birdbath. "Or here, under the bench!"

Lily giggled.

"What's that I hear?" Whitby said, stopping only a few feet away, seeing her as plain as day. "You must be hiding in the hedge!"

She giggled again, and he lunged around the birdbath. "Found you!"

Lily screamed and took off, and Whitby ran after her, throwing his arms around her and tickling her ribs until she bent over, clutching her side. She laughed and screeched until he stopped and slapped his hands over his ears.

"Great Scott, Lily. My head."

She straightened. "You're getting too old for this, aren't you, Lord Whitby? One of these days, you won't want to play with me, and you'll be very dull like James. Very *old*."

"James isn't old."

"Well, he's certainly dull," Lily said spitefully.

Whitby felt honor-bound to defend his friend. Or perhaps he was inclined to help Lily understand that her brother was a complicated man. If he was reserved, he had his reasons. "He's dull because he doesn't play hide-and-seek? Surely he's interesting in other ways." Whitby could certainly think of a few.

"He doesn't play anything. Like I said, he's practically an old man. As bad as my father was."

Whitby narrowed his eyes at her. His tone became serious with a gentle reprimand. "I doubt that, Lily."

She shrugged casually, and he could see she regretted the remark, for her father had been a cold, cruel man. To compare anyone to him was beyond exaggeration.

Whitby bent forward to speak to her at eye level. "I promise I will never stop playing with you, Lily, because I have no intention of ever growing old."

"Everyone grows old."

"Not me." He straightened and rested his fists on his hips. "I will stay young forever. Young at heart at least."

Lily smiled. "Then I shall grow up and catch up with you in years, and then we can get married. I should like that."

"Married! Good heavens, Lily, what are you thinking? I am the worst rake in the world, and you, darling, are a child."

He tugged at one of her braids and turned to walk back to the veranda for more coffee, which he sorely needed. After running around just now, his headache had returned with a vengeance.

He rubbed the back of his neck as he walked, oblivious to the fact that Lily had run off without a word in the other direction with tears in her eyes.

Chapter 1

Wentworth Castle, Yorkshire
October 1884

WITH THE LATE-AFTERNOON SUN BEAMING in through the lace curtains, bathing her room in bright, shiny light, Lady Lily Langdon sat at her desk, tapping her foot impatiently on the floor while she tapped her pen in a similar rhythm upon the letter she was trying to write. She gazed at the clock on the mantel, ticking away in the silence, while the sunlight reflected off the silver-and-gold plated face.

She was anxious and edgy. She couldn't pretend not to know why. She knew enough about her own emotions to understand it. It was the first day of her brother James's annual shooting party. The guests had been arriving all day, and in a very short time, she would be dressing for dinner in one of her elegant gowns and donning heavy jewels.

She'd already chosen the right gown for the evening—her dark blue satin Worth with the black velvet roses emblazoned on the hem. She need only select the right earrings to go with her sapphire necklace. Then she would be ready to venture downstairs and meet the guests in the drawing room.

Lily continued to tap her pen upon her desk, still feeling frustratingly anxious. It was not something she enjoyed, mingling in a room full of strangers. Of course, they wouldn't all be strangers. Her family would be there, and friends of her family, some of whom she had known forever....

Perhaps that's why she was anxious.

A knock sounded. She rose from her desk chair, crossed the room and opened the door. "Mother...."

Her mother, Marion, the dowager duchess, stood in the corridor with her hands clasped in front of her. She wore a long-sleeved black day dress, buttoned stiffly around her neck. Her dark gray hair was pulled into a tight bun at the back of her head. "Lily, I must have a word with you."

Lily stepped back and invited her into the room.

While her mother gazed around at everything— the pile of unfinished letters on the desk, the modern novel lying open on the bed—a sense of inadequacy swept through Lily.

She quickly moved to close the book and turn it over, face down, wondering if she would ever be able to disregard the enduring weight of her mother's disappointment in her. Lily's mother had never understood Lily's romantic nature, in particular when it made Lily take exception to her duties, for Marion was a strict, humorless woman, and she would never even consider questioning her own duties.

Marion sat down on a chair, while Lily sat on the sofa opposite. They gazed at each other uneasily for a few seconds before Marion spoke.

"Lily, as you know, the guests have been arriving throughout the day."

Lily nodded.

"As it happens, there is a particular gentleman who arrived not more than an hour ago—a young man I encouraged Sophia to invite, as I believe he is a charming and respectable young man. He is Lord Richard, the Earl of Stellerton's youngest son."

A youngest son. Lily squeezed her hands together in her lap. There was a time when her mother would only consider an eldest son as husband material—for Lily was after all the daughter of a duke. But Lily was twenty-one now, and not exactly without her share of knocks and scratches. She suspected her mother was becoming desperate.

"How old is he?" Lily asked, grasping frantically for calm, intelligent questions when all she really wanted to do was leap out of her chair and say, "I don't want to be shepherded."

But she didn't leap out of her chair because she supposed she did want guidance. She was afraid of trusting her own judgment when it came to men. She knew how foolish one could become when blinded by passion, for she had become infatuated with someone once—Pierre, a charming Frenchman with an enchanting accent. That man had turned out to be something very different from what she believed him to be. Yet, for a brief week or two, she had fancied herself quite in love with him.

And then there was Whitby. Always Whitby. But he did not see Lily as a woman. He saw her as a child or sister. She had learned that to hope for something more where he was concerned was unrealistic and foolish.

So yes, she needed guidance, because she wanted to get on with her life.

"Lord Richard is twenty-six," her mother replied. "I met him when he arrived, and I can say, without hesitation, that he is very handsome."

Lily lowered her gaze. "You know I don't consider looks to be the most important quality in a husband."

"Well, you did at one time," her mother said flatly, revealing the embers of resentment that still smoldered over Lily's recklessness with Pierre.

Lily wondered if she would ever be able to make up for that misstep.

"Is he expecting to meet me tonight?" she asked. "Is that why he came?"

"Yes. Like you, he does not enjoy London during the Season, and he is looking for a quiet country girl."

That sounded promising.

"What do you plan to wear this evening?" her mother asked.

"My blue Worth with the black velvet roses."

Her mother's gaze drifted toward Lily's dressing room. "The blue Worth...." She pondered it for a moment. "Perhaps something more traditional. What about the green gown you wear with your cameo?"

The green gown was certainly more traditional. It

had long sleeves and a lace neckline that was far less daring than the blue gown. "If you think it would be more appropriate...."

"I do. Lord Richard is a highly regarded young man, and he has just taken the chaplain's position on his father's estate. His father seems to think he has a bright future with the church and might one day become a bishop."

"He sounds perfectly ideal." Lily crossed her ankles and squeezed her hands together on her lap. "But what if he finds out about what happened with...?"

It was difficult to say Pierre's name. She didn't like to think about how foolish she had been. "Lord Richard might not want me," she said. "Having me for a wife might hurt his chances of becoming a bishop."

Her mother frowned and spoke in a firm voice. "That is water under the bridge. No one knows but the members of this family—"

"Whitby knows."

Her mother said nothing for a moment. It was no secret that she had always detested Lord Whitby, ever since the first moment she'd laid eyes on him. He was the one who had befriended James at an early age and had exerted more influence upon him than she'd ever been able to do.

When she did speak, her voice was strained. "Yes, unfortunately he does, and I wish that were not the case. If I had had any say in the matter three years ago...." She stopped herself. "I suppose that is neither here nor there. The point is, Lily, you must move on. You were young and you made a mistake, but thankfully there were no lingering effects from it."

Her mother was of course referring to the matter of Lily's virginity. She still possessed it.

"But what if Lord Richard approves of me and wants to marry me? Would I tell him what I did?" An image of Pierre's dingy boardinghouse room flashed in her mind. She thrust it away. "I can't imagine keeping something like that a secret from my husband."

Her mother's brow furrowed. "Why ever not?"

Lily experienced the confusing mixture of frustration and sympathy she always felt when her mother said things like that, for she had never loved Lily's father. She had probably kept many things about herself secret from him.

But since James had married Sophia, Lily had seen for herself what was possible in a marriage. There were no secrets between them. They loved and trusted each other completely—something she never could have imagined when she was growing up. And now she wasn't sure she would want to jeopardize such a future for herself. She wanted openness and honesty in her marriage, just like James and Sophia had in theirs.

Oh, and passion, of course.

Yet, if Lord Richard or any other prospective groom knew about her reckless behavior with a Frenchman at eighteen, there might never be a marriage....

Lily flinched. She sometimes felt as if she were teetering on a narrow precipice, and one day soon, she would fall to one side. But which side would it be? Would she end up closed off like her mother, or open and loving like Sophia?

She felt her chest constricting under the pressure to

choose the right side, before she merely lost her balance and toppled whichever way the wind blew.

"Wear the green dress tonight," her mother said.
"And the cameo. It is so becoming on you."

"Thank you, Mother." Lily stood and walked her
mother to the door.

Later, however, while she sat at her vanity watching
her maid, Aline, do her hair, she found herself wondering what *another* man might think of the green
dress and cameo. She suspected that man would prefer
the blue one with the more daring neckline.

As she considered it more, she reconciled herself to
the fact that Whitby would probably not even notice
what Lily was wearing. He would be noticing the
other women, as he always did. Which was why she
had to forget him.

If she had a farthing for every time she said that....

Lily gazed fixedly at herself in the mirror for a
moment. She thought of her childhood suddenly and
heard the distant sound of her own laughter as she
dashed about the garden, playing tag with Whitby.
His visits had always been a bright, shining light in an
otherwise dark existence, when she'd lived in a house
without laughter.

Her heart ached suddenly with grief and a painful
longing for those singular moments from the past. She
laid a hand over her heart.

"Are you all right, my lady?" Aline asked.

"Yes, I'm fine," she replied.

But she was not fine. Not really. She hadn't been
fine for a very long time.

She wished she could travel back in time and find

the girl she had once been. The girl who had known how to skirt the shadows. The girl who was not afraid to act upon her passions.

Was that girl gone completely? Or was there still a part of her alive somewhere, deep down inside? Lily leaned close to the mirror and looked carefully into the blue of her eyes.

Chapter 2

$\mathscr{A}$T QUARTER PAST FOUR IN the afternoon, a liveried footman with clean white stockings and
shiny buckled shoes hurried down the steps of Wentworth Castle to open the coach door for one final
guest—the Earl of Whitby, the duke's oldest friend.

Wearing an impressive dark brown wool overcoat
and matching hat, Lord Whitby stepped out of the
coach and smiled up at James, who had just emerged
from the house with Sophia at his side.

Whitby walked up the steps, pulling off his gloves as
he approached. He stopped before James and Sophia,
his shoulders rising and falling with a deep sigh.

"Well. Another year has gone by, and another
shooting party is upon us. Where does the time go?"
He reached for Sophia's hand and kissed it. "Duchess,
you look stunning as always."

She smiled at him. "Oh, Edward, give me a hug."
She pulled him close and wrapped her arms around

his shoulders. But when she stepped away, she glanced with concern at James.

Whitby had expected such a reaction from her. He was unshaven, exhausted, and he was conscious of the fact that he had lost some weight since they'd last seen him.

James eyed Whitby curiously. "You look like hell, my friend. What the devil were you up to last night?"

With one booted foot raised on a higher step, Whitby tapped his gloves on his thigh and looked toward the moors in the distance. "The usual, I'm afraid. Colchester had one of his theater parties at his country house. It went a little late."

"You slept during your travels here, I hope," Sophia said.

"Yes, I did manage to get some rest."

Which was not entirely true. Whitby had in fact sat awake all day, worrying about his sister, Annabelle.

But he did not want them to know that. They would ask why, and then he would have to tell them. And he was not ready to talk about it.

Sophia linked her arm through Whitby's and led him up the stairs to the front door. "Well, there will be no such wild, late night parties here, I assure you. We will all retire at a decent hour like the mature, responsible adults that we are. Lights will be extinguished at precisely ten o'clock."

Whitby laughed and glanced over his shoulder at James, who was following behind them. "Who is this impostor leading me into the house? Or has your wife finally given up her American ways?"

Smiling, they entered the grand hall, their laughter

echoing off the gray stone walls and the high cathedral ceiling.

"And how are the boys—little Liam and John?" Whitby asked. "Getting into trouble yet?"

"Gracious, yes, and growing faster than weeds," James replied. "Just the other day, Liam rode the pony without either of us holding on to him."

"Rode the pony on his own. He's only two, James—and heir to a dukedom, may I remind you? Your mother couldn't have been pleased."

James smiled. "We didn't tell her. We thought it best to spare her the anxiety."

They walked past a shiny suit of armor on display at the bottom of the stairs.

"Well, now that the pleasantries are out of the way," Whitby said, "let us skip to more important matters. Is Lady Stanton here?"

Sophia stopped and slapped his arm. "Lady Stanton is a married woman, Whitby. Shame on you for asking."

"We are friends, Eleanor and I." He grinned. When Sophia smirked at him, he surrendered to her proper influence. "All right," he said. "Tell me who the unmarried ladies are. I suppose they and their mothers are waiting to wrestle me to the ground."

Sophia shook her head at him while James looked on, amused and unsurprised. She listed off the names while they climbed the stairs and escorted Whitby to his room in the east wing.

"I promise I will dance with each of them," he said as he entered the Van Dekker room—the guest chamber they always reserved for him when he visited. The green velvet curtains were pulled open, held back by gold braided tassels. His trunks were already waiting for him, stacked in the center of the room, as his valet had taken an earlier train.

Whitby shrugged out of his coat and tossed it onto the canopied bed—a massive structure made of old English oak, with a headboard that duplicated the turrets of the castle itself and bed curtains tied back at the posts. "There will be dancing, I presume?"

"Of course," Sophia said. "Tomorrow night. Tonight, we will gather in the drawing room at seven and dine at eight, then we'll play some cards afterward."

She and James paused in the doorway.

"We will leave you to get settled," James said.

As soon as they were gone, Whitby sank onto the cushioned bench at the foot of the bed and pinched the bridge of his nose. He inhaled deeply a few times, feeling shaky and winded after climbing the stairs. He probably should have eaten something.

Reaching into his breast pocket, he retrieved his flask and quickly unscrewed the cap. He took a sip and forced himself to swallow.

His valet walked in just then and saw his pained grimace. The man stopped suddenly in the doorway.

Whitby held up a hand. "Don't say anything, Jenson."

Jenson, who had been Whitby's valet for more than ten years, walked to the bed and picked up Whitby's coat. "I had no intention of speaking, my lord."

Whitby watched Jenson hang the coat in the corner wardrobe.

"It's a sore throat," he explained, not knowing why he felt he needed to explain himself to his valet. But what could he say? He'd lost his father at the age of eight. Jenson, now sixty-one, had occasionally filled the role of father figure.

"Another sore throat, my lord?" Jenson said, disbelieving.

Whitby shook his head at him and downed the rest of the contents in the flask, finally feeling the welcome, numbing relief it offered.

It was close to seven-thirty when Lily stopped in the doorway of the crimson-and-gold drawing room. Inside, the heavy drapes were drawn, and the room was lit invitingly by dim lamps and candles. A few young ladies were seated on the sofa with their mothers in nearby chairs, while some of the gentlemen stood next to the piano. They were laughing over something.

Another group of guests, including Sophia and James, stood before a crackling fire in the hearth.

Lily wondered if Lord Richard had arrived yet. She would be glad to get the introductions out of the way.

At that moment, she felt someone approach from behind, and before she had a chance to turn, a large hand wrapped around her elbow. "Lily. Thank God, you're late, too."

She turned and found herself gazing up at Lord Whitby, dressed in formal black and white dinner attire, his golden hair thick and wavy. He was smiling down at her, waiting for a response. She noticed he looked thin.

Tongue-tied as usual, she gazed up at him and felt instantly lost in the deep blue of his eyes and the playful allure of his smile. He was so beautiful.

She wished she didn't feel that way about him every time she saw him. She wished her stomach wouldn't erupt into a wild flock of frenzied butterflies. She wished she could just see him as a brother.

"What do you say we sneak in together," he suggested, leaning close, "and no one will be the wiser? Come on."

He placed his hand at the small of her back and guided her into the room.

She went with him, more than a little aware of the fact that she'd not yet spoken a single word. She cursed this effect he had on her. The same thing had happened to her the last time she'd seen him—a few months ago at one of the London balls. He had flirted with someone else that night, as he always did. That particular night it was the Lady Violet Scott, who had been sure that Whitby was going to propose to her. Lily had not enjoyed herself that night.

"There," he said. "No one even noticed us." He nodded at the footman who immediately approached carrying a tray of champagne. Whitby took two glasses and handed one to Lily. "Cheers," he said, then he took a few deep gulps.

Once that was done, he gave her his full attention. "So how are you, Lily? You look well."

She swallowed hard and tried to smile, but a nervous shiver was scuttling through her. "I'm fine... thank you. Fine today. Are you fine?"

Someone should smother me with a pillow....

His eyes glimmered with amusement as he leaned forward ever so slightly. How charming he was—charming and handsome and full of life and exuberance. His lips were moist; it was intoxicating just to look at him. Lily became filled with the old familiar longings from which there was no reprieve.

"Fine, very fine, thank you," he whispered in reply.

He was making fun of her. She should have laughed along with him. She should have tossed her head back and slapped his arm. But she couldn't. Her stomach was wrenching into a knot. She felt as if she'd just been dropped onto her behind on the cold, hard floor.

At that instant, James and Sophia appeared beside them.

"I thought you might have forgotten about us," James said.

Whitby turned away from Lily. "Heavens no. I simply wanted to look my best and thought I should take my time." He glanced over James's shoulder. "I see Spencer is here. I heard he has a new shotgun he wants to show off."

"Indeed, he does," James replied. "Come and say hello to him. He'll tell you all about it."

Without so much as a glance back in Lily's direction, Whitby followed James across the room.

Lily watched him for a few seconds while the butterflies in her tummy continued to swarm, then she sipped of her champagne. When she looked up again, Sophia was staring at her.

"Are you all right?" Sophia asked.

Lily pasted on a smile. "Yes, of course. Why wouldn't I be?"

Sophia shrugged. "No reason. Your face just looks a little flushed."

Wishing she didn't feel completely mortified, Lily raised a hand to her cheek. "I was late. I had to hurry to get here. And perhaps Aline tied my laces a little too tight."

"Lily, my dear," her mother said, joining them. "Come and meet the other guests. There are a few you don't know."

Lily followed her mother to the other side of the room, privately humiliated over the fact that she was still shaken from her brief and utterly insignificant encounter with Whitby. She had promised herself she would forget him. She had wanted to feel nothing, but the reality was very different. Unfortunately, whenever she saw him, she felt everything—every nerve in her body, every emotion in her heart, every impossible wish and every agonizing desire.

Her mother led her across the room to the gentlemen who were gathered by the piano. There were a few familiar faces, but some new ones, too. One in particular stood out—a young, dark-haired man who was not unattractive. He was watching Lily with apparent interest.

Lily's mother made the introductions, and sure enough, the young man was Lord Richard—her potential future husband if her mother had her druthers.

Lily smiled politely, then listened to the conversation rather than joining in, while at the same time stealing discreet glances at Lord Richard. A few times their eyes met, and he gave her a smile. She began to feel more at ease. Her pulse slowly returned to its normal pace.

A short while later, the conversation was clipping along, and Lily was smiling brightly at all the people in the group. She forgot about her flushed cheeks. She forgot about Whitby. She did not look across the room, perhaps because she was very aware of Lord Richard's interest in her, watching her and evaluating her. She did her best to be charming and friendly, laughing at witty remarks that were made, gazing with interest at whoever was speaking at any given moment. Then, when the dinner gong rang and the time arrived to proceed into the dining room, she smiled candidly at Lord Richard before taking the arm of her elderly neighbor, Mr. Horton, for they were to line up two by two according to precedence.

They entered the vast, formal dining room, lit by dozens of candles set in silver candelabras, spaced evenly down the long length of the white-clothed table set for thirty guests. Colorful bouquets of flowers trimmed each place-setting and filled the room with the delightful fragrance of a summer garden. Before long, everyone was seated, and the extravagant service began.

Lily sat at a diagonal across from Lord Richard, so they were unable to speak to each other directly, but it was a fine opportunity to observe him and see how he behaved with the others around him. He seemed very polite. Occasionally he smiled at Lily, and she smiled back.

On other occasions, she found herself gazing up at the other end of the table where James, Sophia and

Whitby were laughing and engaging in more animated conversation. Whitby was seated next to Lady Stanton, who was very beautiful and evidently very amusing. Everyone laughed at the things she said.

Lily forced her gaze back to her plate and resolved to keep her attention on the people sitting beside and across from her.

After dinner, the ladies returned to the drawing room for coffee, while the gentlemen went to the library for claret and cigars.

"It's nice to see Lord Richard here," Lady Stanton said to Lily's mother, while the coffee was being poured. She leaned forward to pick up her cup. "He has become quite handsome of late. Indeed, I believe he would be a very good match for the right young woman—a woman who enjoys country life." She directed her smiling gaze at Lily, who said nothing as she picked up her coffee cup and stirred it with a spoon.

"He is indeed an upright young man," Lily's mother said. "Any young lady would be fortunate to catch his interest. Very fortunate indeed."

Lily glanced across at Sophia, who was watching her. Sophia smiled warmly.

Later, after the gentlemen had joined the ladies in the drawing room, Sophia approached Lily who sat alone on the settee by the window.

"You look lonely over here," Sophia said, sitting down and touching Lily's knee.

"No, not at all. I was enjoying watching everyone else talk."

With a quiet, gentle voice, Sophia said, "You know,

Lily, there was a time when you enjoyed social gatherings like this. You used to long for excitement and a new face now and then. A handsome face." She gave Lily a knowing, sidelong glance.

Lily managed to reach the edges of a smile, though she felt little joy to go along with it. "That was when I was young and innocent and knew nothing of the wicked ways of the world." She spoke with mocking humor, though there was more than a little truth to it, and they both knew it.

"So, what do you think of Lord Richard?" Sophia asked, thankfully changing the subject. "Your mother thinks he would be a very good match for you."

"I am sure she's right," Lily replied. "I'll look forward to getting to know him over the next few days."

Sophia stared intently into Lily's eyes. "Will you?" The skepticism in her voice was unmistakable. Sophia had always been direct. "Or would you prefer to get to know someone else?"

A thick cloud of uneasiness descended upon Lily as she sat speechless on the settee.

Sophia knew.

How long she had known, Lily had no idea. She remembered telling Sophia three years ago that she had once fancied Whitby when she was a girl. Lily had thought she was over him at that time. She had sincerely believed she was. In fact, she had thought of him very little over the year prior to that.

But something had changed lately. Lily had gone to London in May and thrown herself back into the scorching crush of the Season. She'd seen Whitby over and over at balls and assemblies after not having

seen him for almost two full years—the years after
Pierre, when she had retreated from society in general. She had skipped the London Season altogether
during those years.

But when she saw Whitby again last May, she had
remembered all too clearly the day he had come with
James and Sophia to fetch her out of that horrible
boardinghouse and bring her home and save her from
certain doom. He had carried her down a flight of
stairs and taken her into the safety of a private coach.
He had not judged her—like she'd felt the others had,
especially her mother after she had arrived home.
And she couldn't blame them. Even Lily had judged
herself and continued to judge and condemn herself. But Whitby never had, nor did he seem to judge
her now. It was all forgotten. He never mentioned
it. Though he never talked to her about anything of
consequence....

Sophia took hold of Lily's hand. "You know you
can trust me, Lily, don't you?"

Lily nodded.

Sophia squeezed her hand a little tighter. "I like to
think that we are close, and I believe that we are,
but there is something you have been keeping from
me—and everyone else, for that matter—for a very
long time. I believe you care for Lord Whitby, but
you haven't wanted anyone to know."

Lily looked down at Sophia's hand upon hers and
said nothing for what seemed like an eternity. At last,
she sighed. "You are very intuitive."

Sophia's shoulders relaxed, as if she'd been preparing to coax it out of Lily with a large conversational

pump.

"How long have you known?" Lily asked.

Sophia glanced around the room to make sure no one was listening, then spoke quietly. "I've known since the day you told me three years ago, when I was first married to James. But since then, I thought you were over him. I continued to believe that, until you left London unexpectedly when everyone thought he was going to propose to Lady Violet. But when James and I returned home, you never mentioned him or asked about him, so I thought perhaps I was wrong. Until tonight."

Feeling exposed all of a sudden, Lily asked, "Am I that transparent?"

"No. If you were, your mother would know and Whitby would know, too. He has a very keen awareness when it comes to women expressing their interest."

Yes. Lily knew how clever he was with women. She had been watching him for years. "Does James know?" she asked.

Sophia shook her head. "No. I've mentioned my suspicions to him a few times, but he has never believed it could be true. Perhaps because you're his sister, he has a hard time imagining you being in love—with Whitby, at any rate, since you've known him forever. James most likely sees the two of you like a brother and sister."

"But we're not."

"No, you are not, which is very clear to me."

Lily couldn't begin to express the elation that came from knowing that someone saw her as something other than a sister to Whitby. "I think you're the only one who sees it that way," she said, still finding it impossible to imagine anything coming of it.

Sophia grinned with gentle compassion. "Only for the moment."

Lily's heart bounced a little in her chest. "What are you saying, Sophia?"

"I'm saying what you think I'm saying. Perhaps the time has come to see if there can be more between you."

Lily stared dumbfounded at Sophia. She had been talking herself out of loving Whitby for so long, she couldn't even begin to comprehend the possibility of any other fate.

Her thoughts went immediately to all the reasons why she shouldn't. "But mother despises him."

"James doesn't."

"But Whitby's so much older than I am."

"Twelve years," Sophia replied. "A mere obstacle, easily circumvented."

Lily felt her eyebrows lift. "Easily circumvented?"

"Yes." Sophia glanced discreetly around the room again. "Life is too short, Lily. You've cared for Whitby for a long time, and you haven't seemed able to care for anyone else, even though you've tried. If you want him, you should pursue him and see what comes of it. Then at least you'll know whether or not the two of you are meant to be together."

Lily laughed out loud, then put her hand over her mouth, afraid she'd attracted the attention of the other guests. "Just like that? Pursue him?"

"Why, yes." Sophia was looking at Lily as if she

couldn't understand what the problem was, which was very typical of Sophia. She had a tenacious will, and every Englishman knew that Americans had hard noses for getting what they wanted. Lily supposed she could do with a few lessons in diligence from her sister-in-law.

Lily dropped her gaze to her hands again. "But James is right in one respect. Whitby does see me as a child, and a sister. If he sees me at all."

"You don't know that."

"Yes, I do. He barely notices me when there are other women around—women who know how to flirt with him. In fact, he barely notices me even when there *aren't* other women around. Just tonight, he was far more interested in hearing about Lord Spencer's new shotgun than he was in talking to me. Whenever we're in the same room together, it's like I'm invisible."

"Have you ever tried to make him see you?"

Lily scoffed at the suggestion. "By doing what? Jumping up and down and waving my arms over my head?"

"No, silly," Sophia replied quietly. "He's a man. You're a woman, and a very pretty one. All you need to do is flirt with him, but don't be too available. Don't chase after him. A good flirt will manipulate the man into thinking he's chasing after *her*. And perhaps wear a more daring gown. Surprise him, so that he has no choice but to finally see that you've grown up."

Lily gazed pensively at her mother sitting before the fire. "I was going to wear my blue Worth tonight, but Mother thought I should wear this. She thought it would be more suitable to meet Lord Richard."

"Ah, yes," Sophia said, glancing over at him. "Lord Richard."

Lily looked over at him, too. He was talking to his father and a few others. "He seems very nice. I certainly won't discount him." Lily sat up straighter and studied her hands.

"Neither would I, if I were in your shoes. But you know, if Whitby sees that you have captured the interest of another man, it might be just the thing to make him notice you."

Lily began to feel uncomfortable. "I wouldn't want to use Lord Richard or mislead him in any way."

"No, no, of course you wouldn't do that," Sophia said. "What I'm saying is that you are young and unattached, and this is the time to test the waters with different men. I think you should try to get to know both of them over the next few days. Do you think you can do that?"

Lily's lifetime dream came to her mind—the vision of Whitby leaning down to kiss her, his lips touching hers lightly at first, before he pulled her into his arms for a more passionate kiss.

Her heart began to race with excitement. "Do you really think it's possible?"

"I wouldn't be having this conversation if I didn't."

The blood stirred in Lily's veins, sending a burst of excitement from the top of her head down to the tip of her toes. Sophia was confident. She believed it could be done. Could Lily believe it, too?

"I don't have a daring gown," she said. "Even the

blue Worth has a conservative neckline compared to what some of the other women are wearing."

Sophia smiled wickedly. "I have a few. And my maid knows how to use the sewing machine. We could easily alter one to fit you for the dancing tomorrow night."

"But what about Lord Richard?" Lily said. "I don't want to do anything that might spoil my chances with him. To be realistic, I must remember that the chances of Whitby actually falling in love with me are slim."

Sophia patted Lily's knee and smiled. "Don't worry, Lily. I suspect if Lord Richard is like most men, he'll approve of your new look. They both will."

Love According to Lily – Available Now

Books by
Julianne MacLean

HISTORICAL ROMANCE

The American Heiress Trilogy:
To Marry the Duke
Falling for the Marquess
In Love with the Viscount

Can This Be Love Trilogy
(American Heiress Spinoff):
Love According to Lily
To Annabelle, With Love
Where Love Begins

Love at Pembroke Palace Series:
In My Wildest Fantasies
The Mistress Diaries
When a Stranger Loves Me
Married By Midnight
A Kiss Before the Wedding–
A Pembroke Palace Short Story
Seduced at Sunset

The Highlander Series:
Captured by the Highlander
Claimed by the Highlander
Seduced by the Highlander
The Rebel – A Highland Short Story
Return of the Highlander
Taken by the Highlander

The Royal Trilogy:
Be My Prince
Princess in Love
The Prince's Bride

Western/Americana Historical Romances
Prairie Bride
Tempting the Marshal
Adam's Promise

Time Travel Romance:
A Time for Love

CONTEMPORARY FICTION
A Curve in the Road
A Fire Sparkling

The Color of Heaven Series:
The Color of Heaven
The Color of Destiny
The Color of Hope
The Color of a Dream
The Color of a Memory
The Color of Love
The Color of the Season
The Color of Time
The Color of Forever
The Color of a Promise
The Color of a Christmas Miracle
The Color of a Silver Lining

ABOUT THE AUTHOR

Julianne MacLean is a *USA Today* bestselling author of more than thirty novels, including the contemporary women's fiction *Color of Heaven Series*. Readers have described her books as "breathtaking," "soulful" and "uplifting." MacLean is a four-time Romance Writers of America RITA® finalist and has won numerous awards, including the *Booksellers' Best Award* and a *Reviewers' Choice Award* from *Romantic Times*. Her novels have sold millions of copies worldwide and have been published in over a dozen languages.

MacLean has a degree in English literature from the University of King's College in Halifax, Nova Scotia, and a degree in business administration from Acadia University in Wolfville, Nova Scotia. She loves to travel and has lived in New Zealand, Canada, and England. MacLean currently resides on the east coast of Canada in a lakeside home with her husband, daughter, and mother. She invites readers to visit her website for more information about her books and writing life, and to subscribe to her mailing list for all the latest news: www.JulianneMacLean.com